MY NAME IS
VICTORIA

Lucy Worsley

Illustrated by Joe Berger

BLOOMSBURY
LONDON OXFORD NEW YORK NEW DELHI SYDNEY

KT-377-244

Bloomsbury Publishing, London, Oxford, New York, New Delhi and Sydney

First published in Great Britain in March 2017 by Bloomsbury Publishing Plc
50 Bedford Square, London WC1B 3DP

www.bloomsbury.com

A CIP catalogue record for this book is available from the British Library

ISBN 978 1 4088 8201 6

Typeset by RefineCatch Limited, Bungay, Suffolk
Printed and bound in Great Britain by CPI Group (UK) Ltd, Croydon CR0 4YY

1 3 5 7 9 10 8 6 4 2

To Alexandra, Beatrice, Deirdre and Joanna,
my own ladies of Kensington Palace

All the characters in this story – including Sir John,
Miss V, Lehzen and the Princess Victoria – are based on
real people. If you've read history books about the
childhood of Queen Victoria, you might think you know
what's going to happen.

But appearances can be deceptive …

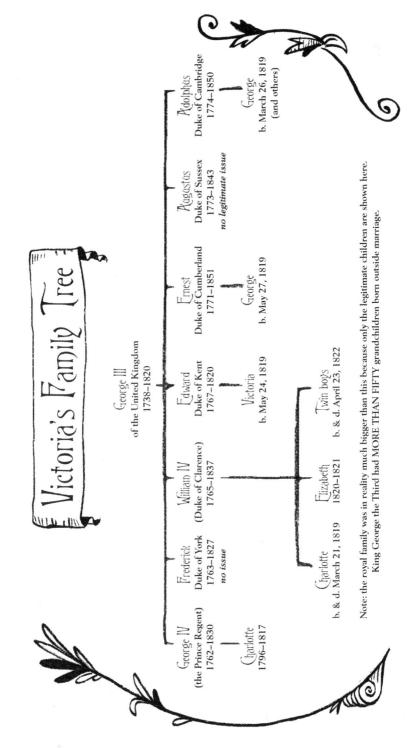

Victoria's Family Tree

George III
of the United Kingdom
1738–1820

George IV
(the Prince Regent)
1762–1830

Charlotte
1796–1817

Frederick
Duke of York
1763–1827
no issue

William IV
(Duke of Clarence)
1765–1837

Charlotte
b. & d. March 21, 1819

Elizabeth
1820–1821

Twin boys
b. & d. April 23, 1822

Edward
Duke of Kent
1767–1820

Victoria
b. May 24, 1819

Ernest
Duke of Cumberland
1771–1851

George
b. May 27, 1819

Augustus
Duke of Sussex
1773–1843
no legitimate issue

Adolphus
Duke of Cambridge
1774–1850

George
b. March 26, 1819
(and others)

Note: the royal family was in reality much bigger than this because only the legitimate children are shown here.
King George the Third had MORE THAN FIFTY grandchildren born outside marriage.

Contents

Part One: At Kensington Palace

Part Two: Ramsgate

Part Three: At Kensington Palace

Part Four: At Arborfield Hall

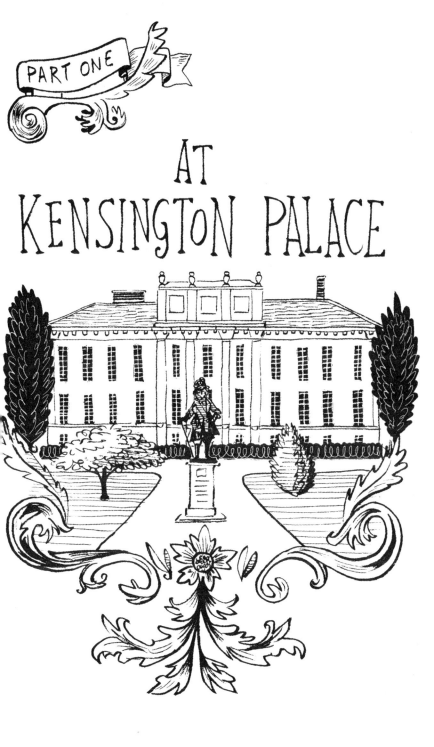

PART ONE

AT
KENSINGTON PALACE

Chapter 1

Journey to the Palace

'Goodbye, Miss V.'

I struggled to reopen the carriage door, for Edward had already clicked it shut before I had had the chance to say farewell properly to my mother. But I was too late. Her stooped back was already disappearing towards the entrance of our house, Arborfield Hall. She had one hand raised to her spine, as usual, as if she found it a great effort to walk.

I gazed after her as she went, giving up my struggle with the handle.

'Have fun!' said Jane, my sister, who did at least manage to reopen the door. She climbed up the step to smack a kiss on to my cheek. 'Goodbye, Dash!' she said,

3

kissing him too and almost smothering him under her ringlets. 'Come back soon with lots of stories.' She jumped back down on to the gravel. 'Maybe you'll have exciting adventures that you can write down into a book of your own,' she added as an afterthought.

'Goodbye, Jane,' I said, although I don't think she heard me. Exciting adventures were the last thing I required. Of course she meant well, but Jane never understood what I might or might not want to do.

I thought she had gone, but here she was bouncing up once more upon the carriage's step. 'Mother *will* miss you, you know, Miss V!' she said. And then, this time, she really did disappear, darting back across the gravel to the house.

I am called 'Miss V. Conroy' because Jane, as the elder, is 'Miss Conroy'.

I am always 'Miss V' so that people will know that I'm not the first Miss Conroy. I was disappointed when my mother told me I would have to carry my 'V' with me, like a limp or an affliction of the speech. I thought I should like to slip through life as 'Miss Conroy'; it sounds more discreet, less noticeable. People always wonder what the 'V' stands for, and they try to find out … I hate that. I hate people knowing about me.

I am good at keeping secrets. I like to be neat and

discreet. I like to sit quiet as a mouse, escaping notice. Hopefully escaping criticism. And that's how I felt that morning when my father jumped into the carriage beside me, and with a jerk of the vehicle we moved off to begin the whole day's journey to London.

Of course my family might use my Christian name; that would be perfectly correct. But my father says that even when I was only one week old, my nursemaids reported that I was already a well-behaved young lady, a 'miss', not a normal, noisy, messy baby.

As our carriage rolled out between the gateposts, it occurred to me that perhaps at our destination for the first time people would call me 'Miss V. Conroy' seriously, and not as a joke. I decided I must prepare myself for the possibility.

I'd been up to London before, of course, with my father, in his blue-painted carriage. But we visited the shops and once the theatre, never staying more than one night. Certainly we had never stayed for several days, as was now the plan. I had packed very carefully, as always, and it had been hard to create space in my trunk for the great number of novels I thought I might need. I was a little anxious that the straps might tug loose and that my trunk and hatbox might fall off the back of our carriage. I kept trying to glimpse them out of the window. Dash was

5

worried too, I could tell, as he sat between my ankles. I rubbed his ears to reassure him.

'Don't worry,' my father said. 'Edward will keep the luggage quite safe.' My father had always had an uncanny ability to read the minds of other people. 'And you will be kept quite safe too, you know,' he added.

I tried to raise a little smile to show that I believed him. I thought, as I often did, of my mother's injunction that I should smile more.

But to be truthful, I didn't quite believe in the new Edward. He was a recent replacement for the old Edward, who had been my friend. All our footmen abandoned their own names and became 'Edward' when they entered my father's service at Arborfield Hall, but they never seemed to stay all that long. I was glad when the last-Edward-but-one had left, for he had been a lazy telltale. The new Edward was so new that I couldn't yet tell if we would be friends. I hoped so.

The thought made me sigh. I wished I had more friends, lots of friends, like my sister Jane. But in truth there was only Dash. It was kind of my father to allow Dash to come with us when it would have been more convenient to have left him behind.

'Now then, Miss V,' my father said, resting his hands on the round brass knob that topped the cane standing between his knees on the carriage floor. He was leaning forward so that his chin almost sat upon his knuckles. As usual, his eyes were twinkling, amused. 'I think,' he said, 'that you and I must have a little confidential conversation before we arrive. I want things to go quite pleasantly, you know.'

I lowered my eyes to my own hands on my lap. 'Pleasantly' was far more than I hoped for from this visit. I wished merely not to disgrace or draw attention to myself.

'You must be excited to be taken to stay at a palace,' he went on. 'And it'll be easy. All you have to do is to play with another little girl. All the girls in London would be glad to take your place! Eh, Miss V?'

In truth I found the prospect as much terrifying as thrilling. This wasn't just any little girl! How would we 'play' together? Could she even play the piano? Would she expect me to entertain her with witty conversation? That would be awful, for I had none.

I glanced up doubtfully.

My father caught this and gave me one of his sharp little nods of encouragement. 'Come on! You can count on me!' he said. 'You can always count on a Conroy,' he added, with a tap of his cane on the floor, 'which means I know that I, in turn, can count on *you*.'

Of course, he was right. Of course I was a lucky girl, and I was fortunate to have a father like him to help me. I'd get through it somehow. With Dash's help too. He was a great icebreaker. Again I stroked his silky brown ears.

My father sat back on the padded seat, quite at ease. There was a pink carnation in his waistcoat. He was watching me with his usual quizzical look. My mother, Lady Elizabeth Conroy, didn't notice much because she was always so tired. But my father noticed everything.

'I know that you're a shy miss,' he said, cocking his head to the side, 'but so is the Other Party.'

'You mean –'

He nodded sharply and flashed his eyes towards the box where Edward sat next to the coachman. Of course. *Not in front of the servants.* I'd been brought up hearing these words every mealtime, every time the conversation got interesting.

'The Other Party …' I hesitated. 'May I ask, please, Papa, how I should address her when we meet?'

'Certainly!' he said. But then a furrow wrinkled his pink forehead. 'I thought your mother would have told you that.'

He leaned forward on his cane and beckoned me nearer to him.

'She is, of course, a princess,' he said very quietly. 'And

8

you must say, "Your Royal Highness". Never say "Princess", that's not correct when you're talking to her, always "Your Royal Highness". And wait until she speaks to you. And you know your curtsey?'

I bent my chin again, right down to my chest. My mother *had* said something vague to me about curtseys earlier this morning, but it had been in her usual dreamy manner. She had not been well recently. In fact, I could not remember her being perfectly well in my whole life.

For a second, I had to blink hard to clear my eyes. This had been one of our mother's bad mornings, when she had gone straight from her bed to recline on the chaise longue in the window, hardly stopping to dress herself properly on the way. On days like these she seemed reconciled to staying put there in her nightgown until dinnertime.

'Of course you know your curtsey, don't you, Miss V?' she'd murmured, not turning her head, as I'd crept across the carpet towards her to remind her of our departure. Well, I thought I knew my curtsey, but I wasn't entirely sure. And I hadn't dared to ask her for clarification.

Now I reminded myself fiercely that it had been a great step for her to have come down from her bedroom to see us off at all.

'I ... think I know how to curtsey, Papa.'

It was the wrong thing to say. His eyebrows shot

9

forward and his hands tightened on that brass knob as if he wanted to hurt it. 'My God!' he said. 'My dearly beloved family have cotton wool for brains. Sometimes I think the good Lord has sent them specifically to try my patience.' He fell to looking crossly out of the window, and silence reigned.

I waited, mute, a careful hand on Dash's head to warn him that now was no time to wriggle or bark.

Eventually my father's eyes wandered back inside the carriage and I tensed myself to take the pressure of his gaze. Surely he would not be cross today, with all the excitement and strangeness of departure. I was sitting demurely on the seat, knees squeezed together, my hair smoothly looped up at each side of my head – not falling forward in torrents of ringlets like the fashionable girls wore – waiting anxiously for the storm to pass.

I was right. He was smiling again.

'Well, Miss V,' he said. My father's temper tantrums never lasted long. 'You certainly have more common sense than the rest of them.' By this he meant not only my mother and Jane but also my three boisterous brothers.

'You at least are quiet and obedient,' he said. 'And I know,' he added a little more kindly, 'that you'll miss that wretched little hound of yours. What's his name, again? Is it Splash?'

'Dash! It's Dash!'

Upon hearing his name, Dash sat up straight and raised his tiny chin as if to look my father in the eye. Dash! He was such a good dog, so well trained, so quiet and clean. He really was a comfort to me as we went about our daily business at Arborfield Hall: the shrubbery walk, piano practice, needlework. When I was sitting behind the curtain in the library with a volume of Sir Walter's in my lap, it was Dash who would first hear and warn me of the tread of the housemaid with the coal scuttle, giving me time to hop up neatly and put the forbidden book back. It was Dash who kissed me before I went to sleep at night.

But what did my father mean about my 'missing' Dash? Surely he wasn't going to be sent back to Arborfield Hall? Before I could ask, he spoke again.

'Well, young Dash!' My father prodded Dash with his cane. 'How are you going to enjoy being a royal dog? That's a distinguished canine band to be joining, and no mistake!'

I was speechless. What could he mean? I felt the shameful crimson rising up my neck, as it so often did.

'Oh, *Lord*!' he said as he saw me blush. 'Confound it! Can it be that my dear wife has failed to explain?'

He knocked his cane once or twice on the floor in his

11

exasperation. His eyes always seemed to flash theatrically, like those of the enchanter we had seen in last year's pantomime. 'Miss V, my apologies, but I thought you knew. The dog is to be your gift to the Other Party, of course.'

'But ...'

My breath failed me. Give away my dog? To this unknown girl? I gripped my hands tighter together. Dash could sense that something was wrong. He knew his own name, the dear, dear hound.

'It's just a senseless brute, Miss V,' he said, with vexation. 'And it's of the utmost importance that you make a friend of this ... erm, this child you're going to meet today,' he went on.

Despite my efforts, I felt a fat tear welling up in my eye. I tried to pretend it wasn't there. I felt utterly incapable of reaching for my handkerchief.

'Oh, come, come, my dear!' he said, pulling out his own handkerchief and shoving it roughly into my hand.

'Perhaps I have miscalculated,' he said quietly, as if to himself, and once again his gaze seemed drawn away from me, out of the window. I felt sore inside. I loved Dash desperately, but then I loved my father even more.

'I thought that you would be a good girl, Miss V,' he said. 'Equal to this task. You can do it, eh? You can give up your dog in order to make a fine first impression? The party has asked me specifically for a dog, exactly like this one! Come, come, don't let me down. Otherwise I'll have to send you back to the country and find myself a new Miss V from somewhere else.' He gestured vaguely out of the window, as if daughters were to be picked up anywhere. 'And I'm sure I won't like the new one half as much.'

Now his attention was trained back upon me, like a beam of light concentrated by a prism glass. As always, when he *really* looked at me, I felt the warmth of his gaze.

'You're a brave little miss, aren't you?' he said cajolingly. 'And you know that it's your duty to win this little girl over, don't you? To make friends with her?'

Reluctantly, I sniffed and nodded.

'My post depends on you, Miss V!'

My father was the comptroller to the Duchess of Kent, the princess's mother. He often spoke proudly of his position in a royal household, and the advantages and connections it brought to us.

'You know that the Duchess of Kent is our patroness? And that's why we can live at Arborfield Hall and drive in a carriage, and why in a day or two, when I have a moment and when one or two bills have been dealt with, I'll be able to buy you another little puppy to replace that one.'

The thought of another puppy was horrible.

'But I love Dash,' I coughed. 'And he loves me!'

'You'll have another puppy, my dear, but the first chance to impress the princess will never come again,' he said. 'I regret it, but it really is for the best that you give her your dog.'

At that he folded his arms, throwing himself back on his seat and returning his gaze to the passing fields and damp meadows.

And so, as we sat in miserable silence, all thoughts of home wiped from my mind by this catastrophe, my hand crept down again to rest on Dash's head. I tried not to think of his life with another girl. I tried to not think of the wet, whiskery kisses he gave me, nor of his cushion, his bowl or his little felt toy mouse that I had last night packed lovingly into the corner of my trunk.

How could I endure our stay in this horrible place where Dash, my only friend, was to be taken from me? How could I possibly return to Arborfield Hall without him? And how on earth could I make friends with his thief?

Chapter 2

The Face at the Window

I hardly saw what was passing outside. Dash, now locked securely in my arms, gave out a whimper from time to time. It was almost as if he knew, clever dog that he was, that he was about to be torn away from the mistress who had loved him so well.

When I did look up at last, we were in crowded streets with tall houses, white like wedding cakes, on either side. There were avenues with trees, and a bustling high street. Then we were passing a grassy green and drawing up at a gate in iron railings.

The iron of the gates was wrought into the pattern of a golden crown.

We heard the new Edward exchanging a word or two

with some guards, and then, after a jolt that made Dash wince, we were creeping forward again into what seemed like a small town of red brick. Our own home, Arborfield Hall, was not a large house, but it was built in the up-to-date Gothic style with plenty of pretty decoration and beautiful coloured glass. Kensington Palace, on the other hand, seemed to be an enormous, sprawling building, but sadly out of fashion with its boring rectangular windows and grimy brick walls. It looked rather like my idea of a prison.

At last we creaked to a halt in a cobbled courtyard. The sound of the horses seemed to echo three times around the high walls before it faded away. Edward jumped down with a thud.

'Remember!' my father said, his eyes twinkling at me once again over the top of his cane. '"Your Royal Highness", that's what you should say! And I know that you have the cleverness to bring this off, Miss V. You won't fail me. Will you?'

His confidence forced a tiny smile to raise the corners of my mouth.

Now Edward opened the door and reached a hand to steady me as I stepped out. I lost my footing for a second on the cobbles, and Dash squirmed free of my arms to make a circuit of the courtyard with his light bound.

My eyes followed him around the enclosing walls of dull dark red.

There were lamp posts in the courtyard, just like a street, and the front doors of many different households. I knew that other members of the royal family lived here too, although the princess's household was the most important. An old lady in a mob cap was sweeping the dirt from the step before one blue door and sending it flying down on to the cobbles below. But otherwise the courtyard was deserted and silent. The biggest door of all was marked by a portico, and lay straight ahead.

I checked that all the little buttons were straight on my navy blue travelling cape, and settled my bonnet forward so that my vision was restricted to a narrow tunnel ahead of me. This, my mother had told me, was the correct way for a young lady to pass through life, gaze lowered, shielding herself from the hungry eyes of other people.

My father was evidently pleased. He took the crook of my elbow. 'Cool as a cucumber again, eh, Miss V?' he said softly. 'That's my girl. We can carry it off. Always trust John Conroy for that.'

And so, because of my bonnet, I could only see a thin vertical slice of building as he guided me towards the door, and perhaps that's why I looked up. A movement

17

had caught my eye. One of the upper rectangular windows, towards the top of my field of vision, had bars across it like a cage.

With a tremor, I saw that the courtyard was not as deadly quiet as it had at first seemed. At that shrouded, barred window, a little white face was hovering. And it was watching me. I felt the two eyes boring into me with what felt like such malevolence that I gasped and glanced down instinctively to make sure that Dash was safe at my feet.

But when I looked up again, the face had gone. Was it a girl's face or a ghost's?

Perhaps I'd only imagined it after all.

Chapter 3

A German Welcome

We stepped in through the heavy front door beneath the portico, where another lady, not young, but matronly and plump, stood waiting for us. She was wearing a dark gown and now came forward with her arms outstretched. In one hand was a lace handkerchief that she waved about to give further force to her words. It was as if her hands talked as well as her mouth.

'Sir John!' she cried out, before releasing a great torrent of speech. 'We are so glad to see you again! This household of women needs a man, you know. You were cruel to leave us for so long! *So* long it has been!'

She had a strange, guttural way of speaking. I wondered

if she were German, for I knew that the princess's mother and many of her attendants were from the princely states across the North Sea.

'But, dear lady, my dear Madame de Späth!' my father exclaimed. His voice was muffled. He was bowing over to kiss her hand, gallantly, fulsomely, while she whinnied and giggled at the attention. 'I have my own ladies, you know, at Arborfield Hall, whom I must go home and see sometimes. I cannot always be here. And this is one of them. May I present my younger daughter, Miss V. Conroy?'

'Ah … yes … this is the young lady of whom you spoke?' The lady seemed a little doubtful; her hands wavered in mid-air. I tried to take up as little space as possible on the marble floor, as if to slink back into the shadows of the vast and echoing entrance hall.

'Yes, indeed!' said my father with confidence. 'I have brought her to Kensington Palace for a visit, just as I promised. I believe that she will be a great comfort to Their Royal Highnesses.' At this, I drew myself up a little straighter. I did not imagine that I would be much of a comfort to anyone, but if my father thought I could do it, I would try.

All of a sudden, Madame de Späth smiled, and her handkerchief fell still at last. When she stopped fussing and fluttering, she looked like a grinning wooden doll with rosy apple cheeks, and I felt a bit more comfortable.

'Well, my dear,' she said, 'even if you have no other good qualities, you have bravery to come among us in this strange life we have here. Come and meet your new playmate.'

I could not help smiling back as I bobbed down into a curtsey. It seemed safest. At first I had thought this lady a servant, but she seemed rather a grand one, as if a colleague or an equal of my father.

But then, despite her friendly smile, Madame de Späth's eyes moved quickly onwards, away from me. That often happened. I am not … impressive. I am always the least in any gathering, the last to be noticed, first to be dismissed. But that's just the way I like it. My sister, my father, even Dash: they all love attention, and as far I'm concerned, they're welcome to it.

'And this must be the new … *schatz* for the princess,' she said, bending to give him a fluttery pat on the head. All at once my mouth turned dry once more. I knelt to clip Dash's lead to his collar.

'Yes.' I spoke so quietly that I'm sure she could barely hear me. 'This is Dash. He's a very good dog.'

'He's also a very pretty dog, isn't he?' said the German lady, looking at him closely. 'Does he bite?'

21

'Never!' This time my voice came out as a loud squawk, so incensed was I.

She laughed. 'Just as pretty as the little lady who has brought him!'

She boldly put out her hand, and I had no choice but to place Dash's lead into it. I would rather have put my hand into the fire and watch it be licked with flames, but I felt the weight of my father's own hand on my shoulder. It lay there heavily.

And then my darling traitorously frisked around the old lady's skirt as she turned to lead us up an enormous staircase. I lowered my eyes to the steps, quite unequal to the task of watching him skip away from me so blithely.

Concentrate, I told myself sternly, *upon just what your eyes can see. This is no time to cry. You can count on a Conroy.*

And so, blinking hard, I gradually came to notice that the broad stone steps were not quite clean, and that cobwebs were draped over the oil lamps that should really have been lit on such a dim and gloomy afternoon.

'Have care!' the dumpy little figure said from the shadows ahead of us. 'The marble is slippery, and Lord knows we cannot get the maids to sweep the steps.'

'Madame de Späth,' said my father, 'let us not have that conversation again now.'

22

'*Ach so*. But later, Sir John, later. I have had so many bills come in while you have been away, and no means to pay them, as you know. You are the comptroller of this household, or at least so you always tell us, so the care of this should fall upon YOU.'

She chattered on plaintively in the same vein. The weary arch of my father's neck suggested that he'd heard such complaints many times before. In fact, he stealthily turned back towards me and stuck out his tongue so suddenly and so foolishly that, despite the traces of tears in my eyes, I almost laughed out loud.

As we continued to climb, I thought that as well as being not quite clean, the great building seemed unnaturally still. Apart from Madame de Späth's wheezy breath, I could hear Dash's claws tapping and my father's confident, prancing tread. But there were no other sounds, and we saw no one. A smaller, winding staircase followed the big one, and then we were in a carpeted passage. It was a little like the maids' passage at home, with sprigged but stained wallpaper and a dirty carpet.

Madame de Späth at last halted in the corridor outside a low and dingy door and gave it a smart rap.

Again I settled my bonnet forward on my head and straightened my shoulders beneath the dark blue wool. This was it. We had arrived.

But nothing seemed to stir inside the room.

We waited, my breath coming faster and faster, even though we were doing nothing but standing there silently.

Madame de Späth put her ear to a panel of the door, and then nodded her head. Despite the lack of an answer, it seemed that we were free to enter, and she slowly started to turn the knob.

Little did I know it, but that pause in the dirty passage was the last moment of my old life. I was nervous as I stood on that threshold, but I had no idea of the surprises that would lie ahead.

Chapter 4

A Parrot and a Princess

'*Vickelchen!*'

Hardly had we crossed the threshold when the hoarse, violent word came hissing out of the dim room. Madame de Späth must have sensed me shrinking back into the passage, as she gave me a little encouraging nod over her black bombazine shoulder. As she had certainly appreciated Dash's beauty and character, perhaps this lady could be trusted.

Our German guide passed on into the room containing this strange harsh voice, and now I could see that it held scarcely more light than the dingy passage. The windows were swathed with curtains, and dimly behind them I could see the impression of bars. Perhaps this was the window of the very room that had given me the idea that it was haunted.

Inside was a maze of musty furniture bearing dusty curios. A high glass dome was placed over an arrangement of faded flowers. It was so cluttered and murky that at first I did not see the tall, thin lady, also dressed in black, standing still on the hearthrug. But Madame de Späth bustled forward to introduce me.

'This is my compatriot, the Baroness Lehzen,' she said. Was she the possessor of that awful grating deep voice? I hung back, timidly hanging my head. I felt my father's hand sharply in the centre of my back, pushing me forward so abruptly that I almost tripped.

'My daughter, Miss V. Conroy,' he said. 'We usually call her Miss V, for short.' In speaking he had emphasised our surname with a smile in his voice. It did the trick. I pulled up my spine in preparation to make a curtsey.

'*Vickelchen!*'

It was the voice again, harsh, sinister … but surely it came from behind me?

It couldn't be the tall, thin lady speaking after all. There must be some third person in the room. I whipped around to look, but saw no one. Bringing my eyes back to Baroness Lehzen, she gave a quizzical smile, and I saw all

the lines on her brown, monkey-like face heave themselves up and settle into new patterns.

'I see, Miss V. Conroy, that the parrot has discomfited
you. I do apologise. It belongs to our mistress the duchess.'

Now she used her hand to guide my eye, and I saw
another dome under a cover. I had taken it to be the twin
of the one with the flowers. The two German ladies
exchanged a couple of words that I couldn't understand.
Madame de Späth handed Dash's leash back to me, and
together they crossed the carpet to lift the cover.

Inside stood a malevolent grey parrot. He regarded me
coldly out of one dull eye, turning towards me a profile
that seemed to me to be identical to that of the Duke of
Wellington, who was always in the newspapers.

'Don't be afraid,' Madame de Späth was saying. 'Come,
come, he wants to meet you!'

'Now, now, ladies!'

My father had somehow slipped into the position he
adopted in any room, the position of command, with his
back to the fireplace, legs apart and palms rubbing heartily together. 'I have not brought my daughter here to play
with a bird.'

Baroness Lehzen turned towards him, and I saw her
giving him a long, cool gaze.

'Oh, there'll be time for Miss V. Conroy to meet

the family,' she said. 'Plenty of it.' She clapped her hands together in an impatient gesture. 'Time!' she repeated. '*That* is the one thing not in short supply at Kensington Palace.'

Ever since we had entered it, the atmosphere of the room had seemed strange, although I could not have said exactly what was amiss. But now, with the baroness's words, it suddenly occurred to me that these people might indeed be short of something: money.

This was not at all my idea of a palace in which a princess might live. In novels and tales, royal surroundings were usually much more splendid. Here the furniture seemed so faded, the dust so thick. There were only a couple of coals glowing meagrely in the grate, despite the chill of the afternoon and the rain outside. Dash had seated himself in a noble, protective position at my feet, like a little lion, but I could sense his body quivering. I had thought it was fear of the parrot, but perhaps it was the cold.

'Vickelchen!'

Again that strange name, but this time the word was spoken in the deep, husky voice of Baroness Lehzen. Was someone else present? This mysterious room must contain yet another surprise. The baroness had looked like she was addressing the sofa that stood near the window, so I swivelled my eyes towards it. As we stood in silence, I heard a rustle. From behind the sofa, very slowly, the top of a head emerged. A head with brown hair like my own, blue eyes like my own and a tiny little pursed mouth.

I knew immediately that this was the white face I had seen down below, watching me arrive. From the girl's hostile expression, I guessed that I was on her territory and that she did not want me there. All at once, I wished I could disappear.

The two ladies now turned towards the little apparition and sank, as one, into curtseys. She crept round the end of the sofa, and I could see she was wearing a pretty blue-and-white striped dress. But it was undeniably grubby.

'Your Royal Highness.'

My father had spoken. He was in a profound bow. So, tentatively, I too attempted to curtsey, the deep curtsey I imagined to be proper for royalty. But I found myself somewhat at a loss as to how to execute it properly, and ended up merely bobbing down towards the carpet and almost falling over.

'Why does she curtsey in that ridiculous manner?'

The little apparition had a powerful voice, with the same German inflections as the ladies who were perhaps her servants or nurses.

'Your Royal Highness!' my father said quickly. 'I beg leave to present my daughter, Miss V. Conroy. She is quite new to court life and does not yet know our ways. But you will find her quick to learn and eager to please.'

'You may call me Your Royal Highness.' Was the girl talking to me? It was hard to tell, for she was pointing her nose in the air and avoiding my gaze. 'Indeed, you *must* address me so. You may never call me Victoria.' At that she turned suddenly and caught me looking at her. I hung my head at once.

I managed to stammer out a 'Yes, of course,' then tentatively added a 'Your Royal Highness' on to the end.

The girl's words had been confident, but spoken in such a strained voice, with such hectic emphasis and energy, that they seemed to indicate extreme nervousness and excitement. I saw her little frame almost quivering with anxiety and emotion. To my surprise, I felt protective towards her. I wanted to stroke her and calm her, as I stroked Dash.

'Quite right!' said the amicable Madame de Späth, as if the little girl's pronouncement had been normal, indeed laudable. 'Your Royal Highness the Princess Alexandrina Victoria of Kent is your name, and you must never allow other girls to become too familiar.'

'What other girls?' said this supposed princess crossly.

30

'YOU never allow me to play with any other girls. Until today.'

My eyes now were firmly fixed to the carpet, but from what I had already seen, she did not look at all like my own idea of royalty. She was tiny, rather like the younger sister I did not possess. Her face was sulky and looked almost unhealthy. *I'm not surprised that her face is too pale*, I told myself, *if she lives in this dingy room*.

'Now, now, dear girl …' said my father, becoming a fraction uncomfortable. I waited, confident that he would find a way of telling the little girl that her words had been rude.

'Do NOT call me your "dear", Sir John!'

The little body produced quite an astonishingly loud sound.

To my amazement, my father bowed at once. 'My apologies, Your Royal Highness,' he said. 'Now, you will remember that I did promise you another girl to play with, as you have long requested, and here she is. Your wish is my command.'

She folded her arms and screwed up her eyes to examine me narrowly. 'I did not want you,' said the princess directly. 'I wanted a real little girl, not some relation of Sir John's. I only agreed to have you because he promised me a puppy. Is that it?' Coming out from behind the sofa, she pointed at Dash with her little toe. I feared that she meant to kick him.

It was hardly possible that my spirits could sink any lower. But I realised, of course, what I was expected to do. My father's gaze was drilling into me.

I did not attempt to curtsey again, fearing further ridicule. So I simply stepped forward. 'Your Royal Highness,' I said, 'I am delighted to make your acquaintance, and I have the pleasure of bringing you your new dog, Dash.'

With a great tearing pain in my heart, I handed his lead over, handed dear Dash himself over, to Lord knows what.

Chapter 5

They're Spies!

The Princess Victoria and I were crouched behind the sofa. I knelt on the floor, my heels tucked under me. No one had proposed that I should take off my cloak, and indeed I did not suggest it myself as the room was so far from warm. I also had a distinct need of the water closet, but these strange people did not seem to think it necessary to offer their visitors such things.

Over near the fireplace, the two German ladies and my father were chatting together in a hearty manner.

'You wanted to play, Your Royal Highness,' my father had said, rubbing his hands so hard the knuckles cracked. 'So play!'

Given such an instruction myself, I would have stood

uncertainly, wondering in what manner to begin, but the little princess did not pause for a moment. She had grabbed my elbow and pulled both Dash and I behind the sofa. And there she'd seemed to look at Dash properly for the first time.

All at once, her face had changed. From pale and peevish, it lit up like a lamp. Her little mouth dropped open. 'Oh!' she breathed. 'He is beautiful!'

At that Dash arched his back and pulled his lips back from his teeth, just as if he understood her words and was smiling. He did it so quickly and sweetly that, to my surprise, I heard a small giggle slip out from between my lips.

My poor crumpled heart unfurled itself, just a little bit.

Soon the strange princess was caressing his long ears and trying to trick him into rolling over so she could tickle his belly. Dash, forever docile, was squirming in delight. I could not help putting out my own hand to the soft white hair of his stomach, and in doing so I drew near the princess on the carpet. We were hidden from the room by the sofa. I now saw that the dark green velvet curtain was looped over a corner of it, making a kind of tent against the window.

The princess caught me looking around in bemusement.

'This is my playroom,' she said.

'Here, behind the sofa, Your Royal Highness?'

'Indeed, yes.' She dropped her voice and spoke to me very confidentially across Dash's belly. 'They can hear us, but at least they can't see us here.'

'Who do you mean? Those German ladies?'

Barely in time, I remembered and corrected myself.

'I mean, do you speak of the German ladies, Your Royal Highness?'

I was worried that she would reprimand me for forgetting her title, and perhaps, even worse, that my father might overhear her doing so. And perhaps her eyes – which were a bright blue, but somewhat bulging – did widen a little. But she was clearly eager to seize her own turn to speak.

'Madame de Späth is my nurse. Of course, I'm too old to need a nurse now, but she helps look after me, and sorts out my clothes, you know. That kind of thing. And Baroness Lehzen is my governess. But they are both spies.'

Although the Princess Victoria spoke exceedingly quietly, I had noticed before that people have an uncanny ability to hear their own names spoken, even over a buzz of general conversation.

'Louder, girls!' called the tall, thin governess. 'Play

together with more volume, please, so that we may hear you.'

The princess rolled her eyes.

'What a DELICIOUS dog!' she said shrilly. At the same time, she gave Dash such a volley of tickles that he barked. As she did it, I noticed that her fingers were red and raw where she had been biting her nails. There was also an unhealed sore on her lip.

The burble of adult conversation resumed. 'Lord!' she said, returning to her former tone. 'Your clothes are very dull. You look like a nursemaid.' She cast her eye critically over what I had thought that morning to be a neat, trim outfit.

'But anyway,' she quickly ran on, not giving me the chance to respond in any way, 'I didn't want you to come here to Kensington Palace. I thought you'd be just another of Sir John's spies. But I'm quite glad you're here now.' She sniffed. 'I have no brothers and sisters to live with,' she went on, 'and never had a father – he died when I was a baby. And I am not on comfortable terms, or at all intimate, with my mother. It is a very melancholy life that I lead.'

She gave a theatrical sigh.

I could only gape at her. She had left me quite astonished by her flood of personal information. I should never have revealed such things to a stranger; *I* had been brought up properly. But it was clear that this was no ordinary little girl, and not just because she was a princess. She seemed to have no notions of ladylike behaviour or discretion. My father had quite a job on his hands looking after her, I could see that. But then, it was only fitting that such a brilliant man should be chosen for such a difficult and important task.

Not knowing quite what to say, I asked if I was correct in thinking her mother to be Her Royal Highness, the Duchess of Kent.

'The Duchess of *Spent*, more like.' Now something like a convulsion passed over her face, and that chubby lower lip dropped open again. It was a silent giggle. 'She spends all her time on a sofa like this one. "Oh, Vickelchen, I am *spent*!" she says. Yes, she means tired, but also …' There was another silent peal of laughter. 'She also could mean that she has *spent* all our money. She is a spendthrift. Or so says Sir John, master of everything.'

'My mother, too, likes to lie upon a sofa,' I said lamely. It was all I could think of to say. It had given me something of a start to hear my father talked about like this, casually, by a third person. I had never really imagined much about his life when he was away from Arborfield, and I had not considered that strangers might know him well. I had only wished he would spend more time with us at home. Maybe then my mother would not be so sleepy.

'But … Your Royal Highness, why do you call your ladies "spies"?'

This question had been nagging me ever since she had first used the word.

'Ah, they're part of the System, of course.'

'The System?'

'Why! You really don't know anything, do you?' She laughed out loud this time, opening her mouth a bit too wide. I could see a gap in her pink gums where a tooth had fallen out, and there was a powerful, unclean scent of gumdrops from her breath.

It crossed my mind to say that I certainly didn't know why a person in her right mind would live behind a sofa, but when in doubt, silence has always been my policy. I looked down at the floor. When we'd been playing with Dash, I had felt I could almost come to like her. But now she was just making me feel small.

She sighed, unable to wait more than two seconds, it seemed, before leaping into any conversational void.

'They call it the Kensington System,' she said with emphasis, but speaking once more in a furious whisper.

'They think I don't know what the word means, but I do. The System means that I'm not allowed to sleep in a room by myself. I'm not allowed to meet other girls. I'm not allowed to see my relatives. The System is why I'm never allowed to be alone but must always have Späth or Lehzen or my mother with me. I'm not even allowed to go downstairs without holding someone's hand, in case I fall and hurt myself, they say. Well, it hurts me, I can tell you, to be so muffled and mollycoddled and spied upon. That's what hurts and upsets me! They say I upset myself, but they … *bring it upon me.*'

As she spoke, her tone grew more and more violent. Her little chest was heaving for breath, and I noticed that her hands were gripping the blue and white skirt so hard that I thought it might rip.

'Lehzen, Späth, they do their best, but they're just *his spies*!'

She hissed the last words so aggressively that it was as if the malignant parrot had spoken again.

'But …' I groped for words in my confusion. 'But, Your Royal Highness, whose spies are they? Who has created the System?'

'Oh, you are a fool,' she cried softly. 'They're the spies of your father, of course. Sir John Conroy.'

39

I felt my own mouth fall open to mirror hers, in an 'O' of astonishment.

I gathered my breath to tell her at once that she must be mistaken, that my father was kind and good, but her passionate words had attracted unwelcome attention.

'Your Royal Highness!'

The adult conversation had stopped. The room was completely silent.

'Young ladies! Come out from behind the sofa at once!' The words rang out in Lehzen's booming tones. 'You have become overexcited, Your Royal Highness, have you not?'

I believed that the little princess was being melodramatic with her talk of spies and a mysterious System. And of course she was quite mistaken about my father. What a ridiculous claim to make! But as we rose together to our feet, I could see that my companion was panting hard, still fighting for breath, and terribly upset. My own heart was pounding too, for we had obviously done something deeply wrong for Madame Lehzen to yell at us like that.

I gave a sheepish glance sideways at the princess. On her face was hostility, yes, and crossness, but something else too. She gave me a private little moue of the mouth as if to say that she didn't blame me for the scolding.

'You can keep your dog,' she whispered as we crossed the carpet. 'Just let me play with him sometimes, will you? That will keep Sir John quiet.'

Again, I opened my mouth to say that my father wasn't her enemy. But I was too late. The adults were watching us intently. So I closed it silently, swallowing my words.

Chapter 6

'What Is the Kensington System?'

With our introduction to the princess brought to this abrupt and distressing end, my father said a courtly goodbye to the two German ladies and led Dash and me from the room. It had been agreed that Dash should accompany me so that I could get out his bowl and his biscuits from our luggage.

'Well done!' my father said, as we groped our way down the gloomy staircase once again. 'I think that passed off quite well. There was plenty of conversation, wasn't there? Although it did get rather heated. What did she say? No, don't tell me now. The walls in this palace have ears. We'll wait until we are in our own apartment.'

The long day had been so dark and strange and

uncomfortable that I was near fainting, and in great need of warmth and cheer. He noticed and suddenly swung me off my feet and carried me down the final flight.

'You weigh no more than a feather, Miss V!' he said. 'And you're cold! What a fool I am to have sent you to fight the good fight on poor provisions. An army marches on its stomach, you know.'

Of course I did know, for my father was fond of referring to his military days in Gibraltar in service with the dead Duke of Kent, this princess's father.

In no time at all, we were out in the courtyard once again, dodging the raindrops and laughing. He took Dash and me along a cloister, round a corner, and I saw the mob-capped old lady again, looking at us through her opened window.

'My daughter,' my father called out, as he whisked me along upon his strong arm. 'My daughter is here, but she feels faint. Excuse me, dearest lady, I shall return very shortly to pay my respects!'

Then we reached a snug little door. It led to an apartment much less grand than the suite where we had just been, but considerably more cheerful.

As I found my feet on the warm, yellow carpet, I saw that there was a lively little fire, and cushions on the couch. It was a welcome sight. 'Here are our quarters,' my father said. 'This is where you'll live during your visit. Normally I'm all alone – how delightful to have company! And here's tea! Edward has already brought in your trunk and taken it to your own room.'

I looked around with intense interest, eager to see this new realm in which my father was king. I smiled when I saw a shiny piano. 'Yes, I have had it tuned especially for you!' he said. 'You must play for me in the evenings. We shall be very cosy.'

Our domain turned out to be quite a rabbit warren of little rooms, panelled in wood, very dark, but warm and blessedly clean. My father introduced me to our own housekeeper, Mrs Keen. He explained that she looked after him when he was at Kensington Palace, and would now look after me too. Mrs Keen clearly kept this particular corner of the palace in very good order and had filled a vase with early tulips and placed it in the little attic where I was to sleep.

Then I came down to a muffin, and to the warmed slippers that my father had placed upon the fender.

'Now,' he said. 'You did well. I think you won the confidence of all three ladies.'

I looked down at the floor. I felt that the meeting had been awkward and uncomfortable. Surely life in polite society wasn't always like that?

He noticed my confusion.

'The princess quite took to you,' he said. 'I have seen her behave … well, far worse than that. And this is important, Miss V,' he went on, 'because the friendship of the family will help your brothers to get good positions in the army and your mother and sister all the leisure and pretty dresses they require. I have a decent understanding with the princess and her household, but I must always be watchful for opportunity. You will help me. We must deploy our forces to best advantage. Now, what was she saying to you behind the sofa?'

He was right to consider that fun and dressing up were essential to the happiness of my sister Jane, just as endless leisure and a lack of what she called 'bother' was what my mother required of life. On the other hand, I myself only wanted to feel useful somehow, to someone. And, of course, to be well supplied with novels.

'Dear Papa,' I began tentatively, 'what is the Kensington System?'

'The System!' He banged his teacup down on the table. 'Now what does she know about that?' He leapt up and began pacing about, all his previous good humour gone in a flash.

'Well, Papa, Victoria … the Princess Victoria … said

45

that she is kept away from other people and kept under watch, and that she does not like it. And, Papa, she said that *you* are responsible.'

Up and down the hearthrug he went, like Dash on a rainy day when we hadn't been out.

'Well, there is some truth in that,' he eventually muttered. 'But I can't think where the little minx learned of what we call it.'

'But, Papa!' Now I was dismayed. 'I don't believe it! It can't be true! Why would you want to lock up a little girl? I know you wouldn't do that. She's even younger than I am.'

'She may seem younger,' he said distractedly, 'but she is eleven – the same as you.'

He paced on and on. I wondered why he hadn't answered my question. Perhaps he was angry with me for even raising the possibility that he might lock up a little girl, even if she was strange and pert. A princess locked up! It did *sound* romantic, too romantic to be real.

Eventually he paused before my chair, looking down at me in a manner I could not interpret.

'Can I trust you, Miss V?'

'Of course, Papa.'

I lowered my gaze, hoping that he would go on.

46

'Well, there is a system of sorts here at Kensington Palace, and it is true that the princess leads an … unusual … life.'

My breath caught in my throat. I could not believe this! The bars at the window? The sense of strain and captivity? The surveillance? No, my father would never do such things.

He must have seen my worried expression. He laughed and flipped out the tails of his coat to squat down by my chair. He took my cold hands to warm them between his.

'Listen, Miss V,' he said. 'You know you can trust your father to tell you the truth. Here it is in all its ugliness. This isn't a pretty story to please young ladies. It's a serious business.'

I waited for him to go on, trying to look as serious as I knew how.

'As you are aware,' he said, after a pause during which I could see him searching for the simplest words in which to put the problem, 'there is great uncertainty about what will happen when the king dies.'

I nodded eagerly, keen to show my understanding. He meant King George the Fourth, who had been on the throne for as long as I could remember and whose father had been the mad, blind, ancient King George the Third.

'Now, the king has no children. You know this, don't you? But he does have a large number of *brothers*, and one of them was the Duke of Kent, my kind and unfortunately deceased master – and the Princess Victoria's father.'

At this he emitted the deep, respectful sigh he always gave when he mentioned this dead duke. After a moment, he went on.

'And so the Princess Victoria, as the king's niece, is very high up the line of succession. She may be queen one day. But she has cousins who are jealous of her high position and who would like the throne for themselves. Her cousin George, for example, is just one week younger. And there are other cousins too. These people wish our princess ill. They would rejoice should any harm come to her. Should any *harm* come to her, you hear me?'

He paused, as he could see I was struggling to take it all in.

'Are you saying that some people … would want the princess out of the way, and that they might try to hurt her?'

'I knew you would understand, Miss V!'

I smiled. Of course that crazy princess had got it all wrong. Her guardians weren't trying to spy on her or keep her locked up. They were just trying to keep her safe.

'And that's why your becoming her friend is a grave responsibility,' my father continued, looking perhaps more solemn than I'd ever seen him before. 'I am trusted to be near her. I hope that if you continue to please, Miss V, you will be trusted too. We need to know what she's thinking and feeling, just to keep her safe, of course. But we must see how this visit unfolds before we shall know for sure if she'll come to trust you, if you can be really useful.'

He had his fingers raised into a tent, appraisingly, as if he was hoping that I would pass the test but was not quite sure.

'Very few others are admitted to the princess's presence,' he explained. 'There's danger everywhere. The princess's mother is not well and is unable to care for her properly. But I, and Madame de Späth and Baroness Lehzen, we must keep her safe. It is a sacred duty. And I hope that I might be able to count upon you too, as a true Conroy, to help us in this vital work.'

I had an inkling of such things – the great cares of state, the great dangers and decisions that fall upon royal shoulders – for I had read about them in stories. I had never thought that they would touch my own life. Surely girls were just to be seen and not heard? That was what my mother had said.

I was good at being seen and not heard. But this was a completely new challenge.

There was much to think about as I finished my tea. One cloud of worry had passed, at least. Of course my father was wise and good. I had been foolish to doubt him for one instant. But, staring into the fire, I realised that I now had a new worry. I knew that I could not let myself fail the task that he had given me. I too must give all my attention to this vital work of keeping the heir to the throne safe and well. Whatever might happen. Whatever might happen.

Chapter 7

Lessons

That first night I was so tired I could hardly keep my eyes open long enough to examine my new attic bedroom at Kensington Palace.

It was far from palatial, but it was certainly snug. Much smaller than my room at home, it was nevertheless nicely furnished with a blue jug and basin, a fine glossy quilt and a window looking down upon gardens far below. They were dripping in the March rain, but I thought drowsily as I went off to sleep that they must be green and pleasant in summer. I imagined Dash and I walking in them together, just us two. He'd like that. The parks and gardens all around meant that at Kensington Palace we didn't seem to be in London at all. I could not decide if this was delightful or a tiny bit menacing – as if no one would come if you screamed.

The next morning, the rain still falling, my father put up his umbrella to escort me across the courtyard to the princess's apartment. In that murky, dark green room we were soon seated around the circular rosewood table and Lehzen (as the princess seemed to call her) made us read from Shakespeare.

This was to be the first of the regular morning lessons I'd been told to expect during our stay at the palace. But the work was hardly taxing, certainly nothing like as hard as that I'd done with Miss Moore back at home.

'… *and our whole kingdom*,' read Victoria, '*To be … contracted* – is it? – *in one brow of woo?*'

Lehzen looked at me.

'… *and our whole kingdom / To be contracted in one brow of* woe,' I said quietly. 'It's like the entire nation is frowning. The king who speaks is distressed because his brother has died.'

After a while, I noticed that the baroness would always have me read first, and then have the princess follow me. It did not take me long to suspect that *I* was in fact giving the lesson. My father had explained that it was necessary for the princess to lose that Germanic tinge to her speech, and that I was to help her to do it by speaking good plain English that she might copy.

In the afternoon, we once again went behind the sofa, and the princess showed me her dolls. The dolls were numerous and finely dressed. At home I also had dolls, if not half so many. It had been a good while since I had played with them, for I had come to spend my time with Dash, my piano and Sir Walter Scott. I had forgotten what a lovely thing it was to play at make-believe, and soon we were deeply engrossed.

Victoria, it seemed, could do nothing without making a lot of noise and action, and she upturned an ebony box so that its contents of tiny dolls' furniture gushed out on to the floor. From among the mess she picked up and hurled aside one bent and bald-headed doll that had lost its clothes. The naked wooden figure aroused my pity, and I picked it up to cradle it. I longed to freshen up its pink cheeks and give it new hair. 'Poor old doll!' I said. 'This one needs some love.'

I watched her carefully to see if she would notice that I hadn't said 'Your Royal Highness', and to my relief she let it pass.

'Oh, that nasty old thing,' she said at once. 'He doesn't belong. It's the German SPY appointed to watch the others having fun.' She grabbed it and tossed it back into the box, snapping down the lid.

'There,' she said, with some satisfaction. 'I wish I could shut Späth and Lehzen into a box, instead of having them always hanging about and watching me.'

I bent my head down to the dollies, adjusting their little dresses, so as to avoid having to comment.

I was supposed to become her friend. But if she hated my father, would she believe me if I explained the truth that they weren't spies, that she was at risk and needed protection?

An uncomfortable chill gradually made itself felt in the pit of my stomach as I realised that I had so many secrets to keep. It would not be easy.

'Be careful!' Victoria said sharply. 'That gown belongs to Thumbelina's baby sister. Can't you see it's too small to go on? And you've got it upside down as well.' I quickly returned my attention to the more pressing business at hand.

At four o'clock, Madame de Späth opened the door to a tall, fat footman. She gave him her usual excitable welcome, addressing him as Adams and whisking her handkerchief across a small table before she would allow him to set down his tray. He had brought in tea and bread-and-milk. Princess Victoria's was served in a tarnished, if not outright dirty, silver basin, and mine in a plain china dish. But it was cold and sour.

'Why aren't you eating, Miss V?' Victoria asked. I could not answer that the tea was stone cold, weak and disgusting, that the milk looked almost blue and had black specks floating in it.

'I'm not hungry,' I said.

'Well, you are almost as thin as Thumbelina,' said the princess. I glanced up at her, surprised. She had spoken almost protectively. 'Here, you can have my bowl. You do look like you need feeding up.' I forced down a couple of mouthfuls to please her, and it was worth it because an eager little smile came out for a second or two to brighten up her suspicious face.

When I got back to our own rooms after tea, my father was on the hearthrug, pacing up and down.

'Well?' he said sharply, as I came in. 'What did she say? What did she do?' I stood still in the middle of the room, racking my brains, frozen in the act of taking off my bonnet. I scarcely knew where to begin.

'Well, Papa …'

He was standing and waiting and watching me, and I began to panic.

'Well, this morning we read Shakespeare – *Hamlet*, you know – and then later on we played with the dolls …'

'Come, come, Miss V! You can do better than that. Come on, let me take this.' Now he was taking my bonnet and swinging my cloak over his arm, and leading me towards the fire. 'Are there any matters of high import to report? Any compromises to the princess's safety?'

I pondered the matter carefully, sinking down to the sofa and holding out my hands to the flames to warm them while I thought. It was a difficult question, but I felt a small thrill of pride that he was interested in what I had to say. This was not like an Arborfield teatime, where it had always been Jane who amused him while I sat silent and dull.

'Well …'

She had used the word 'spies' again about her German ladies. Could it be right that she did so when they were only there for her own protection?

'I fear that the princess …' I began, but found it difficult to go on. My father was still standing over me, looking down at me, and his silence compelled me to continue speaking. I had observed the same thing when my brothers encountered the still, smooth waters of a pond; they felt a violent urge to throw stones into it.

'I fear that the princess does not understand the System and is afraid of it, and that she might somehow work against it, leading herself into danger.' The words all came out in a rush.

It was the right thing to say. My father's pent up energy

was released. He took his eyes off me and started his swinging walk up and down the carpet.

'I knew it!' he muttered under his breath. 'What a cunning little baggage she is! And how ungrateful!'

I almost gasped out loud at his words. What a way to talk about the princess! But I dared not let my surprise show. He turned back to me, and the bottom of my stomach dropped a little as I saw that his eyes were angry.

'What did she say about me?' he said.

'Nothing today!' I replied eagerly and truthfully. 'She only complained about Lehzen and Späth. She said they were spying on her.'

'Spying!' he said scornfully. 'She does not know how lucky she is to live in a palace and to have so much care taken about her health and her safety. What a little madam.' He swung back towards me.

'Now mind this, Miss V. If she says anything disrespectful or distrustful about me ...' He broke off and quickly corrected himself. 'Or more properly, I mean to say, about her servants or her mother, I need to know it. It is for her own good.'

'Of course, Papa.' I said it meekly. It was with a great sense of relief that I saw him go over to the tea table as if the matter were closed.

The table was set out with cakes and fruit and warm milk. It was so much nicer and cleaner than the princess's own tea in the German household. In future, I decided, I would refuse the food there and wait until I got home to have tea with my father.

Now he was pouring out my milk and bringing it over to me. He patted me casually on the head as he handed me the cup, just as I might myself pat Dash if he had been good. It made me smile.

I was glad that he seemed to have accepted my report of the day's events. My task was daunting, but so far I had been satisfactory. And perhaps even more than that.

Chapter 8

'I Will Be Good'

After a few more days of Shakespeare, I began to wish that we could study something different for a change. My wish was granted when I came into the dull green room one morning to discover that Lehzen had spread a large chart or family tree out upon the table instead of our copies of *A Midsummer Night's Dream*.

She began talking to us of kings and queens.

'What is the chief duty of a good monarch?' she asked.

'Mainly,' said Victoria at once, 'it's to design new uniforms for his army every year. And to insist upon the changing of all the buttons. Gold to brass, silver to gold, that sort of thing.' As usual, she wasn't taking the question seriously.

I had to turn my face aside to hide a smile. Of course she was quite wrong to joke about it, but the idea of the mad ruler of the Kingdom of Buttons sounded like something from the story of *Gulliver's Travels*.

'Your Royal Highness! You know better than that.' Lehzen sternly refused to smile.

'But Lehzen, the king is obsessed with those ridiculous uniforms, and everyone knows it.' It was undeniably true. Even I knew that Victoria's uncle King George the Fourth loved clothes and uniforms and was obsessed with them, as the newspapers harped on about it constantly. However, the patient Lehzen did not give up.

'Your Royal Highness, you are born to a high position. It is important that you understand the responsibilities of such a place in the world.'

At this I sighed. I thought of what these responsibilities might be. I thought of our brave soldiers, the poor people who had nothing to eat, babies whose mothers had died. Surely these must be the things that kept the king awake at night? Not his buttons. But Victoria had not finished.

'My *high position*, as you call it, Lehzen, is not so very high at all. The only person who does what I want is Miss V. Unless I cry and scream, of course,' she said in a threatening manner.

I bowed my head, unwilling either to annoy Lehzen or Victoria herself.

I could see that Lehzen wanted to get off the all-too-familiar topic of Victoria's tantrums. She gestured now to the great chart spread across the green velvet tablecloth, with the names of the latest generations marked in with a pen. Yet Victoria made another attempt to divert the lesson in the direction of her own amusement and turned towards me.

'What of the House of Conroy?' she asked. 'Can we hear about that? Why do you never speak of your mother and your sister, Miss V?'

'Well ...' I looked to Lehzen, to see if she preferred to return to the family tree, but she gave me one of her clipped little nods.

'My mother is an invalid, Baroness Lehzen,' I said carefully. 'She spends her days on a sofa, rather like that one there. And my sister Jane is older than me. She is interested in society and dances and dresses.'

The princess laughed. 'And, as we know, you have no time for such things! I think I should like to meet your sister. Perhaps she could take me to the theatre.'

But Victoria had tried Lehzen's patience long enough.

'And now,' said Lehzen crisply, 'to the family tree of the House of Hanover. You see, girls, that the old king,

George the Third, had fifteen children. An immense number. And his eldest son is our king now, King George the Fourth.'

'Oh, Uncle Georgy!' said Victoria, rolling her eyes.

'That's no way to speak of His Majesty,' said Lehzen sternly.

'But he's so fat,' Victoria whispered to me mischievously. 'And jolly. He gives me presents.' But then her eyes dropped down to the green tablecloth. 'Yet he won't let me and Mother go to live with him at Windsor Castle, and we have to stay in this prison instead. It is so *unfair.*'

Lehzen clicked her tongue, exasperated. But the little pause lengthened. I observed that she was oddly reluctant to go on with the lesson. It did cross my mind to wonder if she secretly agreed with what Victoria had said.

'Anyway,' said Lehzen, gathering herself. 'You'll see that His Majesty's daughter, the Princess Charlotte – your cousin, Victoria – is dead, leaving behind her husband, your Uncle Leopold. It's a complicated business, isn't it?'

'My Uncle Leopold is very kind,' Victoria told me confidentially, as if Lehzen wasn't even present. 'He's my mother's brother. He sends me long letters from Belgium full of all sorts of advice, and invites me to stay at his house when he's in England. I wish we could live with him; even that would be better than being stuck here.'

Again Lehzen redirected our attention to the page, printed with the names and titles of all Victoria's relatives.

'So, George the Fourth, yes, has no sons, and his daughter is dead. This means his brother will be king after him. That will be King William the Fourth.'

'Silly Billy!'

'Vickelchen! Where do you learn all these naughty names?'

Victoria sniggered, and I had to swallow a smile of my own. I suspected that Adams, the fat footman, had a hand in her knowledge.

'But, as you know, King William the Fourth has no children either. And who comes next? It would have been your own father, the Duke of Kent, would it not?'

This had the effect of bringing Victoria back to earth. 'He died when I was a baby, you know,' she told me soberly, 'leaving me and my mother all his debts.'

Once again I marvelled that this family who lived in a palace seemed to worry so much about money – far more so than my own family. Arborfield Hall was not, of course, a great country estate, but it was so warm and comfortable compared to Kensington Palace.

'And who …' Lehzen took off her spectacles, and put them on again, settling them over her ears with a little cough.

'Who is next in line for the throne after the king's brother William?' I said, completing Lehzen's question for her.

She nodded. There was a pause. Then I believe that the princess and I had the same idea at the same time.

'Is it … me?' Victoria asked tremulously.

There was a long silence. We could almost hear wheels turning in Victoria's head. She was transparent like that. Lehzen bowed her head slowly, emphatically.

'I am nearer to the throne than I thought.'

Lehzen gave a sort of savage smile. 'Yes, Vickelchen, you are very near the throne. There is much splendour, but there is more responsibility. That is why we are so careful to protect your health.'

We both sat quietly. I hardly knew where to look. My father had told me some of this, but I now saw that I had failed to understand fully the significance of Victoria's tangled family tree. Victoria was much, much more important – and much more vulnerable – than I had thought. *How well she is taking it!* I thought. If it were me, I would be frightened.

But then, to my horror, I saw Victoria's hands curling

into fists on the table, and those familiar tremors starting in her arms and shoulders. She was about to burst into tears.

'But I don't want to be queen!' she bawled. 'I just want to go to balls and parties, and live like other children do, with a mother and father!'

Floods of tears were running down her face, almost as if someone had dashed a glass of water into it. She had turned bright red, and she screwed up the corner of the family tree and made as if to rip it up.

Lehzen quickly whisked the chart aside.

'There is no "want" about it,' she said sternly. 'Girls in your high position cannot *want* things. They can do only their duty. And how will this outburst go down when your mother hears about it? She might ask Sir John to punish you!'

At that my eye inevitably slid over to the parrot's cage. I had not yet met Victoria's mother, but if she was anything like her pet, she was formidable.

Lehzen's words had the intended chilling effect. All the fight went out of Victoria, and she somehow shrank into herself, looking very small in her chair and trying to hide as much of herself as possible under the tablecloth.

She spoke in a very small voice. 'I will be good,' she said.

Lehzen looked satisfied. But despite my concern for Victoria's state of mind, and despite everything my father had said, I did not like to see her cowering like that in a chair. It was almost like seeing a puppy being whipped by one of our Edwards, the cruel one, who had been dismissed.

I looked at her and tried to imagine that sulky little figure wearing a crown. It seemed impossible that such a thing should ever come to pass.

Chapter 9

Beyond the Garden Wall

After a week of these morning lessons and afternoon playtimes, this new life began to seem almost dreary. No one mentioned when the visit might end. I too began to share the princess's pleasure when we looked down from our barred window and saw something, anything, out of the ordinary. A gentleman coming to call at one of the other apartments, for example, caused a flutter of excitement, and once the chaplain was called to the rooms of an old lady who was sick.

I was told that many, many people lived here at the palace, though they could have been invisible for all the bustle that they added to the silent and deserted courtyards.

One morning, I came into the room to see Victoria's feet elevated over the back of the sofa. She had positioned herself in a handstand there so that she might still be able to see out of the window.

'Miss V!' she said in a strangled voice, as she could hardly breathe. 'A discovery! Come quick, I've found a *new* way to look at the boring old courtyard! Look, it's upside down!'

'Oh, you silly!' I said, coming over to the window. The blood was all rushing into her head, and I knew that she'd get dizzy.

'Come on, Miss V,' she said urgently. 'It's so exciting to see a new view!'

Unwillingly, I climbed on to the sofa, trying to see how she had got into that contorted position.

'Throw yourself over the sofa back,' she panted. 'Come on!'

'I can't! I can't!' I was beginning to laugh, as I could tell that her arms were starting to shake and that she would soon collapse. Her little feet were bobbing about next to me in the air, and throwing caution aside, I seized them and began timidly to tickle them.

A roar of sound filled the air. I almost dropped the princess's ankles. Was she in one of her rages? But no, it was a roar of laughter. 'Don't torture me, Miss V,' she gasped. 'Stop tickling! Help me get down!' Her feet thrashed about, and I gripped them tighter. Slowly, ridiculously, we got her the right way up once more. We were both left helpless with the giggles. As they subsided, and as I straightened my dress, I felt rather surprised with myself. I could imagine Jane tickling someone else's feet until they shrieked, while our mother pulled a pained face and put her hand to her head, begging for quiet. But tickling and giggling was not my usual kind of behaviour at all.

One day several weeks later, towards the end of March, I asked the princess why she never went out. I found her idleness and her indoor lifestyle rather shocking, for Dash had taught me to love fresh air and a morning walk. In our new life at the palace we had neither, and I missed them.

'Out!' she sighed dreamily. 'Oh, I long to go out. To the theatre. Or even just the shops. Or – how about this? – to a grand ball in high society. How marvellous that would be. How cruel it is that I must live under this stupid *System* that stops me from going out.' She fell to pouting and teasing Dash. 'Why, Dashy, why am I to be kept prisoner?'

Prisoner! I said to myself, mentally scoffing at the word, just as I knew my father would do when I reported this conversation later that evening. I knew exactly what he'd say: 'The villains of Newgate are prisoners, not the princess. And she is far too young and babyish for the theatre. She wouldn't be able to sit still. Not like you, Miss V.'

I might have been able to guess my father's sentiments, but expressing them as I knew he would want me to was quite another matter. It was too hard. I found myself glancing around, just to check that he had not somehow slipped into the room behind me to observe my treacherous silence. Of course he had not; I was being silly. I searched around for something encouraging to say.

'But surely there is the garden?' I said rather desperately.

'The garden,' she replied in grim tone, 'is intolerably dull.'

'Ah!' said Lehzen. 'The garden, a fine idea!' She had been reading a book rather than attending to us, but the word pricked her attention. 'The rain has, I believe, quite stopped. You young ladies can go out in the garden this very afternoon. But not beyond the railings, of course.' She added the last words quickly, as if she well knew what Victoria was about to say. 'Not into the park. Don't even ask.'

I was beginning to depend on Lehzen's calm, steady ways. I sometimes suspected her of making a bone-dry jest that sailed right over Victoria's head, but I certainly appreciated the lack of the dramatics that we got with the warmer but more excitable Madame de Späth.

Victoria glowered at me and gave me a sharp little kick under the table. 'What did you have to mention the garden for, Miss V?' she hissed. 'What kind of a simpleton are you?'

But I felt bold enough to stand up for myself. Surely to go into the garden would be good for her health, and it was my duty to think of such things.

'I should be glad to see the pleasure grounds,' I said equably.

'They're not grounds of *pleasure*,' she said. 'They are deeply *dis*pleasurable.'

As very often, although the princess spoke crossly, and naughtily, there was something in what she said that made me laugh. She had such a fiery spirit in her, even if her idea of a pleasant afternoon was to lie on the sofa with a bag of bonbons.

So after our lunch of dull, stale bread with only a thin smear of butter, we went outside.

'Dash! Dash! Dashy!' The princess was running ahead with Dash frisking round her ankles. 'Come on, Miss V,' she called back over her shoulder. 'Race you!'

I smiled and shook my head.

Victoria was wearing a light, rose pink cloak that couldn't possibly keep her warm on this cold day. I had learned by now that if Späth tried to prevent her from wearing an outfit upon which she had set her heart, she would have a tantrum. It was very often easier to let it go.

We made a strange procession, for following on behind me at an even more sedate pace came the enormous footman, Adams, from the German apartment. He was at least six feet tall and rather stout. Accompanying us two little girls he must have looked like a gigantic fairy.

Now he hissed into my ear urgently. 'If Her Royal Highness ... ahem ... makes a noise like that under the windows here of His Royal Highness the Duke of Sussex ... ahem ... there could be unfortunate consequences.'

I understood that Adams was imparting important information. To disturb the reclusive inhabitants of this place, I had often been told, would lead to punishment, or at the very least to a scolding from Lehzen. I didn't want Victoria to get into trouble.

So, sighing, I picked up my skirt and set off after the frisky pair at a fast clip. I very rarely ran. It seemed all too likely to have the effect of attracting people's attention.

But the princess had been whipping Dash into a frenzy of excitement, and he had zipped off into the long lime walk down to the bottom of the gardens. I could hear her yells and Dash's yaps, and behind me the laboured breathing of the outsize footman, who was walking as fast as he could without breaking into a trot. 'Miss! Miss V!' he was hissing, in a powerful whisper. 'Not down that walk. It's forbidden.'

He was too late. The pair ahead had raced along, and indeed had turned off the lime walk, disappearing into the shrubbery. I hesitated for a moment. Should I follow them between the lime trees, along this walk that we weren't supposed to take? Yes, I must. It was my duty to bring them back to safety. Yet as I too rounded the corner and caught up with them in the shrubbery, I came to a stunned stop. I felt my jaw drop open and my eyes pop wide.

This part of the garden bordered on to the park. Some of the shrubs down here had grown thin and weak, as if diseased, and at a certain spot there was no vegetable protection at all between us and the iron garden fence. And just outside the railings, in the park itself, a great host of people were gathering around. There were still more of them coming across the park's wet grass to join the crowd, attracted no doubt by the promise of something to see.

I thought they must have come to see Dash and half smiled. What a darling he was.

73

Some were dirty and ragged, but others were respectable: a lady in furs, some children in sailor hats with a hoop in tow. There were old gentlemen and nurses with perambulators. They were talking excitedly, and indeed a ragged cheer went up from the back of the crowd.

'The princess!' shrilled out the girl with the hoop. 'It's our beloved princess!'

'The hope of the nation!' came a quavery old voice.

For a second I could not think whom they meant. Although I knew very well that Victoria was in theory a princess, she looked so unlike a dignified royal personage that I'd come to think of her as another girl. A very odd one, doubtless, but essentially like me.

But then it came over me like a thunderclap that it wasn't Dash attracting the attention. It was the princess herself. Victoria was playing up to the spectators, holding the corners of her pink cloak, curtseying to the crowd and waving and beaming as if born to it. But of course! She had, in fact, been born to it. This was her natural state.

I wondered what I ought to do, for I certainly could not have endured to step forward beneath the eyes of all those people. I could not even see how many they were because of the surrounding shrubs. And yet I knew, deep down, that this cavorting before the crowd had no place in the System and ought to be stopped.

The decision was made for me by a huge bellow, a roar of rage with hardly any words in it. It might have been 'Disperse!' or 'Away!'

Adams from the left and my father from my right swept past me and picked up the princess, one arm each. They carried her bodily back to the palace, her legs kicking uselessly beneath that inappropriate cloak, and her body writhing in impotent rage. As he went, my father turned back to look at me. His face was dark like thunder. I shuddered to think what he would have to say later on.

The stunned and disappointed crowd still stood there. In the absence of anything better to see, they were all now staring at Dash. Lurking in the bushes, I realised I had to rescue him.

'Shame!' called an old lady.

'Villains!' called an old gentleman.

'This baggage must be part of the establishment,' the nursemaid was saying to the boy and girl with her. 'Look, she's fetching the princess's dog.' My face glowed and my hands trembled as I realised, to my absolute horror, that she meant me. Under their gaze, I fumbled the business of clipping Dash's leash to his collar and was forced to listen to their buzz of chatter for far longer than I thought I could bear.

'It's the work of the evil King Georgy-Porgy,' the nursemaid was now saying to the well-dressed lady.

'He's not fit to be king,' the lady agreed. 'George the Fourth, pah. Nothing like good old King George the Third; he was a kindly gentleman. It's cruel the way the king keeps the poor, sweet little princess locked up in that prison. Little lamb!'

The nursemaid did not answer, and I guessed that she, an experienced manager of children, would not have categorised the princess as 'sweet' or a 'lamb'.

'The gloomy old place looks just like a loony bin, doesn't it?'

'More than looks like – it is one! Lots of nutters they've got locked away in there, princes, princesses and so on.' This was from a fellow who looked like a dustman.

'Mad, mad, all of the royal family. And the king the worst of all, they say, though his blessed royal brothers are not much better.'

'Dash, Dash – oh, please, please come!' I called his name softly, frantic for him to return from the railings, where hands were eager to pat him. I could hardly stand the eyes upon me, and the sense that the crowd had me down as one of the princess's tormentors.

When at last I had Dash under my control, I headed disconsolately back to the palace. The horrible things I had witnessed would not leave my mind. I knew that my father would be furious about this breach of the System.

But another thought chilled me almost even more deeply. I'd heard, for the first time, someone else say what Victoria herself claimed about her situation. She was not alone in her belief that she was being locked up like a prisoner. Other people thought it too.

So the misunderstanding had even spread beyond the palace gates! I wished I was bold enough to go back, to shout through the bars that the lady had got it wrong and that the palace was *not* a prison.

As I trailed back up the lime walk, head bowed, I recommitted myself to my task. With so many mistaken views and misapprehensions out there in the world, I would have to try even harder to keep Victoria safe.

Chapter 10

The Behaviour Book

After I had fully understood that Victoria would never lead a normal life, I felt more and more sorry for her. But she did not make it easy for people to like her. She would happily play at cards until you started to win, and then it would be, 'Don't call me Vickelchen. I am Your Royal Highness!'

But over time there came to be no doubt in my mind that for the most part she was glad to have me and Dash with her. Sometimes, behind the sofa, we would laugh so much that Madame de Späth would bustle in.

'Shush, girls!' she would say. 'Do not disturb the Duke of Sussex!'

'You mean the Duke of *Shush*-ex,' said Victoria,

choking, while Späth's face grew uncharacteristically stern with wrath. We clapped our hands over our mouths and continued to shake with silent laughter until tears ran from our eyes.

Then Victoria would be all aghast at what she considered the drab nature of my clothes, and would drape me in the fringed green velvet cloth from the table and place a crown upon my head. Made from a twisted napkin, it held a ring of candles that she insisted upon lighting.

'It's dangerous!' I cried, as she lit the taper to the last wick. But she clapped her hands and crowed with jubilation.

'Oh, nonsense!' she said. 'You always say that anything exciting is dangerous. Now you look like a real heroine from an opera.'

So I stood there, terrified at first that molten wax from my fiery crown would drip on to my shoulders, while Victoria danced around me, cooing with pride at her creation. Eventually something of her pleasure began to rub off, and I began to swish my green velvet gown around my ankles, and to tilt my head from side to side, the better to model my crown.

I was growing strangely accustomed to the System. It was with a start that I would sometimes recall my initial impression that a trip to the park and a crowd of other children were what the princess needed, rather than a life lived in isolation except for the occasional visit from an elderly bishop.

One day the old lady from the apartment with the blue front door was crossing the courtyard, and Victoria threw down a ball of paper so accurately that it biffed her neatly on the head. The princess squealed with laughter as the mob-capped figure peered about to left and right, trying to work out what had happened.

'Oh!' I breathed, aghast, glancing around to make sure Lehzen was out of the room. I considered it to be in rather poor taste to behave badly towards servants. 'Surely it's not fair for us to tease the duke's housekeeper?'

'Housekeeper?' asked Victoria scornfully. 'That's no housekeeper. That's my Aunt Sophia. You wouldn't think that she was a princess too, would you? She's as mad as a bucket of frogs.'

I could only take Victoria's word for it, because although I often saw the old lady, and although she smiled and inclined her head to me whenever we met, we had never yet spoken. She did not look like my idea of a princess, but then neither did a pallid little girl in a dirty dress falling into screaming, panting rages, as Victoria so often did.

Usually Lehzen or Späth were our constant companions. But Victoria's mysterious mother suffered from attacks of 'the nerves' that sometimes required them both to bustle off to her bedchamber to comfort her, leaving the princess and me to play quietly in the schoolroom. 'Quietly, my sweets, quietly!' was always Späth's parting injunction. 'I am leaving the door ajar,' Lehzen would add. 'We shall hear any naughtiness.'

On rainy afternoons when we were left to ourselves, we would huddle on the hearthrug before the glowing coals in the schoolroom grate. While Dash slept in a heap by our feet, I would read Victoria a fairy story, and watch her eyes glow like the coals as she imagined the palaces and mountains that the tale described. Her mouth would drop open. At peace for once, she looked almost like a little cherub. Sometimes, if the story were long and the rain heavy, she would come near to falling asleep. Once, her heavy head lolled down on to my shoulder. I looked at it, slightly aghast to have someone so close to me, but gradually, slowly, I relaxed, and even lifted my arm to place it round her scrawny shoulder.

And so, as the days passed, I became used to palace life, and I grew almost happy. I lived amicably with Victoria for the morning and afternoon, and then generally had tea with my father, when I would make my report on what Victoria had said and done. Sometimes my father spent the rest of the evening with me too, in our own Kensington Palace apartment, although more often than not he went out and left me with Edward and Mrs Keen. I grew fond of them both, and Edward confided me his wish that one day he might become a butler. He even showed me the letters that his sister wrote to him, encouraging him on in his work. It made me realise, a little sadly, that none of my brothers, nor even Jane, had written to me. Of course I had no expectation that my mother would ever do such a thing.

One day I realised that my father still had not named a date for our proposed return to Arborfield Hall. Our departure had been pushed back once or twice already. So I asked him at teatime when we were to leave.

He didn't answer, but looked up from his newspaper and gave me one of his sharp stares. Apparently what he saw satisfied him. He looked down again and continued reading.

'Miss V!' he said to me at last, through the pages of the paper. 'You are not in a hurry to go home, are you? You are doing so well here.'

I thought it over. It was true. I was not especially looking forward to returning to Arborfield.

'Suppose,' he went on carelessly, 'you were to live here for quite a few months more, maybe years. Would you mind?'

I noticed that although he appeared to be reading, my father had not turned a page in some time. It flashed into my mind that he was anxious to hear what I would say.

'Of course not!' I said at once, keen to reassure him. 'I quite like it here.'

'Good girl!' he said warmly, glancing up again with his flashing smile. With a satisfied sigh, he stretched out his toes towards the fire and went on reading.

Twisting my teacup in my hand, I examined my feelings carefully, like a person who has fallen downstairs and is not sure whether or not she is hurt or just surprised. For I had said what I knew he wanted to hear rather than what I really believed.

But it turned out to be true. I did not mind the prospect of remaining at Kensington Palace. Jane was away on some long country visit; I could not believe that my mother was missing me much.

So our life at Kensington continued, until the fateful afternoon when Victoria was called from our schoolroom to go to meet some bishop or other.

Occasionally distinguished friends of her father, the dead duke, would visit, and she was supposed to go along to demonstrate how many Bible stories she had learned, and other tasks of that nature. I wondered how she performed on these occasions, for I knew that her knowledge was very sparse and likely to remain so just as long as Lehzen let us concentrate in our lessons on reading plays, tracing drawings and making new dresses for the dolls. But then Victoria was not naturally a bookworm, like me. If asked to think about anything serious, she soon grew impatient. If asked about the future, she would say she wished only to become an opera singer or the painter of the scenes in a theatre.

And so I was left alone in the dark green drawing room. I never relished being on my own in there because I was always conscious of that terrible parrot watching me. Even when the cover was on his cage to keep him quiet, I somehow sensed his evil gaze. I knew that he belonged to the princess's mother, who I had still never met. I imagined the parrot as her creature, like the cat of a witch, standing in for her and keeping watch over her daughter and me.

It was merely in order to distract myself from the thought of the parrot that I began to turn over the books on the shelf, and found among them a blue-covered exercise book. I thought it was the history book in which Victoria had been writing yesterday, and I thought I might review our lesson. I took it over to the window, for as usual the oil lamp was not lit.

I smiled as I opened it: the first page upon which my eye fell was covered in Victoria's very slanted and loopy handwriting. *'Today I was NAUGHTY!'* it read. The words brought her to life so vividly it was almost as if she had spoken them out loud.

But seconds later my grin faded from my face, and I looked up from the page in confusion. This was not history, after all. Flipping back to the beginning of the book, I found the first page and recognised Lehzen's hand: *The Princess Victoria. Good Behaviour. 1830.*

It was a diary, of sorts, though it was clear that the emphasis was not on what happened – well, nothing much ever happened at Kensington Palace – but how the princess had reacted.

'Tuesday. Lessons, studied the counties of the British Isles, wrote fifteen lines,' it ran. *'Lehzen said to play the piano well I must practise. I told her that there was no need for a princess to practise. Everyone says I play beautifully already. I was naughty.'*

I turned over a few pages together.

'Saturday. My mother is in bed again. She cannot take me to the opera. Not that she meant to anyway. She always finds some excuse. Lehzen gave me caraway seeds and told me stories of Germany.

'Sunday. Aunt Sophia in chapel patted my head and said that I am a sweet girl. I bit her.

'Monday. I was very, very, very horribly NAUGHTY!'

The word 'naughty' cropped up on almost every page, almost like a challenge to the reader to sit up and pay attention.

And then I noticed something that made my heart stand still.

'*Miss V. Conroy came today. She is horrid.*'

The room was very quiet. I glanced up and around me, like a cat burglar checking that the coast was clear.

All I could hear was the ticking of the clock and the thudding of my own heart. I felt a great tide of blood rise up and course through my cheeks. I was sure they were crimson. But nobody came, nothing stirred, and I returned my eyes to the book.

And the next day: '*I was rude to Miss V. Conroy. She is a SPY.*'

And the next: '*I wish Miss V. Conroy would leave me alone.*'

And the next: '*I love Dash! Today I gave him a bath. He looked adorable. Put him in his blue trousers. Perfect afternoon spoiled only by Miss V. Conroy.*'

I could no longer deny to myself that there was something amiss with my vision. Tears had come between my eyes and the page. I remembered the afternoon when we had bathed Dash. It had been fun, I thought, and I had almost cried with laughter as Victoria wrapped him in the linen towel as if it were a christening gown and he a bald little baby.

The blue book in my hand shook, and a large tear fell down and blotted the page. Aghast at this evidence I had left of my nosiness, I tried to dry it with my handkerchief. I fumbled to put the book back on the shelf, suddenly feeling very cold and very stupid. My legs could scarcely hold me up because of the unpleasant fizzing sensation in my stomach.

I gazed out of the window, feeling my breath coming fast and shallow. With a sharp fingernail I peeled down a cuticle, until a pang of pain ran through me.

My father would be furious, was my first thought. What would he say when I reported this back to him? That the princess herself had accused me, in writing, of being a spy? Could I even bear to tell him that she did not trust me as much as I had thought? For the first time, I considered keeping a secret. But could I really do that? Could I hold out against that terrible pressure when he stood over me, waiting for his report?

'You can count on a Conroy.' He always made a point of saying it as he handed me my teacup afterwards, satisfied that I had made myself indispensible to the princess.

But as well as that, I felt angry with myself. How

foolish I had been to think that Victoria and I were becoming friends. How foolish I had been to think that *anyone* might want to become friends with me. Of course I was not worth it. With scarcely a thought now for the noise I might make, I left the room in a hurry. I even banged the door.

Victoria would not miss me when she came back to find me gone.

Chapter 11

A Friend

That night I lay sadly in bed, looking out between my curtains at the clouds hurrying across the moon. Although I'd tried hard to retain my composure, my father had noticed that I was upset.

'What's up, my little owl?' he'd asked me as we drank tea after supper, he at the table with a pile of papers, me on the sofa. 'No piano tonight?'

I had shaken my head silently at him, not lifting it from my book.

'Are you quite sure that the princess is happy and well?' he asked. I could tell that he was looking searchingly at me, narrowing his eyes. Earlier I had reported that nothing at all had happened that day, the very first time I could remember deliberately telling him a lie.

'Are you quite sure,' he said again, 'that there is nothing you need to tell me?'

If I'd told him that Victoria was suspicious of me, he would certainly have been angry. He might even have sent me away back to Arborfield.

He held the silence, pen raised, listening and waiting. I felt like wolves were tearing my insides apart as I forced myself to lift my chin, meet his gaze and silently shake my head. It was a breach of the System not to tell him, but what she'd written wasn't true. I wasn't a spy! I hadn't let him down! It was best forgotten.

All this was passing through my head when a new horrible thought occurred to me. If Victoria were sitting with us now in our drawing room, watching and listening to my father questioning me, she might well think that she was being spied upon.

What was the truth of it? I did not know.

At very long last, my father had got tired of waiting for an answer.

'Well, have it your own way!' he'd said huffily. 'Sometimes I think I'd get more conversation out of a statue.' And he'd turned back to his book of accounts.

I knew that the duchess's unpaid bills were on his

mind once again, as Lehzen had mentioned them earlier that afternoon.

At the evening's end I had trudged wearily upstairs, allowing a tear or two to flow again once I was alone in the dark of the passage. I blew out my candle almost immediately and tried to sleep. Of course I could not. As I pummelled my pillow, I went over in my mind all the times Victoria had smiled or laughed. What a little actress she was!

My father had sent me to care for her, and care for her I had.

Perhaps, I now thought, I'd cared too much.

I sighed and turned over. The wind really was very high tonight, and the branches of the trees in the garden gave out great groans as they rubbed together.

But that sharp sound, surely, was not the wind. It was the clatter of a slate or tile falling from the roof and hitting the ground below. This was not an unusual occurrence at Kensington Palace, where time and decay were doing their best to take the building down.

All of a sudden, though, the moon was blotted out by a dark shape. My windowpane was being rapped upon imperiously. Someone was there!

'Let me in!'

I froze in my bed. Could this be robbers, or spies?

But would robbers or spies speak with such a girlish voice?

'Come on, Miss V, let me in!'

More rapping. I grew anxious that my father would hear. He had been unutterably furious about the day in the gardens when the crowd had glimpsed Victoria through the gap in the hedge. And now she was breaching the System again, with my father sleeping only just down the passage.

As quietly as possible, I glided across the room and tried to unfasten the catch.

'Shh!' I said in some desperation. But Victoria was incapable of doing anything quietly, especially not climbing in through a window at night. Her teeth were chattering, as she had come in her white nightgown along the leaded roof hidden behind the parapet of the palace.

I had often looked out at the roofscape to each side of my window, wondering if it were possible to get along that gutter to the other peaks and gables and troughs of the palace's many roofs. But I would never have had the courage to attempt it for myself.

'How did you escape?' I whispered in some amazement, for I knew that Lehzen or Späth or Victoria's mother, the duchess, always slept with her in her room.

'Oh, mother is out cold,' she said. 'She has taken her drops. And Lehzen has a sick headache and has gone to the water closet.'

'Victoria, you're so cold you're shaking! And it was so dangerous! Have you been on the roof before?'

'Yes, of course.' She said it with an offhand boldness that I had to admire. 'But not often,' she went on, 'for you know how carefully they watch me.'

Silently I handed her the flowered eiderdown from my bed, and she wrapped it round her. 'Yes, I *know* that my gown is dirty,' she said mockingly. Of course I had noticed a great black streak down her nightgown, produced by some obstacle she must have encountered upon the roof. She had evidently read the disapproval on my face. 'It doesn't matter,' she explained. 'It's an old one. I put it on specially.'

But having wrapped her up warm, I could not think what next to do. My mind was fully occupied in wondering why she had come. For her part, Victoria was looking round my room in interested silence. She was taking in the neat pincushion, the stack of novels, my framed print of Christ washing the feet of beggars. For once, she seemed lost for words. And I still said nothing, although the diary and the pain it had caused me was vivid in my head.

When she did begin to speak, it was characteristically abrupt.

'I know,' she said suddenly, 'that you read my Behaviour Book.'

At that my heart convulsed, and I groped behind me for the mahogany washstand to give me some support. I felt so guilty and mean for having read it. I knew I should not have read a private diary. I had known it even as I picked it up.

'But ... how?' I whispered the words, not daring to look at Victoria. Shame pulsed through me; I could feel it thumping in the veins of my forehead. At the same time I clenched my fists with another, more unfamiliar feeling. Then I realised. I was angry! Yes, angry! She had deceived me.

'Easy!' she said scornfully. 'It was out of its place on the shelf, someone had got it all wet, and you were missing at teatime. You left me all alone, you know. It was like having tea in a tomb. So that's how I know you read it.'

I could not deny it, and she could see it in my crimson face.

I was expecting rage on her part, or maybe cold anger, the type my father showed when something had gone very badly wrong. I found that my hands, all by themselves, had relaxed their clench and raised themselves up to hide and shield my face.

But then there was a gentle tap on my shoulder. She had stepped forward and was holding out half of the eiderdown, as if to put it round my shoulders too. Hardly knowing what I was doing, I accepted it, and together we sank to the bed.

'I wanted to say …' she began, but stopped.

'It's all right,' I whispered quickly. 'It's true my father sent me to you, and I know you don't like him. I'm sorry.'

'No!' she said fiercely. 'You've got it all wrong. All wrong! I mean, I did write nasty things about you in the book, but only because *they read it*. Every day, Lehzen or my mother, one of them or the other or even both, reads the Behaviour Book. It's part of the System.'

I could feel my eyes popping out of my head with surprise. If I knew it was wrong to read a diary, surely these grown-ups must know it too?

'It's a *sham* diary,' Victoria explained. 'I have to put down something that they will swallow. And I have to convince them that we are not friends. If they think that I have a friend or a new sister …'

Here she shuddered, and I felt the pressure of her shoulder against mine.

'… they will take you away.'

'Take me away! But where? And why?'

'Because the System requires it. The System means I must have no friends, be left all alone.' She was angry now. I could feel her fists closing and grasping on the soft eiderdown.

'Victoria, Victoria, don't upset yourself!' I was stroking her hair as I might have done to Dash. But she was gone from me, in one of her strange, passionate fits when no words could reach her. Her eyes were staring at something beyond the patterned paper of the wall opposite the bed.

'Did you know I had a sister once?' Victoria asked suddenly. 'Feodora. My half-sister. Our mother had Feodora with her first husband, before she married my father.'

'And what happened to Feodora?' My hand fell still on her hair. I was on guard once more, for I clearly remembered Victoria telling me that she had no brothers or sisters.

'Taken,' she said glumly. 'She's as good as dead to me. Feodora was my friend. She cared for me and loved me much more than my mother does.'

'Did she live with you here at Kensington Palace?' I asked in wonder. I had never heard of any of this.

'Yes,' Victoria said bitterly, 'until they sent her away. It was ages ago, more than two years. They got rid of her by making her marry a penniless German prince so that she'd have to stay at home with him. She's in Germany now. She writes, but she doesn't love me any more. She has forgotten me.'

I pondered this. It didn't seem particularly likely, but then nothing about this girl's life seemed normal. Victoria's grief was undoubtedly genuine, and I started to stroke her hair once again. Still, I couldn't believe that my father would have done such a thing as to send away Victoria's sister.

Perhaps she sensed this.

'You don't believe me,' she suddenly hissed, with powerful force, 'but it's true. That's why your father is an *evil man*. He got rid of Feodora, who loved me. He drugs my mother – that's why she sleeps all day.' Twisting herself free from my grasp, she was sobbing and panting.

'No, Victoria,' I said. 'You've got it all wrong. He, he *cares* for your safety, you must believe that.'

But she wasn't listening and continued to talk over me. 'I don't know how you can worship him like you do.' Here I could tell that she was rolling her eyes as well as shaking her head.

Eventually she became still. When next she spoke, it was in a much calmer voice.

97

'But you are not like him, Miss V,' she said. 'I do know that.'

She laid a hand theatrically upon her heart and turned to look at me. Then she lifted her fingers to place her palms near my ears, each side of my head, and slowly turned me to face her. Gently, but inescapably, she pulled me nearer until our foreheads touched.

'You are my sister now,' she said quietly and solemnly. 'Never forget it. I love you like my sister, and you are my only friend in all the world.'

I could hardly look back at her because my eyes were so full of tears. A great flower had just opened up inside me.

Despite the strangeness of what she was saying, and my grief at her bitter misunderstanding of my father, a glow spread through my entire body. She had used the word 'sister'. We were sisters! It was as if a gaping hole in my heart was filled up at last.

I could hardly begin to take it in.

I raised my own palms and placed them on top of her hands, pressing them against my head. It was so warm, so delicious to be comforted by four hands instead of two.

Trembling, I opened my mouth to stammer out some sort of reply.

But I was too late. She had broken her grip and was turning away.

'Well, better get back,' she said with a sigh, heaving herself to her feet and leaving my eiderdown trailing across the floor. There was a squawk from the window seat which made my heart jump, but it was only Victoria stamping upon it as she made her ungainly way out of the window once more.

The icy wind was making its way in through the open panes, and the tips of my fingers were still cold, but once I snatched up the eiderdown and wrapped it round me again, I felt warm as toast. Unlike Victoria, who had loved, even if she had lost, this half-sister Feodora, I had never had a friend before.

Chapter 12

The Duchess

The next few weeks passed smoothly and quietly, and I revelled in the new understanding between the princess and myself. Perhaps I deferred to her even more often in our games, and now I never refused the nasty German tea but stoically shared it with her. I stayed longer and longer each evening at her insistence that she could not bear to be alone. I even refused to go with my father when he returned to Arborfield Hall for a few days to see that all was well there and to check that the servants were looking after my mother. The truth, I was surprised to discover, was that I did not want to go.

'I cannot leave, as the princess requires me to be with her,' I explained to him. It seemed rather a rash and self-important thing to say, and certainly my father thought it so.

'What! The little minx needs you every single day, for ever?'

I bowed my head.

'I believe so, Papa,' I said meekly. It did sound rather astonishing that anyone would depend upon my presence. But then I saw his smile and his slow nod of understanding.

'Well, of course I have noticed that you've been spending more and more time over there,' he said, rubbing his chin.

I pulled myself up proudly.

'And that's quite as it should be,' he said, turning decisively towards me and even going so far as to clap his hands together. 'You have made yourself indispensable. You can count upon a Conroy for that. A royal personage must always have a stout shoulder, a companion, someone upon whom to depend. You must stay here at the palace. Your mother will have to make do without you.'

I was reminded how deeply the princess misunderstood his purpose, and it troubled me. But I did nothing but smile shyly, fixing my stare upon the ground.

'And naturally,' he added, 'I will expect a full report on

my return. You must be my eyes and ears, Miss V. Watchful eyes and listening ears – never forget.'

So my father took Edward (who was no longer the 'new' Edward) away to Arborfield with him, leaving me behind with Mrs Keen to keep an eye on me. I enjoyed discussing with her what we should eat and when, and what firewood and candles we required. 'Quite the little housekeeper, you are, Miss V!' she said approvingly. 'I can see why *everybody* relies upon you so much.'

By that significant 'everybody', I knew that she meant the German household across the courtyard, and the princess herself, and it delighted my heart that my special status was recognised.

One day during his absence I came into our sitting room – well, I suppose it was now my own sitting room – to find a strange black cat curled up on the hearthrug. I called for Mrs Keen, who told me that he belonged to the Princess Sophia and that she would take him home at once.

'Oh no,' I said quickly. 'Let me. I shall enjoy being of service.'

I crept up slowly upon the intruder so as not to scare him into running off. He opened his green, glowing eyes and hissed at me for disturbing him. But gradually, after a suitable period of respectful admiration, he consented to my taking him into my arms.

I hurried along the cloister towards the Princess Sophia's doorstep, only to find the old lady standing upon it and looking distractedly in the other direction. When she turned and saw me, she became wreathed in smiles. 'Tiddles!' she gasped, hands outstretched. The powerful black creature hurled himself from my arms and began winding himself round and round his mistress's skirts.

'Thank you for bringing him back, my dear,' the old lady said. 'He is such a good companion to me, and I feared he was lost. Or worse, trying to get into the Kent household to wage war on the parrot once again.'

'I am glad to be of service, Your Royal Highness,' I said, speaking to her for the first time. 'I am afraid we have not been introduced, although I know that you are acquainted with my father.'

'Ah yes, Sir John is a good friend of mine,' she said, bent over to stroke the cat's head. 'And you are a most elegant young lady. It gives me pleasure to see you passing through the palace.'

I could feel a blush rising into my cheeks, and bobbed down into the curtsey that had become second nature.

But now that the courtesies had been executed, I could not let her earlier words pass without comment.

'Did Your Royal Highness imply that Tiddles has already met the palace parrot?' I asked, intrigued.

'Tried to eat him,' said the princess in her loud voice. I believe she was a little deaf. 'Those two animals hate each other. An odd, ugly bird it is. I cannot believe it is a nice pet for a little girl.'

'I believe,' I said, careful of the honour of the German household to which I belonged, 'the parrot belongs to the princess's mother, the Duchess of Kent.'

'Exactly,' the princess said. 'Most unsuitable. And *I* believe she hardly cares for the bird at all, leaving it all to her attendants. Neglectful, I say, shamefully neglectful.'

I left with the impression that the old lady did not approve of the Duchess of Kent. But I liked her love of animals and was glad to have seen a little more of the inner workings of the palace.

On the day of my father's return to us at Kensington Palace, I quietly rejoiced, for I longed to see him again. We expected him after dinner. I made careful arrangements for a tea tray, and laid out his slippers and his tobacco pouch. I hoped he would not be too tired to talk once again about the responsibility we both had to the nation to make sure that the princess grew up healthy and happy. I wanted to share the burden.

As the evening wore on, I flitted about constantly, stirring the fire, setting out the teacups, folding the newspaper just so, running upstairs and down for a book and a handkerchief. Eventually, just for fun, I concealed myself with my book on the window seat behind the curtains, exactly as I had done in the old days in the library at home at Arborfield. Perhaps he would come in to find the room all prepared, and then I could surprise him by slipping out. 'Miss V!' I imagined him saying, in mock alarm. 'Have you done all this for me? Where have you been hiding?'

The thought made me smile. Looking out of the window and through the trees I could just see the lights of the carriages passing along the distant road. The twilit gardens were very beautiful, and for once the reminder of the world beyond seemed almost romantic to me.

Very soon I heard the door opening, a heavy walk and a heavy sigh. He must be here! I hugged myself in delight. Now he was ringing the bell for tea, but I had asked Mrs Keen not to answer, saying I would get him anything he wanted for myself. Just a second more, I told myself. Let him sit down on the sofa.

I heard the familiar creak of its springs.

But suddenly, before I could move, the calm of the evening was broken by a violent hammering at our door.

The door gave on to the brick-arched cloister within the palace rather than a street, and I don't believe I had ever heard a caller knocking upon it before.

'Damnation!'

From behind my curtain, I heard my father stumble to his feet. My limbs were curiously slow to move, and a chill passed over the nape of my neck. It had all gone wrong, I concluded with chagrin. Everything always went wrong when I tried to be spontaneous. I tried to overcome my instinct to stillness and silence, but the hammering had disconcerted me, and I could not gather myself to stand or speak.

In a moment or two, I heard the door creak open and my father's muffled exclamation, 'Your Royal Highness!'

Was the princess here? My heart started into my mouth, and I frantically began to pull on my slippers in order to swing my feet down from the window seat. Too late! The visitor was already in our drawing room. I was trapped.

'Where is it, Sir John?' But this was not Victoria. It was a woman's voice, low, gruff, German-accented. But nor was it Späth nor Lehzen.

'Come, come, Your Royal Highness!' I could tell that my father had been caught off guard. A false tone had crept into his voice, that note I recognised from when he told my mother that of course he never took tobacco.

'Where is it? You promised me!' She was moving round the room, almost trotting, opening drawers and banging them shut. There was the rustle of silk and the clash of bangles or bracelets.

'Indeed I did, indeed I did. It slipped my mind. Here, I have been to the chemist's shop today. Here's the package.'

'Sir John! Be quick! My heart is so faint!' There was a rustle of paper, a drink being poured and a chink that might have been the stopper knocking against a glass bottle. Medicine of some kind, clearly.

There was silence, in which I could just hear breathing and the small sucky sounds of drinking. The breathing slowed. It became inaudible. There was a final rustle, as if the lady had sat down upon the sofa.

'There, my dear!'

I thought that my father must have spotted me behind the curtain and wanted me to come out. I steeled myself, fearing ridicule and embarrassment. But no! He wasn't speaking to me.

'Has it been a bad time, my dear heart? Have the hours been long and the princess noisy?'

Who was it that he was calling his 'dear'? Suddenly it

came to me. This was the Princess Victoria's *mother*, the unseen Duchess of Kent, and my father's employer and benefactor. He seemed very casual in talking to her. Was this really the voice of the mysterious duchess? The surprise made my mouth pop open, and I tightened my arms around my bent knees. What on earth did she look like? Was she as grim and spiteful as her grey parrot?

'Ah, so long, Sir John!' She seemed almost to sob the words out, and I heard writhing about, as if she were uncomfortable on our sofa. Yet it was a far better piece of furniture, stuffed with horsehair and upholstered in pink satin, than the decayed old heap in the German sitting room.

'My head kept me in bed today,' she said confidentially. 'Lehzen sat with me while Späth had the girl, but I could not bear the sound of her crunching those terrible caraway seeds.' I waited, hardly daring to breathe. It would be awful to be discovered now.

'Come, come, Lehzen is devoted to you!' My father was speaking to her soothingly, almost as if she were a girl herself. His voice sounded as if he too were on, or very near, the sofa.

'And that other girl, your daughter, she is not nice.'

Now a jolt ran through my body, and I almost banged my head against the panelling of the window embrasure.

'She slides around the place all silent, like a shadow. My daughter says she has been poking around and spying and looking at things.'

I waited, astonished, for my father to defend me. Did she mean the business of the sham diary? But surely Victoria would not have told anybody about that: she wanted her mother to think it was real. How dare she accuse me of poking around when I was forced to spend all day in what was effectively a lumber room containing a dangerous parrot! And why did my father not spring to my aid?

'Now, now, Victoire.' I remembered that the Duchess of Kent shared the same Christian name as her daughter.

'Now, now,' he said again, his voice swelling and growing into what I thought of as his 'public meeting' voice: oratorical, reassuring. 'You know our fears. My daughter Miss V is sensible, quiet, a little dull, yes, but very solid, very calm. We've talked very often about the ... unfortunate illness, what one might call "the madness", of the princess's late grandfather, King George the Third, have we not?'

'Yes,' she sighed. 'Quite true. He would have been in the madhouse had he not been the king.'

'We know the risk.' He went straight on, as if she had not spoken. 'God forbid, but it's possible that this madness may have transmitted itself through the blood to your daughter. You have seen how she sometimes behaves. But, as you know, we take precautions to guard against this ... malady, madness, call it what you like. We must be constantly vigilant. A quiet life, the conscientious company of a trusted companion, that's the best thing for her.'

My jaw dropped open even further than it had before. Of course! The old king had been quite mad; everyone knew that. I knew that, but I had forgotten it, or at least had never thought of what it might mean for his family. Towards the end, the king had lived at Windsor Castle, talking endlessly to his dead wife, asking for the door to be opened so that he could fly up to the stars, riding his valet like a horse and beating him with a crop.

So madness was ... inherited? Hereditary was the word, wasn't it? And Victoria was at risk?

'Oh, Sir John.' The duchess was speaking again, more quietly. 'Of course I'm just a silly old goose. Of course you're right. I sometimes look at her and the way she stamps her foot and refuses to put on her stockings, and I think I see in her a little of ... the old king. Those same blue eyes that seem to pop out of the head. Those rages!'

Her voice rose once again into a wail.

'Mm, mm. But I think we're safe for now.' I heard the

flicking of pages. 'Miss V is very dependable.' It didn't sound as if he were paying much heed to her words, explosive though they seemed to be. Perhaps he had heard them before, many times. Whatever the crisis had been, it appeared to have passed, and my father had returned to his newspaper.

'I'll go, then,' she said. 'I can see you have no time for me.' She sighed heartily.

I could almost imagine her daughter Victoria sighing in exactly the same put-upon manner, with the sulky downward tilt of her little mouth. I could see now where Victoria had learned some of her wayward habits.

'Goodnight!' he said.

I heard the rustling once more.

'Yes, Your Royal Highness?'

'The bottle, Sir John.'

'Ah yes. Here it is, my dear. And let me escort you back.' He rose too, putting the paper down, and presumably handing her this precious bottle. They both moved slowly out of the room. I could hear them talking in the cloister passage beyond. Once the voices had faded, I finally uncrossed my arms and legs, realising that I had been clenching them painfully tight in the anxiety of being discovered and of what I had heard.

So there *was* something my father had neglected to

tell me! He had told me that Victoria was kept under the System for fear of an assault by rival candidates for the throne. But he had not mentioned this second reason: the fear that she might lose her sanity.

I hared upstairs to my room before my father could return and catch me in my eavesdropper's bolthole. But only slowly did my breath return to normal.

I sat looking out into the garden below, thinking it over, trying to prepare myself to go down and greet my father upon his return from Arborfield coolly and normally. Could this explain my friend's unreasonable insistence that my father was evil and that her friends and relatives were spying on her?

Could she, in short, be as mad as the old king her grandfather? My friend, my *sister*, was she ill? My heart ached. If Victoria *had* indeed inherited a tendency to madness, it would explain so much. And yet it was unutterably frightening and sad.

Chapter 13

An Unpleasant Picnic

The news had shaken me to my very bowels, even though a young lady should never admit to possessing such organs.

'Papa,' I began uncertainly next morning at breakfast, 'why does the king not invite the princess to see him? She would so love to visit her uncle.'

'Because he does not love her,' my father said, breaking open his hot roll.

Lately I had taken to leaving untouched the delicious rolls Mrs Keen brought in each morning, because I had heard Victoria complaining that she had only thin oatmeal gruel for breakfast, made with water instead of milk. I knew that this was partly to save money, partly because the System had decreed that Victoria must not learn to love luxury. I did not like to tell her that our own breakfasts were so much better, and so, to give an honest answer if she asked me what I'd had, I only took old leftover bread, with dripping, for myself.

'But why?'

'No member of the House of Hanover loves his relatives,' my father said decisively, reaching for the butter and not stinting himself.

'But why not?'

'Well, Mouse, you are full of questions today. But I will tell you. It is a family tradition. And then, for another thing, the king hates to think of his own death. He hates to think of the Princess Victoria as queen because that would mean that he is dead and gone. And then again, he *really* hates Victoria's mother. He thinks her foolish, and he's not far wrong there.'

Thinking of what I had heard last night, I squirmed a little.

'Yes, I know that you dislike hearing uncomfortable truths, but there we are,' he said, observing me. 'She is an ignorant, cheating, spendthrift woman. That's why we have the System, as I've told you before, to minimise the damage she can do to her daughter with her ignorant and wilful ways.'

114

I wondered why, if this was my father's opinion, he called her his 'dear heart' and fetched her medicine for her. He was a good comptroller, I was sure of that, but I wasn't sure that comptrollers were supposed to address their employers thus. But I couldn't ask him about something like that. It would be pert.

I turned the conversation back to my friend.

'Yet is it not … cruel for the king to hate his niece the princess?'

'Oh, I don't think he hates *her*,' my father said. 'He just does not particularly love her or want to see her. It's the duchess he truly hates. And in fact we do well to keep the princess away from the king, for he is so unpopular with the people. To the British at large she is an interesting young lady, mysterious, virtuous, untainted by the world.'

It made me smile to think of Victoria, such a lover of both naughtiness and fun, as virtuous and untainted.

But now my father had begun to declaim, as if on a platform to a hall full of people. 'When the time comes,' he said, 'she will emerge from seclusion like the answer to a prayer. She will be everything that her fat and wicked uncles are not.'

I could see it now. It made sense. It just seemed awfully unjust that Victoria had to live the narrow life she led here because of these wicked uncles and the accident of her birth.

'But you have given me an idea, my little wise Minerva,' my father continued, completely oblivious. Putting down his coffee cup, he took a turn around the room, his hands behind his back. 'It is as well that the princess should make an appearance at court, so that people do not altogether forget her, and so the king can see she will be a worthy successor. I think that we should send her to the castle.'

And off he stalked, brushing the crumbs from his coat, clearly keen to execute his plan. I finished my breakfast, reflecting on what an active, clever man he was. In the end it didn't matter that he hadn't trusted me with the secret of Victoria's potential madness. For now I knew the truth I could watch out for it myself. I could help carry the load without his even knowing I was doing it.

He did not always have time to talk, for sure, but not every girl's father could speak with such familiarity of Windsor Castle, or tell a king how to order his social life.

The invitation came in just a few days' time, and the princess was shrill with delight. 'We are going to visit my uncle the king!' she cried, just as soon as I entered the room.

'Oh!' I said, sounding as surprised as if the very idea had never entered my head. 'You're going to stay at Windsor Castle?'

'Well, not really,' she admitted. 'It's only to be a short visit, for tea. My mother says we should have been invited to dinner.'

I grimaced inwardly. I had thought it such a fine thing that my father had arranged the invitation, and now the duchess did not think it was quite good enough. I suspected that nothing would ever please her.

But I knew what would restore her to good spirits. 'Tell me in detail,' I said, drawing her down towards the sofa, 'exactly what you are going to wear.'

'Well, of course, I'll need a new dress,' she began. 'Maybe purple satin? Or, I know! Stiff black satin! With white – no, *silver* zigzig decoration around the sleeves and skirt. I saw one in the colour plates. Awfully chic.'

'Oh, Vickelchen!' sighed Madame de Späth, 'You know it cannot be afforded. Will you cease asking, endlessly asking, and give me a little peace?' She waved her white handkerchief like the signal for a surrender upon the battlefield.

'But you can buy it for me, can't you, Späth, if my mother will not?' the princess wheedled.

'Indeed not, Vickelchen. I have not had my salary

these six months. And you should not speak of such things as money before Miss V. Conroy. It is not polite.'

'Nothing is polite, nothing, nothing that I want to talk about!' Victoria threw herself back over the arm of the sofa and drummed her feet upon its seat, to the detriment of the upholstery. 'I want to talk about money and why we have none ... and how my stomach aches, and the servants' love affairs, and how horrid Sir John Conroy is.'

'Then you are a very impolite little girl, and maybe it will be better that you should never be queen.'

'I don't WANT to be queen! I shall do it badly on purpose.' With that she threw herself right off the couch, pressed her face into its cushions and began her painful, heaving sobbing, all the pleasure in the proposed visit to Windsor dispersed.

It was astonishing how quickly these rages could come over her, and I remembered what her mother had said about the rages of her unstable grandfather. *Mad, mad,* whispered a voice in my head. *Would being queen drive her mad?*

Despite her silly whining behaviour, I was sorry for Victoria. It was so rare that she got to do the things she wanted. But I felt less bad when Späth left the room to return shortly with a white muslin dress with ever so

118

many frills and layers. It turned out that the princess already had a perfectly beautiful dress, waiting unworn, and my heart did one of its frequent flips from favour to annoyance. The next argument was over her lace pantaloons.

'You are too young!' Späth remonstrated. 'It would not be right.'

'But my mother wears them!'

I saw Späth swallow her reply as she turned quickly away, presumably because it was unfit for little girls to hear. My curiosity to see the invisible duchess grew even stronger.

On the great day itself, I presented myself early for duty in the German apartment. Victoria had been squeezed into the despised white dress, and a hairdresser came into the old schoolroom to arrange our hair. Once he had finished Victoria's ringlets, he sat me down. I was not able to see myself in the mirror until he had finished. When I did look, he had curled me all over, poodle style.

I felt extremely uncomfortable and stupid, and unlike myself, and Victoria did not help. 'He has done your hair exactly like mine!' she pointed out in a miff. Indeed, our hair was the same colour and texture, and the hairdresser, through ignorance, had styled us as sisters rather than princess and subject.

Mortified, I seized the comb and did my best to undo his work. 'Oh no, oh no,' cried Madame Späth, attempting to stay my hand. 'You look so pretty as a pair! Why, you could almost be twins!'

But Lehzen, standing and peering down her nose at me, gave me a nod. She turned to the hairdresser. 'I think Miss V will look better with smooth hair,' she said. 'The girls are growing so alike, and people need to be able to tell at once which of them is the princess. Such things are important.'

So the hairdresser used his tongs to straighten my hair once again, and within a few minutes, mercifully, I looked just as usual.

But once the hairdresser had finished, and while Späth and Lehzen were helping him to pack up his things, Victoria came to sit next to me on the sofa.

'I'm sorry about your hair,' she said quietly. 'It did look pretty. And it *is* nice to see you looking pretty and lively, you know. It's not a sin or a crime.'

Once again, I felt that cruel crimson flush rising up my throat. Victoria had spied out my stupid embarrassment all too well. I was aware that in my heart I *did* believe that it was a little sinful to dress up and to show off, but also I knew that I would have to endure such things more often as we grew up. I could not bring myself to thank her, but gave her a mute little nod.

Then I sternly told myself I was not a dummy. I could speak.

'Thank you, Your Royal Highness,' I said primly. 'I shall take your views into account.'

It made her laugh. 'Oh, Miss V,' she said in Adams' comedy washerwoman's voice, 'you ain't half a caution.'

Then she was off again into one of her noisy complaints, insisting that she wanted a pink not a blue sash for her dress, and that her slippers were too small and were pinching her feet.

At length we were decreed by Späth to be entirely ready. She made each of us stand before her and circle slowly around so that she could observe us from all sides. 'Perfect, quite perfect!' she said happily, clasping her hands together in pleasure.

'Today there is something I wish you to remember,' cut in Lehzen's calmer voice. 'You are no longer girls. You are young ladies. Let us hope that His Majesty sees you as such.'

Then the two of them hustled us down into the court-yard. Here a large, old-fashioned and unfamiliar carriage stood waiting for us. Upon its door was painted a crest I

121

recognised: that of the dead Duke of Kent. Inside it was seated a large, bosomy lady with a huge feathered hat and a gown cut a little too low. I curtseyed at once, right there in the courtyard, for I sensed that this was Victoria's mother.

She gave me a lordly nod, nothing more, and extended a braceleted arm towards Victoria to help her in. Then Späth and Lehzen and I climbed in too, and we were off. It was a fine feeling. It was a beautiful spring afternoon, with the chestnuts in bud and flower sellers calling out their prices from street corners. I had never been out with Victoria in the carriage before and, despite the daunting presence of the gaudy duchess, it was delightful. Even Victoria had roses in her pallid cheeks. We were to jog our way west through the town, back in the direction of Arborfield Hall.

But soon we were forced to pause in a queue of carriages near the entrance to the park. Looking out of the window, I observed that a crowd, as once before, seemed to gather out of nowhere. People were clustering all around our vehicle.

'It is the Princess Victoria! Look, the prisoner of Kensington Palace!'

To my horror, I realised that the man shouting out meant me. I gasped, and a strong claw-like hand studded with rings grabbed my arm and swiftly pulled me back from the window. It was the duchess, observing and correcting the mistake.

Meanwhile, the kerfuffle outside had drawn Victoria forward in her seat. She smoothed her blue sash and puffed up her tightly fitting lace sleeves around her arms, and in a moment she was eagerly looking out, nodding gravely to left and right as if dispensing a gift to the grateful crowd. Her demeanour was so dignified and regal it was as if she had almost turned herself into a queen already.

At the same time, though, Victoria's ringlets were so tightly curled and so packed beneath her bonnet that I thought she looked a little like a spaniel, and although her dress was very fine, it really was a little short and snug, as she had put on a great spurt of growth recently.

Yet I could also tell, by the hush and the gasps of pleasure from the crowd, that those who had gathered round our stationary carriage were seeing before them not an over-dressed little girl, but a true princess. She was transformed.

The feathered hat of the duchess was nodding in appreciation as her daughter performed. But Lehzen gave me the gentlest of nudges and breathed into my ear, 'There will be a fortune to pay for this later. She gets so excited and worn out after play-acting the part of the gracious sovereign.'

'Off to the castle to see His Majesty … Yes, the princess is travelling with her ladies-in-waiting.' We heard Adams answering deferential questions from the spectators, until eventually the traffic eased and the coachman flicked the whip to move us on.

But soon I had little attention for what was passing around me. I was seated between the window and Lehzen, facing backwards to the direction of travel, while the princess and her mother had the more comfortable forward-facing seats. The movement of the carriage began to make me queasy. The heat seemed beyond what was seasonal, and my own grey silk dress grew unpleasantly tight and stiff.

As the journey gradually turned into a torment for me, I felt myself repeatedly swallowing, trying to keep down my luncheon. The kindly Späth could see something of what I felt and opened the window for me to receive a little air. Lehzen, on the other hand, was by now deep in a volume of dull-looking memoirs, and the duchess was gaily chatting with Victoria in German that I could not understand.

I stared at the carriage floor in grim misery, dimly aware that Victoria and her mother were pointing out the castle itself across the fields. Then there were the noises of a street of shops, then the louder clip of our horses in the quiet of a park. The park seemed to continue for rather a long time.

'This is the turning for the lodge,' Madame de Späth explained, and as the carriage finally drew to a halt, I looked out to discover that we were outside a huge cottage.

'Ach, we are sent to the farm,' said the duchess. 'We should be received in the state apartments, not the pigsty!'

'It's a little more grand than the sty of pigs,' said Lehzen quietly, snapping shut her book, and she was right.

This so-called lodge was white and gabled, its doors and windows opening on to the smooth turf of the park. It was quite vast, its corners and nooks and turrets seeming to extend for miles to our left and right.

Outside the front door there stood an unusual ramp. It was a strange enough sight to capture my attention despite my nausea. I craned to see past Lehzen's bonnet. Even as I watched, the door to the enormous cottage opened and out waddled an immensely fat man. His head was topped with glossy auburn curls and his white breeches were tight over great thighs like hams.

Behind him a couple of footmen began to help – no, to *push* – him up the ramp. It was heavy work. As he neared the top, a little phaeton drawn by two bays came round the corner of the building at a brisk clip and drew up by the ramp. At once the construction's purpose became apparent. It was to propel his enormous bulk into the high seat of his vehicle.

'Oh, Your Majesty!' The duchess was out of our carriage, twirling her parasol and tripping across the gravel. I was unable to suppress a start. I had not realised that this strange sausage-like man could possibly be *the king*. At that very moment, the man thrust himself headlong into his carriage, and there were grunts from inside as presumably he composed himself on the seat.

The duchess continued to trip towards him, calling out something inconsequential in her manically gay voice.

There was a snarl and a growl from the direction of the vehicle, the words indistinguishable.

The duchess stopped, trembled, and then, as if making up her mind, skipped back to us. We could hear her sharp breathing as she approached the window through which we all anxiously gazed.

'The impudence! The man is a devil in human form!' she hissed. 'Vickelchen! Go quickly. He wants only you. No, he does not want your poor mother in his sight, the widow of his poor dead brother, who has given the family so much. No, no. Never a thought does he give to the care I have for your health, your education ...'

But Victoria was already banging the door open and barrelling across the gravel to the king's carriage. She did not need to be asked twice to do something to her benefit. In no time at all, the two faces, one little, one large, flashed us an indolent, insolent look as the little phaeton flew past and disappeared among the trees of the park.

'Well!' said Lehzen, sucking in her breath through her yellow teeth. 'How our princess takes after our king.'

'The collation,' said the duchess, frantically gathering herself together, just as if everything had gone according to plan. 'He said there would be a cold collation and refreshment laid out for us. We had better go in. They will be expecting me. Madame de Späth, assist me.'

Once the duchess's gown and train were arranged to her satisfaction, and her face composed as best as she could manage, we made a stately progress across the gravel. No one paid me any heed, so I attached myself to the end of the procession behind the three German ladies.

We proceeded in through the front door into a fantastically decorated hall. In one corner stood a stuffed tiger, in another a rich coromandel screen. Incense sticks were burning, making the air dense and sweet, while against the incense fought the heavy, cloying scent of lilies. Brocaded curtains kept out the sun, and we were almost blinded by this entry into rich gloom. It was grander, stranger, than any house I had ever seen.

But inside the room a bowing chamberlain beckoned us on through a French window and out into the back of the house, or cottage, or lodge, or whatever it was. Here, on a lawn, was pitched a red-and-gold Chinese-looking pavilion, and on tables set behind it lay a sumptuous tea.

I continued to bring up the rear of our little party, walking as lightly as I could and fixing a smile to my face to show how much I admired and appreciated everything I saw. I tried to recall how Victoria had behaved to the crowd: dignified, queenly. I felt quite the opposite. My skin must have been ghastly and pallid, like death warmed up.

The ladies scurried to the refreshment table, but I hung back. I still felt so sick that I just wanted to sit somewhere quiet where I could not be seen. Hidden away among bushes and great plumes of pampas grasses were tables and little gold chairs, and here I gratefully subsided just before my legs could give way.

But I was not alone for long. Within a couple of minutes, a stout young man plumped himself down beside me, clutching a glass of lemonade. Its delicate stem seemed in danger of being snapped in his meaty grasp. He looked strong as an ox, blond and somehow glossy, as if he were fed on a diet of milk. I was disturbed to find that I could imagine him picking me up, with ease, and spinning me through the air in his arms. I drew myself up in my seat as if to protect myself from such undignified handling. Earlier on I had heard Adams describing me to people on the street as a lady-in-waiting; I must act like one.

'In the party of the Kents, are you?' he asked in a negligent manner, failing either to bow or to introduce himself. I could imagine Jane's exclamation of scorn at the omission. He nevertheless intrigued me. In his blue coat and buff breeches he was clearly not a footman, yet aside from my brothers, footmen were the only strong young men I had yet encountered. My voice seemed to have deserted me, but I summoned up a croak from somewhere.

'Yes, sir. I travelled with Their Royal Highnesses, and I attend upon them at Kensington Palace.'

He drank noisily from his glass. Entranced, I watched the powerful muscles pulsing in his throat as he swallowed the liquid. I wished that I could have had some myself.

'Ah!' He coughed and laughed at the same time. 'I see! That's why they didn't let you ride with the king.'

'What do you mean, sir? … I'm afraid I do not know your name.'

'His Royal Highness,' he said insolently, 'George of Cumberland.'

I bowed.

'Miss V. Conroy.'

'Oh, you must be the daughter of that old dog, Sir John! I think I met your sister at some crush the other day. Pretty filly.'

'Sir John Conroy is indeed my father,' I said in a clipped voice, bowing my head again. I did not want to encourage him, but nor did I quite know how to extricate myself from his conversation. What with the hazy heat of the afternoon, and the weakness of my legs, he seemed to have some hypnotic power.

'Well, no need to freeze me to Hell for it,' he said more jovially. 'A gal cannot help her own father, eh, even if he is a dirty old devil. Did they tell you why you couldn't ride in the carriage with the king, and what happened to the last young lady?'

'The last …?' Disconcerted, I glanced around us, afraid that this crude and disrespectful talk would be overheard.

'The last ... girl they brought with them from Kensington Palace. It was Victoria's sister, Feodora. A tasty piece she was. Half an hour in the carriage with the old king and Sir John was having kittens! He thought the king wanted to marry her, you see. And we all knew what palpitations THAT would cause.'

His conversation seemed both obscure and yet strangely familiar. Victoria had mentioned Feodora to me. Was this a chance to find out more? My curiosity overcame my natural inclination to stay silent.

'What ... palpitations, sir?' I asked in a whisper.

'Well, if my uncle the king had married that Princess Feodora – and perfectly legitimate and royal she was too, no problem there – then old Uncle King Georgy-Porgy might have had a son, and that would have put Sir John Conroy's nose quite out of joint. It wasn't Sir John's plan to have the king marry and produce an heir, no fear of that. If that happened, his plaything, the Princess Victoria, would be displaced from the throne!'

'Sir ... pray ... you speak of my father.' This was awful. I now felt almost desperate to make him stop with his torrent of slangy, scary information.

'Well, my girl, you should know what sort of a man your father is,' he said with a grunt. To my horror, he leaned in close to me, and I could see the blond hair rising and arching from his forehead, and the creasing of the smooth and lustrous skin round his eyes. He smiled. I realised, with a lurch to my stomach, that he reminded me of a dashing villain in a novel, someone who occupied a hinterland between brutish and handsome.

'He wants his little pet on the throne and will stop at nothing to achieve it. Got rid of Feodora, Sir John did. Married her off to some German princeling, sent her away. She was a risk to the System.'

I gasped.

'Oh, it's no secret, you know. Everyone in the family knows about the Kensington System. Your father's machinations are common knowledge.'

I sat frozen with horror, unable to collect myself or excuse myself, although I wanted to scream.

He smiled. He had obviously noticed my discomfort at last. 'Just calling a spade a spade, old girl,' he said. 'We go in for plain speaking in the House of Hanover, you know. Always have, always will.'

I turned my face aside, for I could not bear to feel his eyes hot upon me. I knew that despite his crude attempts to shock and discomfort me, he was drinking in the sight of me. It was an uncomfortable, horrible feeling. My legs began to tremor under the pressure of resisting his gaze.

I was saved by the clutch of a hand on my shoulder.

'Miss V!' It was Madame de Späth. 'I've brought you some lemonade. That carriage ride disagreed with you, did it not? Your Royal Highness, pray excuse me – you remember Madame de Späth from the household of the Duchess of Kent?'

George failed to reply to her, just looked at her dumbly, stood up and swaggered off across the lawn.

'Are you all right, Miss V?' Späth asked solicitously, taking the seat he had vacated and whipping out a fan to waft welcome air on to my face as I panted and gasped like a fish. 'He is not such a nice young man,' she continued, squinting after my tormentor without waiting for my answer. 'Very good-looking, but very stupid too. I know that you are not accustomed to the ways of young men. And I distrust both him and his father, Her Royal Highness's uncle the Duke of Cumberland. Princess Victoria stands between them both and the throne. Our mistress the duchess takes these things a little too much to heart, but I have heard her say that the Cumberlands wish the Princess Victoria had not lived.'

I leaned forward and put my head between my hands.

'Oh, my dear, he has distressed you!' she went on, turning her attention back to me. 'I run on about politics, while you are not well! What can it be that he has said? Do tell me, my dear. I am old and wise.'

I did not want to speak, but her currant-like eyes invited it so earnestly. 'He questioned the Kensington Palace rules,' I said, 'for the princess's … management.'

'Ach, Sir John is so heavy-handed,' Späth said grimly, almost as cross as I had ever heard her. 'I wish he would remember …' Her words petered out. A guilty look came on to her face, telling me she'd recalled that Sir John was in fact my own father.

She could tell that she had made matters worse.

'Oh, my dear, it is nothing,' Späth said, drawing me close to her solid, motherly shape. 'The king and his brothers hate the duchess, our mistress – and her comptroller, your father – quite unfairly, as she is only a defenceless widow in a foreign country with no family to care for her. They attack and seek to wound her, and those who care for her.'

At this, I managed to look up at her and even to squeeze out a wan smile.

'Us poor Germans!' Späth sighed. 'My mistress the duchess, Baroness Lehzen and I – no Britishers care for us or understand us. They say we are full of vice when we are as good as gold. It is our foreignness they hate. Us, they do not really know. They have never taken the trouble.'

I placed my hand on my chest as if to show that I believed her words and intended to pat them into my heart. 'The young man,' I whispered, 'merely sought to distress me with an unpleasant lie. I know that you and Lehzen and my father serve the duchess and the princess faithfully and well.'

I believed that despite the corners he had to cut and the risks he had to take for the good of the princess, my father had her best interests at heart. Well, I wanted to believe it.

Chapter 14

A Dumpy, Plain Puss

On the drive back Victoria was full of jubilation, full of chatter about what she had seen and done. She had driven with the king around the lake in the park, and he had given her a diamond bracelet. She showed it to me on her wrist, and I wondered if she would ever take it off.

'He asked me to choose what the band should play,' she said, a hectic red still suffusing her cheeks. 'There were musicians all ready and waiting in the bandstand, you know, for when we should drive past. And quick as a flash I said I'd like to hear "God Save the King"! It was clever, was it not? And then he gave me the bracelet.'

The ladies Späth and Lehzen greeted this with

enthusiastic cries. But the duchess, who had been full of life on the way out, sat silent and chagrined. I suspected that she had not quite recovered from the king's refusal to take her along for the carriage ride. I was glad that Victoria was in her bumptious mood, for no one noticed that my own silence was even deeper than usual.

My head told me to set aside what Victoria's handsome but cruel cousin had said, but my heart was not convinced. And he had indeed confirmed some part at least of what Victoria had said about the mysterious Feodora.

The next day I asked Victoria to tell me more about her cousin. 'Oh, old George!' she said. 'He's quite bonkers. But then all my relations are. His father is the Duke of Cumberland, you know, and a very dark and sinister man.' For a moment Victoria sat silent, and shivered. 'But George is all right, if he can forget for a minute or two that I am ahead of him in line for the throne. I wish I could just give it to him and have done with it.'

'But did you not like being with your relatives yesterday in Windsor Park? One day you will be there, with them, the whole time.'

She turned to me, and I saw her eyelashes flutter down over her cheek. She was thinking, and looking down at her hands.

'Of course, I like it at the time,' she said. 'I like people noticing me and praising me. But then afterwards I feel so … fevered. I cannot sleep. In the end, Mother gave me some of her drops last night. I hate those drops.'

She said it so simply and so sadly that I felt my own shoulders droop as if under a great weight of sorrow.

Since the dreadful day when Lehzen had revealed Victoria's position in line of succession, I had never heard her say anything positive about her future. I could see that she feared what was to come.

'Anyway, you shall meet George again for yourself tomorrow,' Victoria said, with new energy. 'Apparently my mother invited him to tea when she saw him yesterday.'

The news filled me with foreboding, and Victoria noticed.

'What's wrong?' she said. 'He's a great chump. He hasn't been chumpish with you, has he, Miss V? Why are you set against him?'

I shrugged my shoulders.

'I know!' Victoria crowed. 'Perhaps he's fallen in love. Is he in love with you, Miss V?'

It was such a ludicrous suggestion that I rolled my eyes. I managed to gather up enough spirits to biff her playfully over the head, and soon we were cheerfully arguing about whether we should pick our own flowers for tomorrow's tea table for George Cumberland and his father, or whether Späth would decree that we could afford to have some bought.

The next day, the shutters were opened for once in the big upstairs drawing room, the one we never normally used except for hide and seek. The covers were drawn off the red silk furniture, and the vast cavernous space lost its usual appearance of a junk shop. It almost looked like a drawing room in a palace – albeit a shabby and cobwebby one.

Strong, blond George was accompanied on his visit by his father. The Duke of Cumberland turned out to be a distinguished-looking old gentleman. He stalked into the room like an elderly vulture. The hair was sparse around the sides of the dome of his head, but he had enormous mutton chop whiskers along the edges of his jaw.

'Miss V. Conroy,' murmured Lehzen, as she presented me, 'companion to the young Princess Victoria.'

He merely glanced at me and grunted. In his desultory look I saw no kindness, no interest. Instead, I glimpsed something buttoned-up and fierce. I was glad when he soon became ensconced with the German ladies and the duchess, telling them some long and boring story in a booming voice, while George wandered over to the window seat where I sat with Victoria and Dash.

'Hello, Vicky,' he said absently to the princess, swinging Dash up into the air. This gave me pause for thought, for I did not trust this young man, and I did not like to see Dash in his hands.

'Fine little puppy!' he said, seeming to examine Dash, though once again I felt his eyes passing over my face and figure. I looked down, trying to avoid his gaze.

'I see you enjoyed your ride with the king the other day, you hussy!' He spoke to Victoria in a loud, jesting tone, but she seemed not to mind. She twisted her diamond bracelet on her wrist. I could sense that she was blossoming in the warmth of some male attention.

'Would have done you good to walk and lose a bit of fat,' he muttered into Dash's ears, so low that only I could hear. He did have half a point. We were now both exactly equal in height, but Victoria had also been putting on weight prodigiously. I think it was because they rationed her food so severely that she would wolf up anything she could get, including mountains of bread and butter. I darted a quick look at Victoria, but she seemed serene. She had not heard, or had not guessed his meaning.

'George!' she said. 'I have had a fine idea. Have you

ever looked at the chart showing how we are related? Lehzen showed it to us once.'

'Oh, the old stud book, you mean?' He was nonchalant. 'What of it?'

Now he was twisting Dash's ears, and I could see that my darling was not happy with this, although he was too well behaved to complain.

'Well, it shows that our fathers were brothers.'

'Yes, of course I know that. Good God, it is almost like talking to the royal librarian. Your information is astonishingly full and accurate.'

But she was smiling up at him, laughing at herself and showing pretty little dimples that were rarely to be seen on a normal day.

'Well, you know that I am to be queen, as things stand, after Uncle William. And you could be king, you know, if you married me!'

He came and stood close to us, Dash still in his arms, and he looked down at her. He was not smiling now, not even looking politely blank. I remembered what Madame de Späth had said about his wish to be king himself. Now I could see a dull red mount up the flesh of his throat, and the sickening-looking white of the knuckles that grasped Dash.

'Don't flatter yourself,' he muttered. 'Don't imagine

that I would ever marry such a dumpy, plain puss as you are. You are mad as a hatter to suggest it. I know why they keep you locked up here in this grim old prison of a palace. Madness, you know. It'll come and get you soon enough.'

He spoke quietly enough for our chaperones not to hear him, but precisely and clearly enough for both of us to be quite sure, this time, of his meaning. He wished to humiliate and to wound. I saw the tears start in Victoria's eyes, and again she shrank back like a whipped dog.

If I could not be brave on my own account, I could do it for my friend.

'Sir!' I said sharply. 'Remember to whom you speak!' And with that, Dash dug his sharp little teeth into our persecutor's hand.

Instantly there was rage and confusion, George shouting, Dash barking and the duchess demanding to know what was happening. I was on the floor, my arms wrapped around Dash, and Victoria was clinging to George's arms, pulling him back while he attempted to aim at Dash a sharp and deliberate kick.

'Sir!'

It was a voice of doom, strong, deep and loud. With a single step, it seemed, my father had swooped forward and almost picked George up by the slack in the back of his coat between his shoulder blades. George's great hammy hands hung, almost uselessly, by his sides, while his face got redder and redder, his eyes popped and his lips moved soundlessly, emitting only a faint *pop-pop-pop* of saliva.

From where had my father come? We did not know. But I did know I had never been more grateful to see him in my life.

The duchess was all flap and flutter, and came bustling over to see what had happened. But I think that all three of us realised simultaneously that the scene was not to our credit, and we subsided, each of us studiously avoiding the gaze of the others. My heart was thudding almost as loud as thunder. I felt full of mortification, but there was … something else there too, a sensation in my heart that was hard to identify.

I got it at last. I had been brave! I had spoken up for my friend. I felt a righteous glow and looked up with the intention of speaking, of denouncing Cumberland once again.

But at that very moment, my eye met my father's, and what I read there instantly quelled any final thoughts of self-justification.

George found himself dragged to the tea table, while Victoria and I were told to take Dash outside to run off his energy.

'He is a liar, a liar!' Victoria said to me under her breath as we walked too fast through the garden. Her fists were once again clenching and unclenching by her side, and her gaze was fixed on the path ahead. 'I know I am not mad. I know it.'

Neither of us had before dared to mention the word 'madness'. It was too deep, too dangerous.

'Believe nothing that he says,' I said, linking my arm through hers and bringing her to a halt so that she would listen to me. 'And you are *not* plain,' I said, loyally. 'You are as pretty as a picture. I give him no credence whatsoever.' It was true, for more reasons than Victoria knew, and it gave me great relief to say it out loud.

Chapter 15

A Night with the Princess

ell, we had longed and prayed for something exciting to happen, and now it had. What foolish rashness!

I missed our old peaceful life, and I also missed my friend. It seemed that Victoria's spirit had ebbed away after our foray out from Kensington Palace into the world and its consequences. She had once again become the lonely little ghost that I had known upon my first arrival at the palace. Life returned to its familiar rhythm, but our circle felt smaller, the prison seemed tighter, the passage of time ever slower.

'It is so stupid, the System!' Victoria whispered to me one day, while Lehzen was taking stray seeds from our seedcake and feeding them one by one to the parrot. 'Nobody wishes me ill. You saw that yourself when we rode to Windsor Castle. The people were *pleased* to see me. I'm not in any danger. I am locked up here for nothing.'

I saw the nervous, strained look in her eyes and the anxious, repetitive movements of her hands.

'Locked up,' she muttered again, 'locked up, locked up.' She drew her knees up upon the sofa and hugged them. I sat down next to her, reaching out a hand towards her arm, but she whipped her head away. '*Lehzen,*' she screeched suddenly and shrilly. 'Put the cover on. He's *looking* at me again.'

Lehzen turned from the parrot in some surprise, and we both stared at the miserable figure bent almost double on the sofa.

'That was not a ladylike way to speak,' Lehzen said, after a pause, in her measured tones. I expected a retort from Victoria, but this time none came.

Not for the first time, I wondered if the risk to Victoria's mental health came not from her grandfather, but from the System itself. I wondered how I could ever find the strength to raise such a concern with my father. But then, I was beginning to feel that it was my duty to do so. The words that expressed my fears fought their way up my throat each night when I made my report, but still I swallowed them down again. Perhaps tomorrow, I told myself.

But there was no chance. The very next day, Späth went away on a visit, Lehzen had a cough and the duchess had one of her nameless illnesses. Instead of asking for his usual report at teatime, my father told me that because of these three things combined I should go across to sleep that night with the Princess Victoria in her bedchamber. Because, of course, she could not be left alone.

It felt very strange, as evening drew down, to gather my hairbrush and my nightdress from my own bedroom, and then, instead of climbing into bed, to walk in carpet slippers behind my father across the cloister and court-yard. Odd, but a tiny bit exciting too. Victoria and I would be unsupervised! What games might we get up to? What dresses might we try on? If she hadn't been so out of spirits recently, I would have predicted a marvellous time.

Adams silently let us in, and I said 'good evening' instead of our usual 'good morning'. The cavernous stair-case was illuminated by streaks of light from the setting sun that were almost green in hue. I felt I could have been in the abandoned marble temple of some long-lost civilisation, like that of the Romans, which had been deserted by human beings for many hundreds of years.

In the corridor of the drawing room we continued

along another few feet to a door I'd never opened before: that of Victoria's bedroom. My father rapped.

'Your Royal Highness?' he said.

Silence.

'Your Royal Highness, Miss V. Conroy is here.'

More silence.

All of a sudden, the door flew open abruptly, sending my heart into my mouth. Victoria must have been waiting, silently, with her hand on the knob, boiling perhaps with rage or fear, intending to surprise and distress us.

Wordlessly, she looked at us, and I saw the distaste in her eyes.

My father stood back to let me enter, and I padded forward. With an ironic, courteous bow, and a twirling, doffing movement of his hand, as if removing an imaginary hat in the most elaborate manner possible, he backed out and closed the door.

'Good Lord, I hate him!' Victoria seated herself on one of two beds in the room. 'I'm sorry, Miss V, but I really do despise him.'

For once, I did not listen. I was fairly captivated by the room itself, and prowled round inspecting it. Its ceiling was high, like the drawing room next door, and again it was luridly furnished with mirrors in heavy frames, an overflowing needlework box, plumes of feathers arranged in vases and a loudly ticking clock. The two beds with their white quilts looked very small and clean amid the junk and the murk. I noticed that one of the beds had a couple of the dolls tucked into it. We had not played with them in a long time, and I thought she had given them up.

'That's your bed,' she said in a dull voice, nodding at the other. 'I wish you joy of it. I'm sorry that you have to be here with me.'

I thought sadly of the night she had come to my room and told me we were sisters. Were we still sisters? I did not know. But then I gathered myself together. *Silly!* I said to myself. *It's not her fault. It's the System's fault. Perhaps she'll feel better soon.*

'That's really quite all right,' I said out loud, stepping this way and that, putting down my things. After all, I was genuinely glad and interested to see this inner sanctum. 'I'm happy to be here. It's nice to see your room. Where are they?'

Victoria had no need to ask whom I meant. 'My mother is in the dressing room,' she said, nodding towards a door in the corner. 'I think she has had too many drops today. And Lehzen has her own room along the corridor. She's been hacking away all evening.' Right on cue, a distant, muffled bark told us that Lehzen's cough had failed to improve.

I lit a candle, the chink of the flint sounding unnaturally loud, and quickly put on my dressing gown. 'Come on,' I said, jumping on to my own bed and squirming about to see if it was comfortable. 'Let's talk about ballgowns. Which do you prefer: rose-coloured or gold?' At that, Victoria also threw herself back on to her quilted bed without bothering to remove its cover, or even her slippers. I had hopes that my ploy might work. This was a favourite topic of conversation, and Victoria had many times described in the tiniest detail to me the first ballgown she intended to wear just as soon as she was sixteen. Every time we talked, its colour, cut and decoration underwent revision.

'Well, I've had a new idea,' she admitted grudgingly. 'Lace. Did you see Späth's *Illustrated London News?* And the picture of the dresses at the ball at Marlborough House?'

We lay back on our beds and began comfortably to chat. As the discussion of the merits of lace continued, the shadows inside the room clotted in its corners until the glow of the candle was the only light. The sky outside the two tall windows darkened to navy blue, and the clock sounded very loud in the silence. We'd left the windows and curtains open, for it was rather hot and heavy.

I hardly remember at what point I fell asleep, but I believe we were midway through a discussion of the best trimming for fans. Suddenly I awoke, and I could tell at once that it was much, much later. The candle had burned out, and the room was still.

Except for a tiny sound. It must have been a repetition of the sound that awakened me.

It was the creak of a floorboard.

I tensed up at once. The linen sheet had slipped away, the air was cooler now, and I felt all the little hairs on my arms stand up on end. Was it the duchess, awoken from her trance and come in to see us? But Victoria told me that the drops from the green bottle made her mother stupid and sleepy. It was yet another thing she held against my father, for, as I knew, he brought them from the chemist himself.

And in any case, it sounded like a heavier tread than a woman's, shifting the floorboards beneath the flowered carpet. I could see the window from where I lay, and through it the gleam of the moon. Suddenly, the moon was blotted out of my vision and a dark shape crossed it. I saw to my horror that it was a man in a black coat, a man with his two hands outstretched …

I felt such terror as I had never before experienced in my whole life. It took all my wits and energy to act and move. But move I did, leaping from my bed and screaming like a maniac.

'Help!' I shrieked. 'Help us! Help!'

It seemed to me, as best as I could see in the darkness, that the figure froze mid-motion, almost like a dancer.

'Help! Lord preserve us! Help!'

I flailed about blindly in the dark, feeling for something, anything with which to protect myself. With a crash a glass of water fell from the bedside table.

It was commotion enough. Along the corridor I heard a door open, while Victoria in her corner of the room was saying, 'What? What?' Her voice was still full of sleep. I heard, rather than saw, the dark-clad figure retreating to the window, and out, out across the roof.

I was standing dumbly by my bed, still trembling, when the door crashed open and Lehzen appeared. I gathered my wits as well as I could. 'It was … it was a man, Lehzen!' I just about managed to gasp out the words.

'Has he gone? Has he gone?'

As she spoke, Lehzen was peering out of the window, and then she was back by my bedside, holding the brass candlestick to my blinking face and examining me. 'You frightened him, Miss V!' she said triumphantly. 'You did very well.'

I found that I was brandishing my hairbrush as if it were a weapon and, feeling rather sheepish, I hid it behind my body.

Now Adams was in the room too, bringing an oil lamp and searching behind and under every piece of furniture. A minute later, my father too had made an appearance, wearing his dressing gown and closing the sash window with an angry bang. I wondered how he had got here so quickly.

In the middle of it all sat the princess, bemused rather than frightened.

'What happened, Sir John?' she asked.

'It was an assassin, sent to kill you, Your Highness.' He spoke in a matter-of-fact voice, but he made no attempt to hide the gravity of the situation. 'This is what we had feared. They must have kept a watch and discovered – I don't know how – that your mother and governess had left you tonight.'

Lehzen and he exchanged a long, hard glance. But she was the first to lower her gaze.

I could tell that beneath his sombre manner there was something exultant about my father. Oh, of course! He had predicted exactly this eventuality, and by sending me into the princess's room he had successfully avoided the danger.

'But all is safe,' he said. 'Our security arrangements have held firm. If you had been alone, Your Royal Highness, who knows what would have happened?'

Victoria's eyes had grown very big and round, and she wrapped her arms around her knees beneath the sheets.

'But who could have sent such an … assassin?' she asked in a very small voice.

'Why,' said Lehzen slowly, 'the obvious candidate is the Duke of Cumberland. Your cousin George's father. I wonder if it was him? Or someone else?' Lehzen, oddly, had looked again at my father. She was really staring hard at him.

There was a strange silence. Then she dropped her eyes.

'But …' It was Victoria's voice. It trailed off, then began again. 'Would he kill me just so that George could be ahead of me in the line of succession? George's father was here just the other day, and you all had tea with him!'

'At a tea party!' Lehzen snorted. 'He may be nice enough at a tea party, but this is the man who killed his valet.'

'There was no definitive evidence of that,' said my father in a lofty manner, 'but I think you'll agree – all of you – that what I have told you about security has been right and proper and true.'

All three of us looked back at him, and then at each other. It seemed undeniable. I felt ashamed that I had doubted, only recently, whether the System was good for Victoria. He came over and patted me on the head. 'There is great danger,' he said solemnly. 'Great danger. But you, Miss V, have averted it. God bless you.'

'Oh!' Victoria cried. 'God bless you, Miss V! But Miss V cannot be here always, Sir John. What might happen next time?'

We sat looking at each other in silence. Not one of us had the answer to that. How could we keep the princess safe?

As one, we turned towards my father. Only he seemed to know.

'Your Royal Highness,' he said with a bow. 'Miss V. Conroy will stay with you always. She will never leave you. She will live here, not at Arborfield Hall, and she will keep you safe.'

I felt a deep trembling going right through my body. My doubts about the System had been misplaced; of course it was necessary. But could I really keep Victoria safe *and* sane? I wasn't sure.

Chapter 16

A Sight I Wish I Had Not Seen

he next day, I was walking back through the cloisters towards our apartment and thinking over the midnight intruder. Had he really been sent by the wicked Duke of Cumberland, or not? It seemed so unlikely, but then there was much that was unlikely about our strange lives in this strange palace. I mentally corrected myself at once: this was no longer a strange palace; it was now my home. Of course I could not leave Victoria to return to Arborfield. I had known that even before my father put it into words.

I was musing upon it all so deeply that when the sleek black cat belonging to the Princess Sophia darted across my way, he almost made me trip. He had the welcome effect of shaking me out of my trance. I now noticed that a shaft of late afternoon sun caused the old brick walls to glow red, and that in the beam danced motes of dust. Summer had come upon us unobserved, and it was beautiful. This would not be such a bad place to live.

I decided to take Dash out for an evening run along the lime walks, round the clipped hedges and even among the trees of the park. I was not explicitly confined to the gardens as the princess was, so I plucked up my courage to pass the guards and go out. I wished they would not present their weapons to me with a shout and the clashing of metal as I passed. It made me feel so foolish, although I had grown more used to it than I would have thought possible. And they had not kept out the assassin. Even now, men were installing new bars in the window openings of Victoria's bedroom.

But it was worth running the gauntlet to have some freedom and fresh evening air. Now I felt that I could glide noiselessly and unnoticed between the trees as dusk fell, as the toy sailboats were lifted from the lake, and as the nannies scolded their children homeward.

Dash had a vast amount of energy as usual, more than seemed quite possible for such a small dog. He led me on a great chase through the long grass, beneath avenues of elms and chestnuts and around the snake of the lake. We were approaching the little stone grotto on a grassy knoll where I had heard tell that Queen Caroline, Victoria's many-times-great-grandmother, had liked to sit. It was a useful destination for a walk. It was then, as I drew near, that I heard the sound of angry voices.

Or were they angry? They were speaking in low, urgent tones, and they arrested my attention because they were familiar. Too familiar.

Almost unconsciously, I found myself stepping behind the hanging bows of a low cedar tree and drawing Dash close to me. The little stone grotto received the last rays of the sun, and against the pallor of its white stone I could clearly see the outline of a writhing shape. Or at least it looked at first like the shape of one living creature, but as its form shifted I could see quite clearly that it was two people, a man and a woman. The man, taller, stronger, had the woman locked in his arms, and she was moving, struggling, in a strange way. I could tell at once that this was not play-acting, as Victoria and Dash might pretend to fight, but deadly serious.

And I knew at once what it meant when a man squeezed a woman in his arms like that. When he kissed her on the lips. I was not stupid. I had seen people in the park and on the streets.

And I also knew, with horrible certainty, that I was

looking at my father and the duchess. My mind darted back to the time I had heard them sitting together on the sofa. Had they been too close to each other then, too? Didn't he care about my mother? What about me? Bile lurched into my throat.

I turned instantly upon my heel and scurried back to the palace, not even waiting or watching to see if Dash would follow.

I decided at once to pretend that I had not seen it, and never to mention it to anybody.

Chapter 17

'Pretend All Is Well'

It was Lehzen who noticed that I had something on my mind.

Her lean figure suddenly loomed above me as I sat on the sofa in the princess's apartment the next afternoon, trying to concentrate on my book. The whiff of caraway preceded her as she leaned over with a newspaper to slap at a fly buzzing against the pane of glass behind me.

Victoria was at the pianoforte, separated from us by several overstuffed chairs, a variety of little tables, a potted fern and a broken rocking horse. As usual her playing was more *forte* than *piano*. She was practising scales, which sounded like a giant running up the stairs and back down again. There was no denying that she had a great love for music but, as Lehzen was constantly telling her, she lacked lightness of touch.

Lehzen's deadly aim dispatched the fly. She raised the sash to let in a little more air, but instead of retreating back to the stool from where she'd been turning the pages of the music for the princess, she folded her angular body down on to the sofa next to me.

'What are you reading, Miss V?'

Lehzen, I knew, would never embark directly upon a personal conversation, so I understood that this was just a warm-up question. I showed her the volume of poetry I held in my hand, though in truth I had absorbed little of it.

'Sir Walter Scott … "The Violet" …' she read, talking out of the side of that mouth of hers that never seemed to open itself properly. 'Violet, lavender, mauve … and you, Miss V. Conroy, are looking mauve under your eyes today, and very pale too. Did you not enjoy a good repose last night?'

I looked away from her out into the sun-filled court-yard. Today a ginger cat belonging to one of the sleepy apartments on the other side sat on the step licking itself. It was the only sign of life.

'It was a little too hot for sound sleep,' I conceded.

I had gone up early so that I would be out of the way when my father returned. I had the excuse of our disturbed rest the night before. But then, naturally, I had been unable to sleep and had risen several times in the night to open the window and to fetch a glass of water.

'You are in many ways the oldest and wisest of us all,' Lehzen continued, staring straight ahead at the potted fern and leaning forward to snap off a dead dry frond from it, just as if her mind were quite concentrated upon the care of houseplants. 'But I fear,' she continued, 'that despite having your father to hand you must miss your mother.'

'My mother is not ... like the duchess,' I stammered, uncomfortable with the more delicate turn our talk had taken.

'You mean she is not so passionate, so bold?' Certainly Lehzen was right to note that the duchess was a tempestuous character. But what I had really meant was that I'd observed, despite the drama, that the duchess was deeply devoted to her daughter, while my own mother back at Arborfield had seemed scarcely to notice when I came or went. As far as I knew, she had never asked after me since I had left. And she had still never once written.

I did not want to think about the duchess, though, so

I sat mute, shaking my head. To my horror, tears had filled my eyes.

Lehzen's bony hand was on top of my own. 'What is it, little one?' she was whispering in her deep voice. Victoria had moved on to arpeggios, staring down at her fingers in total concentration. 'What has upset you?'

'My ... father ... I saw ... the duchess ...'

Her unexpected kindness had overwhelmed me, and I could not keep the quaver out of my voice as I tried to swallow a sob.

Lehzen looked grim. Abandoning the pretence that the potted plant interested her, she twisted my unwilling shoulders towards her and forced me to look up at her. 'What do you mean?' she asked sharply. 'Did you see something ... improper?'

From the concern in her eyes, I realised that she had suspicions of her own. 'Last night,' I stammered, 'I ... saw them ... t-t-together.'

It was a breach of the System to mention it, I sensed that. I knew that nothing good could come of this. I had vowed to say nothing. But it was such a sweet relief to share what I knew, even with the desiccated Lehzen.

'What were they doing?' she hissed.

Victoria moved on to a creeping, hammering finger exercise that created a cloud of sound.

'I saw them together. Out in the grotto. They were hugging, or … fighting, or something. It seemed wrong.'

Lehzen's hand flew up to her mouth. '*Lieber Gott!*' she hissed. 'I had hoped there was no truth in these rumours.'

I hung my head, panting. For a moment I wished that she would treat me a little less like a colleague and more like what I was, her pupil. I needed someone to tell me what to do.

She seemed to recollect this.

'Your father,' she said sternly, 'is not the only father in the world to have a … lady friend. It is quite normal. You know that even the king himself has lady friends, many of them. So does his brother the Duke of Clarence, who lives with an actress. It is not uncommon in good society. Even the Princess Sophia, who lives across the courtyard, has an illegitimate son, you know.'

I was surprised to hear this, but it did not really help. I hung my head lower, while tears trickled silently down into the bib of my pale blue summer dress. My own father! I had thought there were no secrets between us. It pained me to think that I was wrong.

She gave me an awkward pat on the shoulder, and in no time at all I found myself cradled against her angular bosom. 'They have no discretion!' she said. 'They will bring down the System if they are not careful. And what will become of us all then?'

I sniffed and hiccupped. 'But what should I do? I think I must ask if I can go home. I must ask my father if I can go home to my mother.' My words came out as half a whisper, half a sob.

'No,' said Lehzen firmly, 'you cannot do that. The princess needs you. We must all be together.' She paused, sighed and continued in a softer voice. 'Madame de Späth and I need you too. We have come to love you, you know. Do not leave us.'

A new fountain of tears started up in my eyes. Lehzen was sitting up straight now and spoke more decisively, handing me a handkerchief. 'I am pleased that you have told me,' she said. 'But nothing good can come of your speaking of it to anyone else. Pretend all is well.'

Then she turned away from me. She muttered something, as if to herself, but with my sharp ears I heard her quite clearly. 'But it is different for me. I cannot allow this to go on.'

Feeling just a little better, I took the handkerchief, dried my eyes and was even ready with weak applause when Victoria's performance drew to its merciful end.

Chapter 18

Where Is Späth?

The following day the weather broke. There were wild winds and clouds once more, shaking the petals from the roses in the gardens and promising rain to come.

I watched my father eating his breakfast and reading his letters, marvelling that his familiar face revealed nothing of his secret life. I could scarcely eat or drink myself. For once, my thoughts returned to my mother, marooned on her sofa. I had begun to realise why he and I were here, at Kensington Palace, so far from our real home. He didn't love her. Perhaps he had never loved her.

'Toast, please, Miss V.'

His words were curt, and he failed to look up as I placed it silently before him.

'Papa, have you heard from Jane?' I asked timidly, as he riffled through the stack of papers in his hand. Although the air was still warm from the recent heatwave, I felt chilly and tired, and a headache hammered in my skull. It had just occurred to me that perhaps he didn't love my sister Jane either, for he scarcely ever spoke of her. And if this were true, could I even be sure that he loved me? I pleased him, I knew, but that was not the same thing.

'Of course not,' he said. He lifted his new eyeglasses to his nose, peering at one particularly closely written letter, brow furrowed. He looked tired and unhappy, not at all like my buoyant papa. 'She never writes. Ungrateful, my family are, ungrateful for all the advantages I have obtained for them. You're too young to remember, Miss V, but it wasn't always like this. It is my hard work that has made our comfortable lives.'

I started at this and shook my head in dismay. I felt very sharply that he could have been talking about me. Here I was, sitting and thinking truly ungrateful thoughts, when that great stack of correspondence showed how busy he was, how much in demand and how responsible.

He must have noticed my small movement of concern and denial.

'Certainly I don't mean you, Miss V,' he said. 'You are my precious pearl.'

And so I was feeling just a tiny bit better when, at ten, I crossed the courtyard as usual to be let in through the grand doorway by Adams, the fat footman. 'Good morning, miss,' he said, as he always did, in response to my greeting.

He led me up the great staircase even though I had now been this way hundreds of times and knew it off by heart. It was as ill lit and chilly as ever on the stone stairs, despite the beautiful day outside.

But something was different about the palace this morning. There was sound and life above us: raised voices in the distance, the drumming of running feet, the banging of a door. Adams' back was impassive, and yet, from the very tread of his feet, more hesitant, less confident than usual. I could tell that something was wrong.

Up in the drawing room, Victoria was waiting for me behind the sofa. We were really getting too grown up to live behind a sofa, I thought, as I sank to my knees on the all-too-familiar carpet.

'What's happening?' I asked, plumping myself down beside her, all my anxiety about my father's behaviour, about the integrity of the System, come back to life. My stomach was a-flutter.

'I don't know,' she said slowly, 'but something's afoot. I have had no breakfast. It didn't come.'

'Victoria, you have chocolate all round your mouth!' I got out my handkerchief, and Victoria obediently tilted her face to let me wipe it away.

'Fusspot!' she sighed.

She had clearly made up for the missed breakfast. We had a secret stash of chocolate hidden in the piano stool, which had been given to me by my friendly housekeeper, Mrs Keen, and smuggled into its hiding place for just such emergencies.

She gave her cheek a final rub but did not remove her eyes from the view out of our window. 'I think I heard Späth and Mamma having a row earlier,' she said.

My heart lurched into my mouth. What could this mean? Had Lehzen said something, then? But if so, why was Späth involved? I had not spoken to her of my troubles. She was so hot-headed I would never have risked such a confidence. I cursed myself. The bottom of my stomach was sinking away down to my soles. There was trouble, and I had a horrible feeling that it was my fault. My father would lose his post, I thought. My mother would be made homeless. I myself might have to leave my friend. I could almost feel the colour draining from my cheeks.

'You look like a ghost!' Victoria said, glancing across at

me to see why I had not spoken. 'Don't take on so. It's exciting to have something happen for once!'

I could see that our lives were so dull that she was greedy for something, anything, to take place. But nothing did for several minutes. Silence once more fell upon the palace. I began to listen for Lehzen's step in the passage, nervous that she would catch us behind the sofa instead of getting out our schoolbooks ready for lessons.

'There!'

It was indisputable, and Victoria turned to me with glowing eyes. We had both heard the slamming of a door and, very distantly, a high-pitched garbled stream of words and imprecations. It grew louder and louder until, with a great crash, the front door beneath us in the court-yard flew open.

Out on to the cobbles was thrown a carpet bag. It was not done up properly, and something white and frilly was spilling out of it into the dust. Next came a trunk. Adams appeared, carefully carrying a birdcage – a small one, not the parrot's. Whose luggage was this? Adams headed off in the direction of the street, and silence returned.

The next excitement was a hansom cab bowling into the courtyard with what seemed like a tornado of noise and dust. This was now certainly the greatest upheaval we had ever witnessed in the quiet courtyard of Kensington Palace. Adams and its driver began packing the luggage, and then, with a flounce, the short, fat figure of Madame de Späth hurled itself into the hansom.

And it drove away.

'Späth?' Victoria was all agog. 'Späth! But where has she gone?' I could see now that her curiosity was turning to fear.

I pleated my skirt nervously. Surely Madame de Späth had not abandoned us? It looked horribly like it. How could we survive within the System without her friendly face? Victoria's stricken expression told me that the same thought had occurred to her too.

We were still on the carpet, craning to see any further developments, when, as I feared, the drawing room door suddenly slammed open. Lehzen was calling out, 'Girls! What is the meaning of this? Why are you not at the table?'

But Victoria's emotions were running far too high to be quashed, and she leapt up and out from behind the sofa like a young colt.

'Where has Späth gone?' she almost shouted. 'What have you done with Späth?'

She stood before Lehzen, panting, clenching her fists and almost stamping her foot on the carpet. Again the fear of her losing her mind entered my head.

Lehzen was glacially calm. 'She and our mistress, the duchess, have had a … disagreement,' she said in an even tone. 'She has decided to return to Germany.'

Victoria was closing her eyes and opening her mouth. I knew that she was filling her lungs to scream and yell. Lehzen gave a flicker of her eyes towards me. I needed no more information, guessing immediately the disagreement's subject. What else could it have been? Lehzen had told Späth that I had seen my father and the duchess together, and the fiery-tempered nurse had made a fuss about it. More than ever I wished I had been strong enough to keep my secret to myself.

I sat down. I could not help it. My insides had turned into icy cold water.

'This … is … the … doing … of … Sir … John.' Victoria could only speak in jagged, gulping gasps between her tears. 'He wants me to be alone! With no one to love me!' She threw herself down on the sofa in a passion of tears. 'He is a monster,' Victoria moaned, 'a devil!'

Lehzen shrugged her shoulders at me, and we eyed each other across Victoria's heaving body. It was as if we were silently exchanging the same words: *This is a fine pickle. What do we do now?*

All of a sudden, the duchess was in the room, scooping up Victoria in her arms and turning upon Lehzen and me.

'Leave!' she snarled. 'Leave Vickelchen and me alone! We do not need spies and traitors around us!' At his mistress's words, the grey parrot gave a terrible scream, like a banshee.

Lehzen simply raised an eyebrow, but I could see that she was shaken by this new and unexpected turn of events.

'Now, Vickelchen, don't be afraid,' the duchess was cooing. 'I will love you myself, of course. You don't need Späth. You are too big to need a nurse. Now, I have some medicine for you. Drink this.'

'Where is Madame de Späth?' Victoria spat out the words. 'I WANT her.'

'I had to give her notice. She said something very wrong, very improper.'

The duchess was stroking Victoria's hair, while her shoulders heaved and strange, awful mewling noises continued to pour out of her.

'She said that Sir John presumed to act towards me in a way that is not proper for royalty and subject,' the duchess went on urgently. 'It is true, I am sometimes so foolish he shakes me or slaps me. But that is because I forget things, or overlook duties, or neglect to pay bills. A strong man like him occasionally loses his temper and forgets himself, and shakes me – like I shake you, Vickelchen, when you are very, very naughty.'

She gradually, gently, reached out an arm away from her daughter, as if groping for something. And then I saw what her goal was. She had brought with her the small green bottle. I observed it, sitting on the little table by the sofa, with extreme distaste. I felt sure that this was the bottle with which my father treated the duchess herself for 'nerves' and 'indispositions' and other vague illnesses. I also felt sure that Victoria should not drink from it.

Lehzen saw me looking at the bottle and gave a sharp shake of the head. *Not now*, she was saying silently. *Not today, not with this other fight going on. Our forces are too weak.* She took me by the elbow and led me through the door. 'Go back,' she hissed. 'Go back to Sir John and tell him what has happened. He will know what to do.'

I trailed disconsolately down the staircase. I feared for my friend, but on top of that, I feared for my father. Did he love Victoria's mother or loathe her? At the very least, he bullied her. I did not think that he would know what to do. I did not know what to do.

My father ... and the duchess. Those two were the very architects of the System, and yet I feared they had built it upon shaky foundations. I decided that everything I did from that moment on must be aimed at protecting Victoria. And I didn't want her to drink from that green bottle again.

PART TWO

RAMSGATE

Chapter 19

A King's Coach

How cold it was, how blowy! The howling wind whipped past me as I stood on the pavement with Dash's leash in my hand. It continued on its way to batter the lonely street lamps and the benches before transforming the spray from the fountain in the cliff-top garden into crazy horizontal rain.

'Go on, then, Miss V! The sooner you go, the sooner you'll be back, and you need to be back soon.'

Victoria was holding the boarding house door half open against the wind, poking her nose out just far enough to feel the force of it.

'Are you sure you won't come?' I tried to make it

sound inviting, but I knew she would refuse to venture outside on such a day.

'You must be joking!' She wrinkled her nose in distaste, just as she had when we were much younger girls, not young ladies of sixteen, and she was refusing to eat her bread-and-milk. But then she smiled. 'You and Dash enjoy yourselves,' she added kindly. 'I know that there have been too many carriages and drawing rooms for you recently. Go on out and perhaps you'll meet a handsome highwayman!'

'*You* might like that,' I said, and she grinned, 'but I would be frightened. Goodbye! See you soon!'

She was right about my need for air. The last few weeks before we had come for our seaside holiday in Ramsgate had been a blur of travel sickness and temporary accommodation in houses great and small. It had been a trial, and I ran off with pleasure into the wind. If I squinted into the gale, I could see the grey tufty waves of the sea far below. Dash was pulling on his leash, for the wind had excited him and he was skipping and yapping like a mad thing.

As we went, I kept a careful watch out for the regular public omnibus on the road to Broadstairs. Its passage would mark the passing of half an hour, and the time for our return. With the visit of the princess's Uncle Leopold, the King of the Belgians, expected later today, the boarding house was busy, almost frantic, with preparations. It would not do to be absent for too long.

It was pleasant to be avoiding the bustle, even if only for a few minutes. It had been a weary business, these last few weeks of our tour, getting Victoria's dresses clean and brushed, and her hair curled, and our long, ever-changing succession of temporary drawing rooms tidy. These were the duties of Lehzen and I during our month-long 'popularity tour' of the nation, as my father and the duchess called it when they thought that no one else was listening.

My father and the duchess were thicker than ever, as they had been since the departure of Späth, oh, more than four years ago. We had all of us never talked about that upsetting scene again, doing our best to forget that it had happened. Uneasily I had watched and waited, doing my best for Victoria, all of us precariously linked by the same purpose: to see her safely to queenship. They had been very clear in public that the point of our recent tour was to educate the princess about her realm. But the journey's real purpose had been to introduce Victoria to those of her future subjects who loved her, or who loved at least *the idea* of a young princess, so as to pave the way for her reign. And I suspected that the tour was intended, too, to win popularity for my father and the duchess themselves. Everywhere they introduced themselves as Victoria's most trusted advisors.

And so our little travelling circus had been traipsing from town to town, country house to country house, to attend parties and to stay in the mansions of great noblemen. Victoria wore ringlets and danced, and I followed her all the time with my eyes, hoping that she would not overexcite herself. She had lost a little weight, and we looked more like each other than ever before. Each evening I took care to dress drably and to have my hair done plainly. It had to be instantly clear which of us was the princess and which her loyal lady-in-waiting. And as much as possible I stayed demurely behind the scenes, taking no part in the entertainment.

The omnibus passed. I turned neatly on my heel and at once headed home, the wind whipping free some strands of hair that obscured my sight. During our tour, we had had the benefit of nightly attendance by a hairdresser, and the duchess had plunged deeper than ever into debt in order to clothe her daughter. But I was happy that at least Victoria had been guided by me towards sky blue or bottle green rather than the pinks and gaudy golds of her natural taste. Now that we were sixteen, Victoria could see perfectly well for herself from the illustrated papers that I was not alone in thinking that young ladies should not dress as the duchess did. Gradually she had come to share my views. I would never say anything out loud, but Victoria was well able to read my mind each evening when her mother appeared in some fringed and tasselled creation with a low décolletage. A fashion assessment was just one of the many things we could communicate without words.

As I drew near the turn where our boarding house stood on the clifftop, a buffet of wind knocked me almost off my feet. This meant that at first I did not notice the barouche, its hood raised, pulling up alongside me. The fine dark horses were showy, and the vehicle itself, although unflashy, was obviously a luxurious and expensive one. Who could be driving such a vehicle in Ramsgate? For a second, the thought of the Duke of Cumberland crossed my mind. Was he still working his sinister magic? Had he sent someone to find Victoria, invading the privacy of her holiday?

As the mysterious vehicle crept alongside me, drawing to a halt, an icy finger of wind found its way beneath my bonnet and down my back, making my spine tingle. There had been no further hint of trouble since that strange night, years ago, at Kensington Palace. I had never forgotten the dark shape of a man seen against the night sky, a memory that still sometimes woke me sweating and trembling from my sleep.

But we weren't in a novel; we were in Ramsgate. My imagination was running away with me again. Of course, this must be Victoria's Uncle Leopold travelling incognito. He had arrived a little early. The conclusion still left my heart beating unpleasantly fast. Despite my recent immersion into society, the thought of having to talk to people I did not know well filled me with dread.

Now the door to the barouche was opening, and a bald, beaky face was looking out at me. King Leopold was gesturing me in, out of the wind. I had met him before. He was Victoria's mother's brother, German like her, although he seemed much more sensible. Among all her relations, Victoria loved this uncle uniquely well. He was quite different and much wiser than the prickly, pompous and even frightening uncles who were the British brothers of her dead father.

Victoria might call him 'Uncle Leopold,' but to me, and to the world, he was the King of the Belgians, so before placing my foot on the step to climb in, I made a low curtsey right there on the pavement. After all these years of practice, I was secretly rather proud of my curtsey: deep, secure and elegant.

'Ah, Miss V!' He had taken up his family's habit of

addressing me in this unstuffy manner. His friendly familiarity, as much as his accent, reminded me that he was not born in Britain. 'Pray don't reveal my presence to the good people of Ramsgate with your court curtseys. You know,' he went on, 'I quite mistook you for my niece herself and was wondering why she was out unattended. But I am glad to see you.'

Shyly, I returned his smile.

'And I am happy to see you too, sir,' I said politely.

He reached out cordially to take my gloved hand and to draw me up into the vehicle, and I accepted gladly. On his previous visits, King Leopold had always asked sensible, useful questions about his niece's health and security. Now that Victoria's uncle King George the Fourth was dead, there was only one life – that of King William the Fourth – between her and the throne. We had to be more careful than ever.

'Come up, come up!' he was saying. 'And your dog too. Sit down, I beg you, and do me the honour of riding with me back into the ... conurbation.' He produced the word with a flourish, as if proud to have remembered it, even though it was a little grandiose for the small seaside town of Ramsgate.

He called to the driver to move us on. 'And how is the Princess Victoria's Miss V?' he asked, turning back to me.

'I am well, thank you,' I said. 'But you will find Her Royal Highness looking a little peaky, I'm afraid. We have only been here a few days to recover after the many public appearances the princess made on her tour.'

Although she had at first enjoyed the late hours and new faces, the gaiety and the attention, Victoria of late had grown tense and snappish. Indeed, towards the end there had been tears and tantrums, and guests left waiting, disappointed, while the princess howled in rage or despair in her bedroom. We were here in Ramsgate, now that autumn had come, for the healthful sea breezes, before returning to the strict seclusion of Kensington Palace and the System.

I saw a look of concern pass across his forehead.

'The tour may have been tiring,' I quickly added, 'but it was worth every effort for the wonderful welcome she received. Such crowds! Even in the Midlands and the North, where we saw the great factories and the pottery works and the moors.'

The frown was gone from his face. 'I hear from my sister's letters,' he said, 'that the tour *more* than achieved its aim of preparing her people for Queen Victoria's reign.'

I smiled. Of course he knew exactly how to go about the business of being a monarch. There was no tricking a reigning king into believing that the tour had been simply for Victoria's education.

'These are hard times for royalty,' he went on. 'Never was there a period in which real qualities have been called for in persons in high stations. The preparation, the dedication, are immense.'

I bowed my head. I knew this all too well. Victoria often read her Uncle Leopold's letters aloud to me, about service and dignity and self-control, and it seemed to me that they contained wise counsel for a future queen. Victoria might laugh out loud at them, and sometimes call her uncle a dry old stick, but I could see what he was driving at.

Lehzen and my father, who were responsible for Victoria's education, were hardly as experienced in government as this man who was himself a sovereign.

As our sombre vehicle bowled past a long terrace of houses, I noticed through the window that a little girl was watching us solemnly from the pavement. Little did she know that she was seeing a monarch travelling incognito through her town.

'And I know the dedication you yourself give to our family,' he continued, cocking his head to the side in order to catch my distracted gaze. I smiled again, tightly, trying not to show just how very pleased I was. 'My sister the duchess,' he said delicately, 'is not always good at expressing her appreciation. But she knows that you and her daughter the princess are most sincerely attached.'

He could not have known that one of my chief duties, as Victoria's companion, was listening to her complaints about her mother. But I did understand that my years of quiet attendance on the Kensington Palace household had won me a measure of confidence from the duchess.

'You are sixteen years of age – that is right, yes?'

I nodded, astonished that he would have taken the trouble to discover such a trivial fact. But Leopold overlooked nothing. Not even my stupefaction.

'Yes, indeed, I keep a close eye on those near my niece,' he added. 'And, even though you are of age, you must think not of marriage, Miss V,' he said in a mock-stern manner. 'I know that young ladies begin to think of such things when they are past fifteen. But the household cannot do without you.'

'Sir!' I said. 'I have no thought of … such things.' I could feel a blush climbing my throat. Maybe one day I would marry, but until I was released from the System such thoughts must remain far away. Parties, visits, holidays were not for me. Until my work was done, until the System was no longer needed, my duty was to my father, and to Victoria. Or at least it was first to Victoria, and then to him.

All at once, it struck me that Victoria, too, must inevitably marry.

'Yes, yes, unlike you, *she* must marry soon,' Uncle Leopold said, divining my thought and twisting a ring on his finger. 'A spouse is, of course, a great comfort.' Leopold's own wife, Louise, was French, immensely pretty, and Victoria held her up as a heroine for her fashionable Paris gowns.

'To be precise,' he said, 'I have it in mind that she should marry her cousin.'

He could have said nothing to alarm me more. I almost leapt to my feet, hurting my head against the soft padding. 'Oh, sir, please, no! He is ...' I felt unwilling to speak the words, but it was important that he should know, '... a cruel bully. And it is thought that he was behind the ... ah, the security breach, you know, when a man got into Kensington Palace.' I did not call it an assassination attempt. I wasn't quite sure how much he knew.

'Oh, not George Cumberland,' he said with a dismissive wave of his hand. 'One of her good German cousins. Albert, I think, my brother's son. Albert has no happy home life. He lacks a mother. I think that he and Victoria, waifs both, could look after each other.'

Now I began to determine his design in speaking to me so confidentially of the family's business. He turned towards me and smiled slowly, and I knew that he had come to the meat of what he wanted to say. No king ever acted without thought, he had told me once, even in the smallest matters.

'Miss V,' he said, 'you should encourage her, when she speaks of her cousins, to think fondly of Albert. He is good, and steady, and quite free from the tainted blood of the House of Hanover.'

Yes, Uncle Leopold, I silently thought, *and although he may be good, he will be your creature, just as Victoria is currently the creature of my own father.* He meant well, of course, but he sought to control her.

But I stayed quiet, restricting myself to a grave nod.

'She listens to you, I know,' he went on. 'She must be married young, for stability. You understand how she requires a strong arm to lean on.'

Oh, how I did! My heart heaved. My Victoria did not often speak of her future, because, as I knew, she was afraid of it.

I turned to look at the sea, thinking of the days and years ahead. I saw a fishing boat coming in towards the shore, slowly but inexorably, just as time passed.

'What do they catch here?' King Leopold asked.

'They served lemon sole at our hotel last night,' I said, 'but the princess is more interested in desserts and cakes.'

I realised that we were looping back now towards the town and the boarding house. The journey would soon be over. It struck me that King Leopold hadn't yet asked the inevitable question about my father. Surely the subject would come up soon. People always asked about him once the pleasantries were over. *Now, Miss V, about your father,* they would generally begin. *Miss V, could you please ask your father for this? Beg your father not to do that? Give your father my excessively sincere compliments …*

'Now,' said King Leopold. 'About your father.'

How predictable people were! I thought. I did not even turn my eyes back from the sea. But the king went on to surprise me.

'Sir John Conroy,' he continued decisively, '*must be kept in check.* That is what I want to say to you. He is very assiduous in his duties, very admirable, but his role is limited in scope. It is not quite as vast as he thinks it is.'

Well, this made a very great change! It was quite astonishing to me to hear my father spoken of thus, and it made me catch my breath. I quickly bowed my head to hide my feelings.

'What a strange man he is to devote himself so closely to the family,' the king went on, interlacing his fingers and watching me closely, 'although I can understand his reasons.'

I could not think what to say. He had caught me quite by surprise. 'He has given them many years of service,' I muttered eventually, 'and been true and honest to his mistress.'

'More years than I like to think about!' he said with a sudden bark of laughter. 'Many more years than the sixteen that you have lived in the world. When your head was turned just now, I could clearly see the similarity between the duke and yourself. You have just the look of him around your forehead.'

I looked up, startled. 'Which duke?'

'Why, the Duke of Kent, of course.' He looked surprised. 'My sister the duchess's deceased husband. Did you not know? Your mother was his natural daughter from … oh, long ago, from when the duke led a riotous life, before he married my sister.'

I had lost all control of my limbs. They felt leaden and immovable. I certainly had not known. He could tell by my fixed gaze at the floor and the intense stillness of my body.

'Oh, my dear, I see I have spilled a family secret,' he said remorsefully, placing an awkward hand on my shoulder. 'But I thought that was why you serve the princess with such sincerity. I thought that was why you are content to live a … well, an abnormal life. Blood is thicker than water after all.'

He was shaking his head now, as if in disbelief. 'Why else would you be such a faithful friend to my niece, giving up your own life to serve her? I had always thought you knew that you are cousins.'

'I had no …' I began to stammer out some sort of response, but trailed off.

Cousins! Was I really related to Victoria? I knew that such relationships were perfectly possible in the royal family: the Duke of Clarence, for example, having had nine natural children with his actress lady friend. Indeed, I had information from very close to home that even in ordinary families husbands did not always love their wives and looked elsewhere.

But if so, my father's involvement with the princess's family was decades older than I had thought. Unpleasant ideas were whirring round in my head. It had been a long time since I had thought of my mother, lying comatose on her chaise, but she came into my mind now. So she too was part of this strange thing called the System.

I scarcely noticed that we were up on the high cliffs once more, passing a row of smart terraced houses wreathed with winging gulls. I began to wish that Uncle Leopold had kept his beguiling, flattering sharing of plans and secrets to himself.

'And now,' he said, 'we must return to the boarding

house so that I can visit my niece.' He spoke abruptly. I could tell he felt awkward at his blunder. 'And maybe,' he went on, 'if the time is right, I will speak to her of Albert.'

'Of course,' I said quietly, bowing my head. 'I see that it must be.'

A little background beat of pain had started up in my temple, heralding the approach of a headache. It seemed that I was deeper in than I had thought. I stared out of the window with glassy eyes, but I hardly saw the fishing boats outside. Victoria was my … cousin? It seemed very strange. And yet I felt closer to her than my own sister. Perhaps I was part of the family of the Kents after all.

'Miss V!'

The carriage had stopped; we had arrived. King Leopold was tapping me on the arm and looking at me with concern. At the sight of his friendly face, my eyes filled with tears.

I forced a smile and gathered myself to descend from the carriage. But my thoughts were still far away. Just how long ago had my father devised the System? And how deeply was it embedded?

Chapter 20

'Royalty These Days Is Debased'

I had not been invited to the family reunion between the duchess, Leopold and Victoria, which took place in the first-floor drawing room of the boarding house, with its panoramic view of the harbour and the tide slipping slowly out over the smooth sand of the beach. But I had heard the gales of laughter and knew that the German family was together once more and happy to be so. My ear, though, was attuned particularly to Victoria's voice, and I heard it less than I expected.

I did not exactly have my ear pressed to the door, but I was sitting in the hallway with a book, just in case I might be called. I wanted sal volatile for my head, and tea to drink, and I had neither. I had spent so many hours in this fashion, and perhaps Victoria had grown too accustomed to being able to call me to fetch and carry, without even rising from her sofa.

Were we really cousins? Is that why we looked so alike? My thoughts churned on. King Leopold had treated me to his confidence today; he took me seriously. I could not help noticing that Victoria, on the other hand, had been treating me rather like her dog. Or worse than her dog, as Dash had been invited into the tea party while I had been left to wait outside. I wasn't her dog; I was her cousin! But did she even know? I dug my fingernails into my palms as I thought of how my father had thrust me into this life without having told me all its secrets. How many years would pass before I knew the whole truth?

But before the tea party was over, my father came strutting in through the boarding house's front door below and began to climb the curving stair. He stopped when he saw me sitting primly on my banquette next to the grandfather clock, and he smiled. In his long face any movement of his eyebrows was particularly striking. He raised them now in his quizzical fashion.

'Patient and faithful as Dash himself!' he said quietly. 'Come up and give me my tea, Miss V.' I was almost annoyed to realise that today, of all days, he had understood at once that my burden of service seemed painfully heavy. I stood up, smoothed down my skirt and led the way to our own sitting room at the top of the house.

Although it was smaller than the drawing room where the duchess and her daughter sat laughing down below, our own sitting room was – in my father's usual fashion – warmer, brighter and more conveniently furnished than theirs. In my angry mood, it once again struck me – as it did every so often – that this was odd. Why did the Conroys live so much better than the Kents? We had a little silver tea kettle, an embroidered fire screen and a velvet sausage to keep out the draughts from the sea wind. But then the duchess had always favoured grandeur over comfort, and had no eye for the domestic details that made life snug.

We sat down to our cakes, and my father asked me how long King Leopold had been in the house, and what had been said. I looked down at my cup, reluctant to answer. I felt that earlier in the afternoon Leopold had been treating me, in the nicest possible way, as his spy. Now my father wanted to do the same thing. I sat, rebelliously silent, stirring my tea and thinking. I did not really want to be a spy for either of them.

'So King Leopold has been nobbling you, has he?' my father said, watching me carefully. 'Did he mention his nephew Albert?'

I gasped, annoyed. I'd had enough of being pumped for information. I decided to say, for once, what was really on my mind. I gathered my breath and spoke all in a rush.

'He said,' I snapped, 'that my mother is the natural daughter of the Duke of Kent! And that you married her just to become part of the princess's family!'

The word 'daughter' emerged from my mouth as a strange squeak. In fact, the whole sentence had come gushing out almost hysterically.

He looked at me in surprise.

'Yes, I am not always Miss Goody-Two-Shoes,' I said huffily, almost under my breath. These days it often seemed that I needed to do something out of the ordinary to make him see me, his daughter, rather than his servant, the dependable Miss V. I knew that he had come to think of me as a cog in his machine. Well, I needed a little oil or I would continue to squeak.

'Yes,' I went on, louder and angrier now. 'I am tired of finding out secrets second-hand. It's as if you don't trust me.'

He seemed positively dumbfounded and sat with his mouth foolishly hanging open. Then he jumped up, strode to the door, quickly opened it, glanced outside and sat down again. It looked like he was checking that there were no boarding-house maids in the corridor, but I also suspected that he was buying himself a little time.

'That's right, Miss V,' he said. 'Although they tried to hush it up, your grandfather was not Major Fisher, as you have always thought, but the Duke of Kent himself. Your mother is not alone in standing among the unrecognised offspring of the royal dukes. I believe that there are more than forty of them.'

'Forty!' I cried. 'But is this not very ... immoral of them?'

'Why, of course it is!' my father said, exasperated. 'Royalty these days is debased, weakened. It's a plant that's dying. And that's why you, and I, my dear, can insinuate ourselves into it. The Conroys are a very old Irish family, that's true, but I – for example – could never have become comptroller to a royal duchess one hundred years ago. But now, today, with my energy and my hard work, I have done so. I have created a fine life for myself and for my family. A royal duchess needs me. And this need, which only I can fulfil, keeps you and me very comfortable. Is that not right?'

I had wanted an apology, and an admission that he had not been straight. Was he trying to throw me off balance with this talk of illegitimate children? But his idea intrigued me. 'You mean,' I began, 'that you and I ... may reach a high position in society purely through our own efforts? Normal people, like us?' He nodded slowly as he watched me take in what he was saying.

'Yes,' he said firmly. 'Even royal personages must win respect through their personal qualities. The old days when they used to receive deference unquestioned are long gone.'

Of course I had heard many people talking against the old king, who had died very soon after we saw him at the Royal Lodge, and more recently his brother the new king, and their loose and immoral ways. 'Debased' and 'debauched' were the words people used when they talked about the royal family. And then, even worse, there were the younger brothers of the two kings. Some of them lived with their mistresses, and one of them was our enemy, the Duke of Cumberland.

'*We* are the people whose age is to come, Miss V,' he said. 'It is our time. The days of royalty are over, but we are the vigorous plants that will thrive among the ruins.'

His eyes glittered, but whether with malice or pleasure I could not tell. I remembered how cross I had felt just a couple of minutes earlier. But reluctantly I admitted to myself that I *could* see what he meant. Why should people rule over us just because of their blood?

'You may be related to the princess,' he continued.

'You may think that it will open doors or win the admiration of others. Not true! I have found that out for myself in marrying your mother. No one cares about her, as she was born out of wedlock. Good society will never recognise a relationship unless it is dignified through marriage. But good society will recognise service and assiduity, and that you have given. And so you have earned its respect.'

He had taken the wind right out of my sails.

But still something remained. An itch at the back of my mind. An anger.

'If all that is true, Papa ... why did you marry my mother?' I had wanted to know the answer to this question for a long time, and only now did I have the courage to ask. Was it to feed like a weed on the ruins of the royal family? I looked away, steeling myself for what he might say.

He did look shamefacedly at the floor. 'Now, Miss V,' he said, 'I guessed that you would be too young to understand, and so you are. Despite your being mature beyond your years. I did not marry her *just* because she was the natural daughter of the Duke of Kent. I married her because we fell in love.'

'In love?' I asked. 'You and my mother were in love?' The words came out almost scornfully. All the hot rage at what I had seen that day in the park, which had been simmering ever since, boiled over.

I had pushed him too far. He slammed down his teacup.

'YOU have no right to question your father!' he shouted. 'You can count on a Conroy to behave honourably. How dare you interrogate me?'

'I'm sorry, Papa,' I said at once, clasping my hands.

We sat silently, both of us staring at the carpet. I was shaking with the shocking violence of his words. How long would the storm last? Not long, not long, it never did. And within a couple of minutes, he was once again pouring his tea.

As I relaxed an inch, and waited, our startling earlier conversation about royalty forced its way back into my mind. I could perceive a glimmer of truth of what he was talking about. Where would the duchess and princess be without our help? Royal blood would not pay the bills. They would be penniless, and given the dangers the princess faced, possibly even lifeless too.

'Now,' he said, smacking his hands together, 'now then, perhaps I was hasty. I know you are a good girl. We must go back to the business of King Leopold. You haven't told me if he spoke to you of Prince Albert of Coburg, and his plans for the princess's marriage. Did he?'

I was stunned into saying nothing but the simple truth. 'Yes. He did.'

'We must never allow that to happen,' he said decisively. 'That would be a great gun in Leopold's armoury. And we cannot have a foreigner controlling who will sit upon the throne of England.'

'But Victoria will sit on the throne, surely?'

Now that there was only the life of King William the Fourth between her and the crown, I thought constantly about when that day might come, and whether she would be strong enough to bear it.

'Well, not if the old king dies before she is eighteen,' my father said slowly. I could tell that he was unwilling to share so much confidence, but my questioning had certainly damaged his composure a little. 'If that should happen,' he went on, 'then her stupid mother, the duchess, will be regent, and the princess will be under her care.'

The word 'stupid' made me blink. I could see that she was not clever like my father was, but the duchess had her own dramatic way of living which made sense to her. And certainly she did care for Victoria. Did she care for my father? I could not tell. It was confusing.

'But I will tell the duchess and the princess what to do, and how to do it. I will know the way to rule. Leopold is thinking of the children that the princess and Albert might have. He wants another damned member of the damned Coburg family to be near the throne of England – and for Victoria's children to be half-German.'

'But what if Victoria herself does not wish to marry this Albert?' I asked tentatively.

'Ha!' he said, almost slapping his thigh. 'You are not foolish enough to think that she has any choice in the matter, are you? A princess can never marry for love.'

I had not thought of this. I remembered Victoria's joke, only today, about meeting a handsome highwayman. She loved romance, the idea of falling in love. But she could never, ever do so herself. How grim!

My father could see this realisation crossing my face like a shadow.

'So King Leopold is not quite as disinterested as he seems with his *good advice*,' he went on, with a low laugh. 'So now we must hope and pray for something quite wicked, Miss V. We must hope and pray that a *certain person* does die within the next two years, so that *another certain person* will become regent. And then John Conroy, commoner though he is, will know what real power tastes like.'

I saw his coal-black eyes glowing, and his colour was up.

My father, always ready with an answer to every question. I turned away from him with a sigh. Sometimes I adored him, sometimes I feared him. Whichever it was, I had no way of escaping him.

Chapter 21

On the Beach

The next morning, Victoria and I went down to the beach with Dash. As usual we left the house with Adams in tow, and as usual he did not take much persuading from Victoria to wait for us in the teashop rather than follow in our exact footsteps.

I watched her running ahead, skipping almost into the foam and out again. I seated myself on a dry patch of sand and ran my fingers through it in search of shells. But I soon abandoned my quest because I fell, once more, to wondering about the future. This romping girl was to have such great power over everyone, myself included, when the old king died.

But then a shriek of pleasure from the sea's edge made

me look up, and I saw her picking up Dash and kissing him because the cold water had splattered his coat. And it struck me once again that at heart she was kind and true. Britain could do worse, I thought, far worse, than have my blood cousin as queen.

Victoria came running back towards me, her cheeks rosy with the wind and spray. She stood before me, laughing, and Dash almost seemed to be laughing too. I resolved that whatever my father might say, whatever schemes he might hatch to take her power, I was on *her* side.

'Get away from me, you two!' I said. 'I know your tricks. You want to spray me, don't you, Dash?' His quivering fur was loaded with water and I knew that in an instant he could shake it off in a shower.

'Frowning again, Miss V?' said Victoria. 'Your face will get stuck like that, you know!'

Then she suddenly leaned forward, ignoring Dash, and put her hands on her knees. She dropped her head, and the laughter turned to a kind of shrill gasp. I did something similar whenever I myself felt faint, but it was so bracing out here, below the cliffs, that I could not imagine how she could be feeling the vapours.

'Victoria!' I said. 'What is it? Have you swallowed sand? It's blowing right up off the beach – just look at it!'

'Suddenly … feeling … a little weak,' she said, straightening up slowly.

I saw that her face had gone dead white.

'Oh, but you're not well,' I said, concerned, taking her arm and threading it through my own. I patted her hand as we strolled back. 'Perhaps you ran too fast too soon after all those weeks in the carriage.'

We took a few paces, but then there was a strong pull on my arm. This time her knees had almost given way, and she staggered.

'Oh, sweetheart!'

Her face seemed strangely sweaty as well as pallid, and I reached out to touch her cheek. Burning hot. 'You have caught a cold,' I said severely. 'That's what comes of not wearing enough clothes.'

She was dressed in a neat navy cloak, but she had smartly refused to bring the muff I'd laid upon on her bed before we set out upon our walk, calling me an old fusspot.

'Fusspot!' she said again now. 'It's nothing. I just need to catch my breath.'

As we stumbled together across the sand, I wondered that the System did not allow Victoria more frequent opportunity to concentrate on her health and strength. This was the first time in the years I had been part of it that the household had taken a holiday. But even my father had been forced to admit, after the tour, that Victoria was run-down and needed a change of air and a rest without the pressure of any princess-ing.

'Home to tea!' she shouted, attempting to push on ahead of me. 'Buns! Scones! Hot milk!'

But again she stopped and dropped her head and seemed almost to be spitting something out upon the ground. When I caught up with her, she was trembling.

'Come on,' I said grimly. 'For you it isn't home to buns. It's home to bed.'

It was late that evening and I was in Victoria's boarding house bedroom. Her bed was narrow and made of iron, like a servant's bed, but it stood near the tall window so that she could see – as she insisted, for she would not have the curtain drawn – the harbour lights twinkling below.

The doctor had gone some time before, and I had crept in to say goodnight. Lehzen sat in the shadows like a sentinel. In the quiet I could hear the rasping of Victoria's breath.

'Ah, it's Miss Caution!' she croaked, beckoning me in. 'Have you brought me sherbet lemonade? Nothing else can save me.' Victoria had been driving the boarding house cook mad with her demands for unseasonable and unfamiliar foodstuffs.

'No, I have not. I've come to see that you're behaving yourself.'

'Pooh! I was naughty with that smelly old doctor.'

Lehzen cackled in the corner. 'You were indeed,' she said, not looking up from her darning. 'You should not have asked him what he thought of the fine new hospital in London.'

'But how could a doctor not have heard of it?' asked Victoria plaintively.

'A country doctor, is how,' Lehzen said with a sniff. 'You should not taunt people who live outside London and know less than yourself.'

'But, Lehzen,' Victoria said more earnestly. 'He says I have just a cold. I am telling you, this is something … *worse* than a cold. I feel dreadful.' She flopped back on the pillows, and it is true that she still looked like a pale, washed-out version of herself.

'Lehzen!' I said in alarm. 'Does this doctor know what he is doing?'

'Her Royal Highness and Sir John have approved him,' Lehzen said grimly, snipping through a thread with her scissors. But this gave me no confidence.

'Well, Victoria, do sleep well,' I said. 'Let me plump up your pillow.'

'Oh, fusspot,' she said, as she rolled over and refused

to accept my help. But there was a smile in her voice. I dropped a small kiss on her shoulder, and I know from her wriggle that she'd felt it and was pleased.

Comforted, I crept quietly away to go to my own sleep.

The next day, the doctor was back in the house before breakfast was over. 'Unnecessary expense!' my father huffed, as he returned to his toast. 'I really think the little minx is putting it on. You haven't been encouraging her, have you, Miss V?'

At that he looked at me sternly over the top of his cup.

'Encouraging her?' I said drily. 'It's my duty to encourage her.' *The Lord knows*, I added silently to myself, *that she needs encouragement to get through these next few years. Whether she becomes queen sooner or later, she needs strength and help.*

'You know what I mean,' he said sternly. 'I hope you haven't encouraged her in her disobedience to her mother and me. Which I fear takes the shape of this pretended illness.'

I stood up, so angry I was trembling a little. 'If you had been on the beach with her yesterday,' I said, 'you would not be accusing anyone of falsehood. She was so weak she could hardly walk.'

At that I flounced out and banged the door. It gave me great satisfaction to think of that final glimpse of my father's face, open-mouthed in wonder and horror.

I took care to hum a little tune as I ran downstairs, so as to discourage the boarding house staff from thinking that anything was amiss, but beneath my grey dress, my heart was beating rather fast. I was worried to hear that she was still ill.

I sought out Lehzen in her cramped, dark bedroom at the very back of the house. 'Lehzen,' I said breathlessly, having knocked on her door with less circumspection than was my usual habit. 'I think that Victoria is really ill, but my father does not seem to agree.'

Lehzen looked up, surprised, from the mirror. She had a turban round her head, and it was quite shocking to see her without her usual frontage of corkscrew curls.

So Lehzen wears a wig! was my inconsequential thought.

But she did not seem to care that I had seen her without her hair. 'She is certainly very sick,' she said grimly. 'I saw the evidence of it in the night. But the duchess is very frightened, and she does not want to believe it. And that local doctor only cares about his fee and wants to reassure her.'

I had known that Lehzen would give me the facts

straight. I could almost have hugged her, but now she had her sharp elbow raised to fasten her locket round her neck.

'But, Lehzen, what ought we to do?'

'We must send for Dr Clark from London.'

'Of course! I must speak to my father at once!'

'Stay.' She held up her hand before I had the chance to withdraw and spun around on her chair to face me directly. 'Sir John,' she said calmly and deliberately, 'has already refused to call Dr Clark. You must consider your own position, Miss V. The System is not kind to those who cross Sir John.'

'But the princess's life could be in danger!'

'So it could. But this morning she did look a little better, and she ate some chicken and some broth.' Then she added quickly, 'I, too, am in favour of calling Dr Clark, but you know that a victory against the System is dearly bought.'

I knew exactly what she meant, of course. She was thinking of Madame de Späth.

I crept back along the passage, discouraged. The boarding house was now alive with the sounds of maids doing the morning cleaning, the few other guests departing for their cliff-top walk and the cheerful clanging of the milk pails being washed downstairs.

Quiet as a mouse amid the bustle, I tiptoed to Victoria's door and listened at it for a while.

Nothing. Perhaps she was resting.

Then there was a sharp whack on my back, right between the shoulder blades. It was the duchess, who had crept up behind me in uncharacteristic silence. It was so unexpected that I almost shrieked.

'Go away,' she hissed. 'Vickelchen is sleeping. She does not want you.'

There was great feeling, even menace, in her voice.

The start she had given me, and the shame I felt at being caught spying, began to prick me in my armpits. I dropped my chin to my chest and curtseyed low and silently, effacing myself as much as I could. I felt the duchess's eyes boring into my back as I retreated along the passage to the stairs, and heard the quiet click as she slipped into her daughter's room and closed the door.

In an agony of doubt, I forced myself to go back upstairs and wait. A few minutes passed. Eventually I could bear it no longer. I sat down and quickly wrote a letter to my sister about our quiet doings in Ramsgate, describing the weather and the little fishing boats and the band that had played on the esplanade. As soon as it was finished – and it was very short – I sealed it up.

'Off to post my letter!' I called out unusually loudly to

anyone who might be within earshot. Nobody replied. I almost ran down the hill to the post office.

'Has this morning's post left for London?' I asked the clerk, breathless.

He shook his head. I quickly handed over two envelopes: one addressed to Jane, and the second to Dr Clark. It contained another letter I had written, begging him to come at once.

The remaining hours of that day seemed to last for centuries. I did not play the piano for fear of disturbing Victoria. I did not offer to accompany my father on his errands in the town, for I felt completely out of sympathy with him. I did not eat at luncheon, for my stomach was too tight and tense with worry to take any food.

As evening approached, storm clouds from the west flew over us and began to race out to sea. After tea, but before the lighting of the lamps, I heard a great commotion start up in the apartment below me. I heard the sound of furniture overturned, and Victoria's voice shouting, 'No! *No!* I won't!'

I froze. The book I'd been reading slipped quietly from my hands, and I half rose from my seat. Fixing myself into this unnatural position seemed to help me to listen intently. What new drama was this? I longed yet feared to know. Plucking up all my courage, I stepped silently to the door and to the head of the stairs. But even as I placed my hand upon the banister, my father came surging up the stairs like a great, unstoppable wave breaking over the beach below. I could see at once that he was furiously, devilishly angry.

'Papa! Is the princess worse?'

He looked at me like a madman, panting, his hair disarranged and his waistcoat gaping open. 'The … little … monster!' he said in a low and menacing tone. 'She does not know what is good for her.'

I shrank back against the wall, clutching at my breast. 'What has happened?' I whispered.

But he charged on, like a bull, into our sitting room. Its door hammered home, and he had not said another word.

I had to see her. I had to. I went on boldly down the stairs and tapped at Victoria's door. Fuelled now by fear, I did not wait one instant for a reply. This time I went straight in.

She was curled up in bed, weeping as if her heart would break. At once I wished I had come sooner. Who could deny that this girl was seriously ill? Her skin had a greenish tinge, and there was a heavy, unpleasant smell in the air.

'Miss V!' she said weakly. 'Look what he tried to make me sign. And he threatened to … beat me, and worse.'

There was a pencil lying on the cabinet by her bed, but I could not see what she meant.

'On the floor.' She mouthed the words, seeming to lack the strength to say them properly.

I stooped. In the dim light I had missed it, but there was a sheet of paper lying half hidden under the cabinet, crumpled and partly ripped.

I tilted it to the window the better to read it. It was covered with writing, but my eyes were drawn to the final sentence, where a space had been left for a signature.

I, Victoria, consent to make Sir John Conroy my only private secretary upon my ascension to the throne, and to compensate him therefore, and to rely upon his judgement.

'He tried to … *make* … you sign this?' In my horror, I forgot for a moment her condition and sat on the edge of her bed. I was trembling, burning with rage.

'Yes!' she wailed, now covering her face with her hands. 'I defied him, Miss V. I defied him. What will he do now?'

Be calm! a voice said inside me. *Don't let your rage out now. Think of Victoria. How can you best help her?*

I took her hand. 'Victoria, whatever happens, Lehzen and I will look after you, you know. You are not in danger while we are here.'

'But you cannot always be here,' she whimpered, 'and he may send you away.'

'What about ...' I tried to find a delicate way to ask. 'What about your mother?'

'She was with him!' Now Victoria's sobs wracked her body. 'She wanted it too! She cannot withstand him; she does not know how. He wants to be a king without a name! And she lets him do it! She is too weak ... too weak. Lehzen says –' here she hiccupped – 'that a queen may be wicked, but it is inexcusable to be weak.'

I looked down at her little body in the bed.

'You may be feeling weak, Victoria,' I said, 'especially now when you are not well. But on the inside you are immensely strong. You are the strongest person I know.'

With that I wrapped my arms around her. Together we lay like that until I could hear the hammering of her heart slowly subside.

'I'm not the strongest person,' she whispered at last. 'That's you. You are stronger than me.' I hushed her and calmed her, and gradually I believe she fell asleep.

Darkness fell and the wind rose, and the house began to stir with the sounds of dinner.

Eventually, the bedchamber door creaked open. A long yellow shaft of light from the passage fell upon the carpet, and outlined against it was a tall, dark figure.

'Is that him come back?' I had thought Victoria to be sleeping, but she was all too wide awake, and I could hear the fear in her voice.

'No, no,' I said, as if to a much smaller child. 'It's Lehzen. Lehzen loves you.'

She looked at us, but with her back to the light we could not see her expression.

'An express messenger has arrived,' she said. 'Dr Clark is coming. He writes that he thinks it might be typhoid fever. Miss V, you are in danger of catching it. You must get up.'

There was silence. I did not move; I cared not for any fevers. My shoulders sagged in relief, and I also felt Victoria collapse a little deeper in my arms, tension leaving her body. But a little core of my heart remained anxious.

Yes, the doctor was coming. Yet it was for less than this that Madame de Späth had been sent away.

Chapter 22

A Revelation of Brutality

I t *was* typhoid. Dr Clark said so at once. He administered strong drugs, and Victoria's hair was shaved off from her head. Great hanks of it had fallen out anyway. A stern nurse was engaged, and the boarding-house maids forbidden from Victoria's room. All the bedding was burned.

The duchess was a broken woman, full of fears and distress and remorse at not having called for Dr Clark sooner. Even my father had nothing to say about the breach of the System. For it was clear, during that long and terrible night before Dr Clark arrived, that our princess had been on the very brink of death.

The following morning, once Dr Clark had seen

Victoria, I tried to raise the matter with my father. 'I hope I did right,' I said tentatively. 'The princess's health, you know, is always on my mind.'

'As it should be,' he muttered. But he turned back to his paper and refused to engage with me any further. I turned away too, in some disgust. We both knew, even if he wouldn't admit it, that I had done the right thing.

Morning after morning, as the convalescence progressed, I went downstairs to relieve an ashen-faced Lehzen from her night watch. Our governess was usually coughing like an old tobacco-stained tar of the sea. I sat by Victoria's bed all day, sometimes reading to her, sometimes just watching the waves through the window. I did not catch the fever. I could feel the strength ebbing from my legs, but that was from long periods of sitting and watching. I would not have left for the world.

The duchess would swoop in and out of the room, once clutching a bunch of unseasonal, hothouse roses and thrusting them into a vase on the mantelpiece and going into raptures about their colour and scent. But on the next occasion she was crying and wringing her hands, and asking God to curse her for being such a mad, bad mother.

The two of them seemed sometimes almost to forget my presence, and Victoria would sometimes berate her mother for getting through her 'drops' too fast, while the duchess would castigate her daughter for not showing her enough affection.

'How I have suffered! What agonies a mother may experience I never knew until now!' she would say, trying to clasp Victoria to her bosom. Victoria's little shorn head made her look like an early Christian martyr cut down from a cross and being consoled by a buxom Mary Magdalene.

Victoria would groan out loud. As the days passed, though, as the medicine worked and as she grew stronger, I could tell that she was sometimes groaning just for show and for attention, as her mother would have done in the same situation. If Victoria spent less time with her mother and more with Lehzen and me, she might snap out of such antics. But it was not to be.

One day the duchess pushed her daughter too far, by marvelling at the generosity of my own father in procuring a little pony cart so that Victoria and I could take some gentle carriage exercise. 'So kind!' the duchess enthused. 'So thoughtful of Sir John!'

'He is only doing it for his own ends!' Victoria cried crossly. 'I will *not* ride in his cart. And neither will Miss V.'

'Victoria!' The duchess threw open her arms in a beseeching gesture. 'How can you be so ungrateful to the man who has almost been a father to you?'

This enraged Victoria. With a toss of the head, she turned over to stare out of the window, presenting only a thin shoulder blade to the room. 'He is *nothing* like a father to me,' she hissed in a venomous whisper. 'Every night I pray that my own father might still be alive, come back to protect me and look after me.'

This in turn enraged the duchess, and for the want of a better audience, she turned to me. 'The Duke of Kent,' she said tremulously, 'is far, far better in his grave. *Never* compare Sir John, who is an angel, to the demon duke. No one knows this better than myself, who has lived under the same roof as both of them. The duke's violent tempers, his extravagant ways ... no one knows how I suffered. When my so-called husband realised that the government had voted us such a small living allowance, how he lashed out!'

She bowed her head and her chest heaved. I perceived that for once this was genuine grief on her part, and she was speaking of something that really had wounded her.

'He thought that marriage to me would bring a bigger allowance; it was only for that that he cast aside his French actress lady friend and wooed me. And when he realised his mistake, he ... hurt me.'

Victoria had turned back to us both, all agog. But then

her features relaxed. 'I don't believe it,' she said. 'You are exaggerating as usual, Mother.'

'He was a violent man!' The duchess was mopping her cheeks now with her handkerchief and breathing heavily. 'The Duke of Kent was a *violent man*. Did you never wonder why he left the army? Where he had occupation and salary? Did you never wonder why we were left at Kensington Palace with no money and nothing to do?'

'Well, surely it was beneath his dignity to have to … *work*.' Victoria said the words with such scorn that I almost laughed. Of course leisure was a fine thing, but I knew that many, many people could not afford it. Victoria had never known such people.

'He was ejected from the army,' the duchess said, drawing herself up in sorrowful dignity. 'He had to leave the garrison of Gibraltar. The men would no longer serve under him for his brutality. There was one whipping too many.'

Now I looked at her in horror. This was strong meat, and I felt that Victoria, in her weakened state, should not have to hear such things.

The duchess caught my worried gaze and took my hand imploringly. Since my calling in Dr Clark, there had been a new understanding between us. I might almost have called it affection. 'That's why Sir John, your own father, has been my saviour,' she said, her voice almost breaking on the word as if she were an actress in a tragedy. 'Where would I have been without him, with no English, no money and a baby girl?'

'I cannot imagine how hard it must have been,' I said quietly.

And I could see her point. If Victoria's real father had been unsatisfactory – and given what we knew of his brothers, the royal dukes, this did unfortunately seem possible – then perhaps my own father had been her only hope. For certainly she could not negotiate life alone, and I knew for myself the power of my father's solid, reassuring, determined presence. It's just that I feared that he sometimes overstepped the mark.

I could see that Victoria, too, was thinking about her mother's situation. I reached out for her hand, and for a moment all three of us were linked in a human chain. For once there was sympathy between us.

'It is hard, my girls!' the duchess said. 'It is difficult being a woman in this world. We lack power; we lack strength; we lack intelligence.'

But Victoria broke the chain. She snatched her hand away and turned once more to the wall.

'I don't believe it,' she muttered. '*I* will have power.

I will have strength. And I will always, always hate Sir John.'

I had a deep, disturbing feeling that she meant it. That little, shaven, shrunken body housed a strong spirit. The princess was a good hater.

Chapter 23

A Ride through the Woods

After some weeks, we did ride out together in my father's pony cart, along the top of the cliff and through the terraces of houses at first, and then down on the hard sand of the beach when the tide was out. Once we trotted nearly all the way to Broadstairs.

'Are you ready for the cart?' I asked Victoria one day after luncheon. 'Or would you rather hear a story?' I had introduced my well-worn copies of the romances of Sir Walter Scott into the sickroom. Sometimes she spent the afternoon on the sofa, imploring me to go on reading aloud to her from one or another of his chivalrous, adventurous tales.

But this afternoon she ignored me and continued

taking her dolls, one by one, from their trunk, laying them out on the carpet and putting one into the dress of another. 'Surely sixteen years is too old for dolls!' I scoffed. 'Do come out for a run.'

'My babies have been such good friends to me,' she said in a dreamy voice, speaking to them, not to me. 'I cannot abandon them now.' She began to twist a new crown from gold foil for a third doll. She seemed to have reverted to a lesser, younger, weaker version of herself.

'Are you feeling wobbly again this afternoon?'

'Yes, I'm afraid so, Miss V,' she said gently. 'I fear that I might never be strong again.' But her attention remained firmly fixed on the floor. 'You see this doll in the coronet here?' she said, indicating a figure in red velvet and gold brocade. 'I wish that was all a princess needed to do, to wear a pretty dress and go to parties. But I know that in real life I must also be despised and bullied and pulled apart. Perhaps it's better to be a doll.'

She looked so young, so small and so sad that I knelt beside her and wrapped my arm round her shoulders.

She sighed and leaned back against me. 'You and Lehzen,' she said, with a smile of great sweetness, 'must go without me. You spend too much of yourselves looking after me, and you need the exercise. Please, do go.' The kind words brought tears to my eyes.

So, abandoning Victoria to her babies, Lehzen and I took the pony cart by ourselves. Lehzen and I had indeed occasionally stepped out of doors together of an afternoon to break our close attendance in the sickroom. Once we had been down to the town to look at hats in a shop, and another time we'd heard the pianoforte being played in the town hall. It was so long since I'd had time to practise, and I'd loved hearing music once again.

Now, as then, I felt myself almost overwhelmed by the sights and sounds of busy people on the street, ladies like Lehzen, young ladies like me, but oh, so different! They were going about their lives, unaware of the System, unaware of the princess living in their midst. The sight and sound of other people was so unexpectedly vivid after the quiet sickroom, enlivened only by the ticking of the clock and the sound of the sea far below.

Today we bowled through the upper part of the town towards the green lanes inland. They were not so green now that the year was on the turn, and there were drifts of leaves by the side of the road. Lehzen's stern profile beside me looked as if carved in wood. As usual, no expression passed over her face as she flicked the whip and dexterously swerved our little vehicle round a slow-moving farm cart that was blocking our way. We were going at such a clip that the speed forced me to hold on to my hat.

It gave me quite a start when at last Lehzen spoke.

'This countryside reminds me of the fields near Hanover,' she said. It was unusual for her to mention her past, and Germany, so I sat quietly, still looking ahead, hoping that she would go on. I had a new respect for Lehzen since her diligent, devoted nights of nursing. 'My father was a pastor there, you know,' she continued.

'Oh!' I said. 'I didn't know. Pray, is he still alive?' Intrigued, I turned myself towards her just a little, to encourage further confidences. At the same time, I had to clutch on to the edge of my seat as our pony picked up speed round a corner.

'Dead, long dead,' she said. 'But he was a good man. I was far from born a baroness.' She spoke almost regretfully, as if being a baroness was a punishment, not a reward.

'And how did you become one?'

'The old king, King George the Fourth, had the idea to make me one. He thought it wasn't right that the princess should be served by commoners. But underneath I am just Johanna Clara Louise Lehzen, as I was born. Like your father, I am not of these mad, aristocratic people by birth. I sometimes wish I had not begun working for the

Duchess of Kent, you know. It is so … tiring.' A feeling came over me, like a refreshing squeeze of lemon juice, that Lehzen would never have said such a thing before the incident of the typhoid. Before, she would have restrained herself, I was sure, in case I reported her words to my father.

'But you cannot leave, Lehzen!' I said quickly. 'The princess needs you too much!'

'I know,' she said, with that odd sidelong smile which transformed her face. 'And you too, Miss V. We are her protectors, are we not?'

Shyly, I smiled back at her. Although it seemed conceited to admit it, and I would never have said the words out loud, I realised that it was true. The two of us, Lehzen and I, counterbalanced the powerful person-alities of Victoria's mother and my father, and made Victoria's life possible. Not happy, not carefree, but possible.

'But, Lehzen,' I went on cautiously, as the little cart entered the shade of a wood and the shadows made the surroundings seem more intimate. 'But recall how unwell she has been. She could have died! And it would have been the fault of my father and her mother!'

'Yes, that would have been a terrible thing.' Lehzen paused. 'It is a terrible thing to see a family … eating itself. When people share the same blood in their veins, it makes their quarrels seem worse, somehow.'

I pondered upon her words. I sensed that something deeper lay behind them. In the wood, twilight was beginning to fall, and while I admired the luminous light that gave the trees an unearthly glow, I also felt a shiver go down my spine.

'A family, Lehzen?' What had she meant by the word?

She did not reply. But all at once I sensed that Lehzen knew the secret of who my mother really was. 'Lehzen,' I said, 'do you know that I myself am the granddaughter of your old master, the Duke of Kent? Out of wedlock, of course. Did you know that I am Victoria's cousin?'

Lehzen twitched her head round, her attention caught by something else. And then I thought I heard it too: the hoofs of a horse somewhere in the wood, somewhere behind us.

But perhaps not. She turned back to the pony and gave me a quick glance.

'Yes, my dear, I do know it. And it has often crossed my mind how unfortunate it is that you are cousins and not sisters. It is unfortunate that your places are not reversed.'

'I beg your pardon?' I thought I saw a fox slipping

through the bracken by the side of the road. 'Did you say that you wished Victoria and I were sisters?'

Lehzen glanced at me again, and turned away. Like me, she preferred to speak to a person without looking at them. 'No, Miss V,' she said. 'It is not so much that. You are close, like sisters. I know you can read her mind. And you look just like each other. But I think that in many ways you would make a better queen.'

I choked. 'But, Lehzen, it is treason to say such a thing!'

'Treason?' Lehzen scoffed. 'That's just a word. You know I have nothing but loyalty to the princess, and that's why I think and say this. Have you never noticed how close to the edge of reason she stands? Like her grandfather, the mad old King George the Third? You never saw him, but it is true. They have the same high colour, the same high temper. When she stamps her foot, she is the spitting image of him. It is dangerous, dangerous to her health.'

She was right. I could say nothing. Silence fell.

'Oh yes,' muttered Lehzen, as if to herself. 'I think that Miss V would sit on the throne more comfortably than the Princess Victoria.'

Once more I was aghast.

'But this is a silly speculation, Lehzen!' I said, pulling myself together.

'You're right, my dear …' Lehzen said.

She glanced backwards again and I followed her gaze.

Yes, there *was* a horseman behind us. The sound was closer now. It was unnerving. But even staring hard, I could see nothing between the trees.

Lehzen lowered her voice, as if eavesdroppers might be able to overhear us.

'It is indeed useless speculation,' Lehzen went on. 'But think of the *consequences*. If Victoria is sick, if she cannot bear it, if becoming queen kills her or destroys her mind, who will take the throne then?'

'Oh!' Suddenly I realised. 'George of Cumberland? But he is evil! Cruel! Stupid! That would be terrible.' A new thought struck me. 'But she must take the throne. What about the law? We cannot live without laws. She has the royal blood.'

This made Lehzen harrumph.

'Miss V!' she said. 'As I said, I was born a commoner, like your father, although I don't care to be bracketed with him. We have made our own way in the world. We haven't been born to high positions; we have made high positions for ourselves. Positions of power. Surely the country should be ruled over by the best person, not the person with the best so-called blood?'

I thought hard about the logic of her argument. Yes,

how happy it would make me, and those others who cared about Victoria, if she did not *have* to be queen! And yet it was all a fancy.

'Lehzen, I don't think we should talk like this. Surely we must believe that Victoria can, and will, make a good queen.'

'I bring it up because my doubts about her strength and her sanity are a heavy load for me to carry, my dear,' said Lehzen quietly. The occasional gleam of evening light through the trees flashed across her face. 'I trust you to help me bear it. You are young in years, but you are also old and wise inside your head.'

I was overcome with feelings I can scarcely describe. It was wonderful to feel needed, wanted. It warmed me inside.

'Oh, Lehzen,' I said, speaking to her perhaps more honestly than I ever had before. 'You know that it makes me glad to help other people, if I can.'

'Ach!' Lehzen suddenly spat out the sound. Her attention was once more fixed upon the road behind us. 'I fear, my dear, that I have made an error. Can you hear that?'

The hoof beats in our wake were growing steadily louder.

'I have brought you to a deserted wood at twilight,

and to the untrained eye you will look very like Victoria in that cloak. I fear that this has been a security breach.'

Now my own heart leapt into my mouth. Lehzen had whipped the pony forward, and with a great jolt the little cart began to bounce even more quickly over the rough road. A low branch snatched my hat from my head, and I let out a cry.

'Leave it!' Lehzen said sharply, whipping the pony again. And now, glancing back, I could see the dark shape of the horseman against the trees behind us. He wore a long, dark greatcoat and a scarf that muffled his face. He looked like nothing on earth so much as a highwayman. And what was that long and heavy item he carried across his saddle?

'Lehzen,' I whimpered, too frightened to scream. 'Lehzen, I think he has a musket with him.'

'*Lieber Gott!*' she said, gritting her teeth. 'Hold on.' I was indeed clinging on for dear life, and the pony, barrelling forward as fast as its little legs could carry it, was speeding us out of the wood. Now we were passing through a meadow, and then, ahead, we could see the blessed sight of the main road. It was busy: there were carts upon it, and we heard the blessed sound of tramping feet. The horseman was left behind.

We drew up at the junction. A great company of

militiamen went marching by ahead of us, taking some minutes to pass, impeding our progress. But we did not care. They could protect us if need be. We sat in silence, staring at each other in horror. I could feel my hands trembling with shock and fear, and clasped them tightly together to still them.

I was certain that Lehzen was thinking, as I was, of the assassination attempt on the princess at Kensington Palace. This looked very much like a second try.

And if that was the case, then the Duke of Cumberland and his son were behind it, no doubt about that: a man and his son who would be murderers if they could. A man and his son who must never, never sit upon the throne.

I felt enormously glad when we saw the comforting lights of Ramsgate ahead of us. But of course I could not relax. My heart still thudded unpleasantly. How could I unwind when we had been in such danger, and when Lehzen – solid, pragmatic Lehzen herself, whom I trusted – had shared her own fears that Victoria would never be strong enough to rule?

Chapter 24

A New Beginning

The next day, on a morning of sparkling sunlight, the dusky woods and our dark fears seemed far away. The more I thought about the mysterious horseman, the less I could clearly remember of him. I certainly could not describe his face. I was beginning to wonder if perhaps we had been melodramatic.

But my father was just as grim at breakfast as he had been over dinner when I told him what had happened in the wood.

'Of course we must go back to Kensington Palace without delay,' he said shortly, when I asked about our plans. 'Security is too weak here. I had in any case been meaning that we should go. The holiday season is over.'

236

'It seems … harsh on the princess,' I said carefully. 'She is still not quite perfectly well.' My memory of Ramsgate would be forever scarred by the painful scenes we'd all experienced here. But to return to the palace, to turn our backs upon the sprightly little tufts of foam on the blue sea, would feel rather like going back to prison.

'Better that she should travel now while the weather is dry and fine for the journey,' he said, ready with an answer for everything. 'In her delicate state she should not travel in wind and rain.'

This was as close as he had come, in my hearing, to acknowledging that she had been ill, and I bowed my head in recognition of the concession on his part.

'And the boarding house bills are running up,' he went on.

Suddenly, with an impatient toss of the head, he rose from the table.

'Yet I cannot think why we are even discussing this in the face of yesterday's security breach.' He strode over to the window. 'And the other day,' he said, staring out at the sea, 'you girls were on the beach without a visible escort. I saw you through this window. I should never have tolerated it. My authority,' he concluded, his voice rising, 'must be heeded on this matter.'

'I shall go and pack at once, Papa,' I said meekly.

* * *

I was to travel with Lehzen and Victoria in the big carriage, while my father drove the duchess in the phaeton.

'I think we might arouse less attention,' said Lehzen, just before we left, 'if you were to wear these, Vickelchen.' Now that there were no more hairdressing secrets between us, she boldly handed the princess a row of false curls. Victoria's hair had grown only an inch since it had been shaved in the depths of her illness.

'Lord love a duck!' cried Victoria in her most rakish music hall manner. 'I'm going to be the belle of the ball!'

She tucked the curls under her bonnet at once, and kept batting them and fluffing them in imitation of a coquettish lady of the theatre. Then she thrust her arm through mine to descend the boarding house steps. 'Come on, Charlie boy,' she said to me. 'Help a girl into her carriage.' Lehzen and I smiled to see her japing around once more.

As we travelled, and it was a delightful journey, Lehzen revealed that there was a present waiting for us at Kensington Palace. Victoria tried to guess what it was. 'A lovely new atlas, is it, Lehzen, for you to use to beat some geography into our brains?'

'No!' I said. 'It's a ruler, the better to smack our fingers when we play wrong notes on the pianoforte.'

'Both wrong!' said Lehzen complacently, and however hard we begged and wheedled, she remained silent.

The journey lasted for two whole days, and Victoria was growing weary and wan by the time we finally reached the familiar road running through the park. The trees had been just budding when we left, but now their leaves were fallen, and drifts of burnt umber and orange covered the walks of the gardens. We passed the guards at the gate, and remembering the horseman of the woods, I shuddered. There was one thing to say for our prison: it did at least make such attacks much less likely.

At the moment we turned into the familiar quiet courtyard, Victoria's aunt the Princess Sophia was out on her step. Probably she was looking for her cat.

'I hope you like it, my dear!' she called out to us in her croaky voice, as we clambered down from the carriage.

I looked at Victoria. 'What does she mean?' I whispered.

But Victoria shrugged. 'Thanks, Aunt Sophia!' she yelled back, rather like a hoyden. 'But I don't know what "it" is yet!'

We were both now burning with curiosity.

And then we saw it. The front door had changed. It was new and shiny and had upon it a great brass knocker.

Then Adams himself was opening the door, just as of old. And yet he too was different: he wore a smart new livery with brass buttons.

He bowed and beckoned.

'Welcome home, Your Royal Highness,' he said.

Victoria led the way inside, and we realised what had been going on. A stupendous amount of building work had taken place. Instead of the crooked passage to the dirty painted steps, an elegant, sweeping low staircase of stone now stood before us. Gasping, we climbed it and found ourselves in a red-curtained saloon: fine, fashionable, with porphyry pillars and a long shining table down the middle.

Like sleepwalkers, we moved forward into the next room, a drawing room with fresh sprigged wallpaper and new plush furniture. An unfamiliar and beautiful piano stood to one side, and a gold-framed pier glass hung between the two tall windows with their swagged and ruched curtains. I caught a glance of us both in the mirror – like as two peas, young ladies for certain. We would not be playing behind the sofa any more.

I could hear my father laughing as he and the duchess came up the stairs behind us. 'Do you like it?' he was saying, eager for praise. 'Isn't it fine? The workmen have done a good job, have they not?'

We all turned to him in amazement. 'It's *heaven*!' said Victoria, her mouth a perfect 'O' of astonishment.

'At last we are to live in a palace,' sighed the duchess, 'and not a rackety boarding house!'

'Your Royal Highnesses both,' my father said, sweeping off his hat and bowing down low before them. 'Let this be a fresh start. I am the first to admit that I am impetuous, sometimes tempestuous. Sometimes more masterful than I should be. But I am sincerely attached to you, and it is my great honour and delight, as your comptroller, to have commissioned these new rooms for you.

'Now that Your Royal Highness is so near the throne,' he said, turning to Victoria in particular, and bowing even lower than before, 'you must live in more splendour and state.'

Victoria was blushing with pleasure, looking almost pretty in her enthusiasm. She was paying no attention to my father, but staring every which way at the elegant new furnishings.

'All right, Sir John,' she said distantly, eventually letting her eyes fall upon him. 'Let us make a new beginning.'

Lehzen and I exchanged a glance that spoke more loudly than words. We kept silent, so as not to spoil the moment. But I knew that we were wondering exactly the same thing.

How had all this been paid for? From where in the world had the money come?

Yes, the new rooms were exquisite, I thought, as my father and I passed back down the staircase. The sight of my elegant pale pink slippers on the marble of the steps took me back, somehow, to my first experience of the cold and cavernous entrance hall, when I had climbed the stairs to the schoolroom for the first time. Of course, the palace was much finer now than it had been all those years ago. But then my heart had not contained this cold little nugget of distrust for my father.

PART THREE

AT KENSINGTON PALACE

Chapter 25

Two Princes

Once they were settled into their grand new apartment at Kensington, the duchess and the princess began planning a ball. I brought the news back to my father in our own little drawing room.

'There are to be ices,' I told him eagerly, 'and musicians. And probably flowers. Victoria has a new book on the language of flowers, and we must consult it before we choose which ones to order.'

'Well,' he said slowly, 'I suppose it is indeed a good time to start introducing the princess to London society. I hope that she is ready for it.'

He interlaced his fingers, as if considering the matter judiciously.

But his frown confirmed my secret suspicion that he was merely cross that he hadn't thought of the idea himself. I looked down to hide my smile, plucking at the tablecloth and tweaking out a crease. By comparison with the splendours over the way, our room now looked shabby and a little dingy, whereas before it had seemed so snug and comfortable.

'I fear that it is a path fraught with considerable risk,' he eventually said, sounding at his most pompous. 'She has been sheltered, so very sheltered, from the roughness of the world.'

'But, Papa,' I said, 'she longs to meet young men, you know. And even if you don't approve of Uncle Leopold's choice of a husband, you must admit that the country and her people will expect her to marry. And soon.'

He went on looking sullenly at the floor. He said nothing, but we both knew that I was right. And also, we both knew that a husband would oust him from his position as the princess's most important advisor. Was this a bad thing? I was beginning to think it might not be.

The guests of honour at this ball, the duchess had announced, were to be cousins of Victoria's, the sons of one of the duchess's brothers from the House of Coburg. This was not Albert and his brother Ernest, of whom Leopold had spoken, but two more cousins, Ferdinand

and August. Victoria was wild with excitement to meet some strange new German gentlemen.

'It would not be wrong for me to marry a first cousin, would it?' she asked me on what seemed like most mornings that month. 'Such things are often done in royal families, are they not?'

'Why … yes,' I said.

The possible consequences of such a course of action, given that the offspring of close relatives could sometimes inherit characteristics such as the madness that ran in the Hanoverian family, made me pause before I answered.

But Victoria failed to notice my hesitation.

'Oh, it will be so exciting when my cousins are here!' she said breathlessly, a bright bloom of colour upon each cheek. 'We're going to dance with men! Of course it's all right dancing with you, Miss V, but you never spin me round fast enough.' She was up and out of her chair now, and practising a waltz step. 'We have firmly settled now that the ball is to be fancy dress – you know that, don't you?' she asked mid twirl. 'And the orangery in the gardens is to be cleared of all that lumber. It will be perfect.'

A clear-out was most necessary, for old chairs and neglected statues had cluttered up the orangery for as long as I could remember. It was to be heated with oil stoves, garlanded with flowers and garnished with a band of fiddlers who were to sit in the alcove to the side while the dancing took place up and down the long airy room.

Victoria's first idea for her costume was to go as a concubine from the harem of a sultan of the East, and Lehzen had some difficulty in dissuading her. Eventually, a Dresden shepherdess became the alternative inspiration for her dress. A dressmaker came to Kensington Palace to fit it, and we all enjoyed her visits. Lehzen had an undoubted talent for making fabric fall and drape, assisting as she did with the pinning, and I remembered that she had made the dresses for many of Victoria's dolls.

'And you, Miss V? What are you going to wear?'

Lehzen looked up at me from her kneeling position at Victoria's feet on the carpet, somehow managing to squeeze the words out of the corner of a mouth that was otherwise occupied in holding a large number of pins.

The question had been a heavy weight on my mind. 'Well,' I said thoughtfully. 'It's so hard to choose. I wonder if maybe I had better just keep behind the scenes, you know, and help out from there? Just to make sure it runs smoothly.'

I really rather longed to cry off from the actual dancing part of the ball, as I hated the thought of making a spectacle of myself. But there was no question that Victoria would allow this.

'Stuff and nonsense, Miss V!' she said roundly. 'Of course you're going to come, and you're going to dance as much as I do.'

'Well, if I must,' I said reluctantly, 'I think I'd just like to wear a normal evening dress.'

'Ha!' she cried at once. 'It's out of my power to accept your suggestion. It is my royal command that you appear in costume.' Imperiously, Victoria began to toss out ideas as she posed and preened in her half-finished shepherdess's dress. 'A Tudor countess!' she said. 'With a white ruff … No, an Indian princess. Or what about … Queen Marie Antoinette? No, that wouldn't be right. Miss V cannot make a more splendid appearance than me.'

'Nor would I want to,' I said fervently.

I refused to commit myself on the matter of my costume and said I would think it over.

When the dressmaker had left, though, and Victoria went skipping off to the piano to choose dance music, Lehzen looked at me seriously.

'I think I must bully you a little, Miss V,' she said. 'Time is running out for your costume to be made. But I have an idea that might suit. What if you were to go as a Grecian maiden, in a very plain white dress?'

I thought about it as I folded up the discarded yards of muslin. The idea did appeal. 'I could perhaps wear golden sandals,' I said. 'That, at least, would please the princess.'

'And laurel leaves wreathed around the head?' Lehzen was wheedling, enticing, and it was working.

'I accept,' I said. A little shiver rose up along my spine. A new dress! Golden sandals! It really might be rather exciting.

Finally the great day arrived. Our house guests from Germany were due at midday, but we were all ready and waiting long before the courtyard clock struck. Victoria and her mother positioned themselves at the head of their new, curving, stone staircase, and my father and Lehzen and I waited a few respectful steps behind.

Looking at the backs of the duchess and the princess as we waited, I felt sorry that Victoria had not inherited more of her mother's undoubted beauty. The duchess had an erect, elegant carriage, and her maid had the trick of sweeping her hair up into a graceful pile. Victoria, on the other hand, seemed to have stopped growing, and she could never stand up still and straight and ready. She kept glancing round, and wriggling, and sighing loudly, her patience soon depleted. Lehzen and I had taken a great deal of care over her hair, yet it was still too short to contrive the ornate and decorative plaits Victoria would have liked.

But the main thing was that the palace was prepared and princes were expected. My chest puffed out a little with pride as the five of us, a team for once, stood *en garde*, putting on a show.

Is this what it would be like when Victoria was queen? I wondered. My father at her back, standing by to 'help' and advise in his own imitable way? And where would I be in this picture? Once Victoria was married, perhaps my job would be done. She wouldn't need me in quite the same way, to tease and to talk to, as she did now.

But I could not imagine ever leaving her. I could see from her back that she was breathing fast and shallow, excited and tense. I knew that occasions like this were thrilling but also arduous for her, her nerves taut, voice shrill.

My father had noticed too. 'Of course, it's difficult at first for an inexperienced young girl to appear in public,' he whispered in my ear. 'But with time and practice and our good care, it will become second nature. She should cast an eye at you, Miss V. You look as cool as ice cream.'

To my surprise, I found that I was. It was the others who seemed on edge. *It's just our duty,* I thought, spreading my weight more comfortably across both feet. *No more, no less. We have to do it, and then it's over.*

But we waited and waited, and the hour of luncheon came and went. At about two, we were all slumped, disconsolate, in the chairs of the new saloon, and the duchess was squirming uncomfortably. I knew she had fastened her stays unusually tight to welcome her nephews, and that she was now slowly sinking into agony.

It was nearly three when Adams rushed up the stairs, knocked in a perfunctory manner at the saloon door, then rushed down to the entrance hall again. We all leapt up and followed him, and resumed our stance on the stairs as he opened the front door, and in came two young men.

It was well worth the wait. They were both dark and slender and exquisite. I could not but feel a flutter of the heart as they came into view, one of them ascending each side of the double staircase in their foreign but extremely elegant officer's uniforms. Each of them had one hand resting negligently upon the hilt of a sword, the other placed over its owner's heart as, simultaneously, they sank into deep bows.

The duchess and princess curtseyed in turn, and then the four Coburg relatives were kissing and laughing and greeting each other. Or at least Victoria and her mother were kissing and laughing and making a fuss in that lively manner they had, while the visitors stood quiet and serious.

'Sir John!' the duchess called in a peremptory manner. 'Come to be introduced.' But there was no chance of this happening just yet. The taller prince still had possession of Victoria's hand. He was gravely cradling it, almost stroking it, staring down at her from beneath his curved, supercilious eyebrows.

She was looking back up at him, back arched, head tilted back, and I could almost feel the delight radiating from her.

Eventually the prince had to relinquish her hand, to go on with the business of greetings and introductions and reception into the saloon. I hardly felt his hand, and I believe he barely saw me as he brushed quickly past, his brows now drawn and his dark face looking stern, almost sullen – but, oh, so handsome!

Victoria too brushed against me as she followed her cousin in towards the table where luncheon had been waiting for us. 'Isn't Prince Ferdinand *beautiful?*' she hissed into my ear.

I could not disagree. My own knees felt almost weak from the sight of him. The introduction of so much brooding handsomeness, so much *man*, into our quiet world at Kensington Palace was going to have quite an upsetting effect.

Chapter 26

The Grand Fancy-Dress Ball

At ten o'clock that night, the warm lights of the orangery drew us across the cold, wet gardens just as fluttering insects are attracted to a flame. We could hear the violins and the laughter spilling out and vanquishing the damp and dark.

My father and I were a little late for the ball. He'd experienced some mishap dressing; at least I had heard him shouting at his valet that he could not appear at a ball in trousers and that his breeches *must* be found. I was waiting in the hallway of our apartment, rebalancing my gilded laurel wreath, made by Lehzen's cunning fingers, on the back of my head.

As he came down the stairs I heard him splutter with laughter.

'Miss V!' he said. 'Are you going in your nightgown?' I could see why he asked, for my white dress was very simple, very long and very straight.

But as I spun round to face him, he came to a halt on the stairs, and the laughter stopped. 'By golly!' he said quietly. 'You have indeed grown into a young lady of excellent taste, my dear. Unusual taste, but that need not be a bad thing. There are so many flashy, showy misses about town today.' He tucked my hand under his arm, patted it, and we set off together into the night.

I wondered how my life would have been different if, like Jane, I were used to going to parties and balls. Would people have admired me? Would I have enjoyed it? I was not sure. Tonight seemed like an ordeal, but I must admit that there was a nervous beat of excitement inside my chest as well.

My mother made one of her rare appearances in my thoughts. When I was little I had imagined that she would dress me for my first ball, that she would send me off, perhaps waving from the porch of Arborfield Hall as I climbed into a carriage with Jane. Everything had changed since then.

As we passed the aged Princess Sophia's apartment,

my father veered off course and pulled me in through the door. 'The old lady would so love to see you all dressed up for the ball,' he said. 'You don't mind, do you?'

I did mind, for I hated people to stare at me. But it was well worth it. I tripped into her small, cluttered sitting room and spun round once or twice, and she almost clapped her hands with joy.

'Those two German princes will be wild to dance with you, my dear,' she said.

'I hardly think that I shall dance with royalty!' I replied, although I could not help but smile at her kindness.

I sensed the adults exchanging a glance over my head. Perhaps they were wondering, as I had, what it would be like if I were a normal young lady coming out into society, perhaps being asked for my hand in marriage by some eligible young man. I brushed the disturbing thought aside, picked up my white mask with its expression moulded into a tragic pose and began to tie its strings around the back of my head. The ball was a masquerade and we had to hide our faces.

'Papa, I think we should go,' I said. 'Would you be so good as to help me fix my mask?'

But the old princess had not finished admiring me and insisted on seeing my shoes. Only then did she let us depart, with one final injunction:

'Take good care of her, Sir John! She is too precious to fall into the hands of a scoundrel – and there are so many of them about these days!'

'A rich railway magnate would make an excellent match,' my father replied. It seemed a strangely inconsequential thing to say, but I had no time to ask him what he meant, for we were off at a fine pace.

Stepping into the lighted ballroom was a mixture of agony and ecstasy. I stiffened my spine and drew myself up tall as I could, as if to face an ordeal. A strange footman, not Adams, bellowed out the words, 'Sir John and Miss V. Conroy!' to the heaving crowd. But it was nowhere near as bad as I had expected. To my relief, very few people looked up, and among those who did I saw one or two smiles of welcome. Stepping forward into the crowd was like launching ourselves into a warm new world, a world of swirling skirts and music and dozens of candles.

I could soon see that the entirety of the room's attention was focused upon the dancing area, and there – yes, it was true – there was Victoria, whirling round in the arms of Prince Ferdinand. Unlike the other guests, he had come in normal dignified evening dress. And I thought there was something rather arrogant about that. Victoria's shepherdess's hat, and the mask across her eyes, hid the upper part of her face, so that to most observers her name would have been unknown. But I could see that her small mouth and apple-shaped cheeks, so like my own, held an expression of utter delight.

It was at that moment, seeing her transported as if in the arms of an angel, that a cold premonition fell upon me. Was she falling in love? Did she not realise that she would not be allowed to choose her own handsome prince?

Although it was hot in the room, I twitched my bare shoulders as if there were a chill.

My father swam through the rich, perfumed air of the ballroom like a fish in its native element. Everywhere he went he called out greetings, shook hands, bowed and showered joviality upon the guests. Fantastical characters – ranging from bishops to ballerinas to devils – swirled around the floor, or else flirted and gossiped on the side-lines and tried to guess each others' identities. I thought I spotted Prince August spinning along in his brother's wake in all the gold-frogged splendour of a hussar's uniform.

My father went to stand near the duchess at the head of the room, and together they proudly surveyed the scene. For a moment, it was hard to remember that they were not a married couple, so well did they suit each other in good looks and high colour and high spirits. For a moment, the grinding dullness and stifling boredom of the System seemed to be firmly in the past. They looked like proud parents at their daughter's first dance. The thought, the sight, made me feel a little sick.

The music swirled to a climax and a close, and by chance I discovered Victoria and her partner coming to a halt just a few steps away from me. I raised an eyebrow at her over the prince's shoulder. I knew that she would know what I meant. Was he a good dancer? Was she enjoying herself? 'Oh yes!' she mouthed, vigorously nodding her head towards the prince. As their limbs disengaged, she nevertheless kept his hand tight within her own, as if she never meant to let him go.

I giggled, pulled into her pleasure despite my concerns. But then the crowd tugged us apart. I myself had no partners lined up, and during the intermission I was too timid to take any steps to get one. I wiggled my way discreetly through the crush and sat down next to Lehzen on a little gold chair. But hardly had I taken my seat when a tall Pierrot was bowing down before us and asking me for the pleasure. I felt myself blush and glanced at Lehzen. But she gave me an encouraging nod and one of her lopsided smiles. So I stood up, smoothing down my long Grecian gown, and consented to take his hand.

A moment later, we too were whirling round the floor.

It was faster, much faster, than the dancing lessons Victoria and I had shared in the seclusion of the dingy old drawing room, and the fiddles played far more furiously than the old musical box that had provided our staid country ditties.

This Pierrot, grinning behind his mask, seemed to have immense strength and power; he grasped my waist and spun me round as easily as a child with a top. I could see only the wet pinky-white of his eyes and the startling red of the inside of his mouth when he opened it to laugh. As we danced, a huge wave of excitement began to run up and down my spine. But whether it was caused by the music, the brush of Prince Ferdinand's coat sleeve as he passed with Victoria in his arms, or the powerful grip of my partner, I did not know.

Another tune came to a close, and now, in my giddy state, drunk with waltzing, I actually needed the strength of his arm to prevent me from falling over. My partner steered me expertly through a screen of potted plants into the alcove facing the one where the band played. Here he pushed me down upon a garden bench, which had presumably been brought inside for the duration of the cold weather, and plumped himself down next to me.

'By Jove!' he said, panting a little. 'What a remarkable filly you have become!' I tweaked my skirt down modestly over my golden sandals and cradled my bare upper arms with my hands. I was not entirely comfortable with his tone, and I had a feeling that his voice was familiar. I wondered what steps had been taken to prevent uninvited guests from gaining admittance, as the masks made it impossible to know who was who.

'May I know your name, sir?' I asked. I began to wish that we were still dancing, or, even better, that I was dancing with someone else. A beautiful new tune, soaring and dipping like a skylark, had begun, and it now seemed an awful waste to be sitting here backstage and away from the rest of the ball.

'Oh no!' he said, laughing so that I saw a row of gums and perhaps even a little bit of his dinner caught in his back teeth. It was not a pleasant sight. 'Tonight we are all mysterious,' he said in a superior manner. 'Except, of course, for Prince Ferdinand. The rules don't apply to him, it seems, though it is most impolite to ignore the dress code. The scoundrel! He longs to have all the royal ladies of Europe in love with him. What abominable boldness to show his face to the public as he works his wiles.'

'What do you mean, sir?'

With a lurch of the stomach, I feared that I knew already. For it hardly took my expert knowledge of

Victoria's character to deduce what must also have been embarrassingly obvious to everyone. Somehow, between lunch and dinner, Victoria had fallen in love with this handsome prince and was not even trying to hide it.

'They make a grotesque pair, don't they?' He laughed again, slapping his thigh this time and treating my question as if it were hardly worth considering.

He smiled down at me, and suddenly the black mask and the strangely blank eyes behind it seemed to present a sinister aspect.

'Little and large, heh?' he said. 'Fat and thin. The beast and the beauty. The most beautiful prince in Europe, they say.'

He paused, as if expecting contradiction, but I could think of no more beautiful prince than Ferdinand.

'Well, Prince Ferdinand is her cousin,' I said defensively. 'It would make a fine match. Keeping it in the family.'

'God!' he snorted. 'I see that this fine prince has neglected to inform his cousin or her household that he is *engaged*. Engaged to be married! Already! To the Queen of Portugal. Not dancing like a man with an engagement, is he?'

'I don't believe you!' I said shortly. But the floor seemed to sink away beneath my feet, and I swayed again and reached for the arm of the bench. I felt a tremendous emptying out of all the happiness I had felt only half an hour earlier, almost as if I were a jug and someone had poured all the water out of me at once.

'Well, my priggish little miss!' He cackled again, and I wondered how much of the fruit punch he had consumed. 'I told you once before what a scoundrel your father is, do you remember? And have you had the chance to find it out for yourself by now?'

Suddenly it clicked. There was something memorably piggish about those pink eyes, the fair skin of those strong hands, the power of his tall but stocky body. George Cumberland was older now, a real young man, but still the same unpleasant person.

'Sir!' I stood up abruptly and awkwardly, gaining my balance with difficulty. 'Thank you for the dance, but I must now return to my governess.'

I strolled away with what I hoped was nonchalant ease. But inside I was trembling violently. I almost groped my way across the dance floor, apologising to the couples whose path I impeded. Sinking down next to Lehzen, I whispered the dreadful news.

'George of Cumberland is here!'

She turned to me, her face a picture of worry and disgust.

'And he says that Prince Ferdinand shouldn't be dancing with the princess like that, for *he is engaged to another lady*.'

Lehzen took my hand and squeezed it. She could tell by the droop of my shoulders that I was angry and deflated. 'Let us not take the word of that liar,' she said consolingly. 'We must investigate more carefully. And don't be disappointed. There will be other balls, my dear. This is only your first one!'

'I know. I am not disappointed for myself,' I replied. 'But will there ever again be a ball as perfect for Victoria?'

Watching her happy face as she flew around the floor, still in Ferdinand's arms, I think that we both doubted it.

Chapter 27

The Morning After

The next morning I was first to appear in the drawing room of the princess's grand new apartment. For some considerable time, I sat there alone at the desk in the corner, writing notes of thanks for the duchess to sign to the tradesmen who had brought the fruit and the ices and the decorations. The ladies had long since abdicated such responsibilities to me, and I almost enjoyed the labour as I could indulge my passion for being neat and orderly. But some of the bills had already arrived in the morning's post and seemed to me to be very steep. Again, I wondered where my father had found the duchess all this money.

From time to time I lifted my head from the paper

and shook myself in my seat, as if to shrug off the effects of the late night and my disturbing thoughts. I had gone to bed reasonably early, sated with the ball, but I knew that my father, and presumably the princess and duchess, had been up into the small hours.

I was just finishing the address on the final envelope when I heard the confident clack of a man's boots on the boarded floor from the direction of the door. The sound made my heart lurch unpleasantly, but only for a second. I told myself that I had every right to be here in the palace drawing room, and that the duchess would be well pleased with the work I had completed.

As I pushed the sheets and envelopes together into a neat stack, I looked up to see the younger prince standing before me. Prince August. He shared his brother's long face and nose, but on him the effect was mournful rather than deliciously tragic. He gave an extremely low continental bow, straightened himself up, then sighed breathily.

'I trust, mademoiselle,' he said, 'that you slept well?' Sinking down into a nearby sofa, he sighed again. 'I fear I cannot say the same for myself.' He raised the back of his wrist to his forehead. I wondered if this was an invitation to me to gush with sympathy or to rush for coffee and seltzer water. But I felt in no mood to pander to anyone else's sensitivities.

'I did, thank you, sir,' I said, bowing a little from the waist without rising. I shuffled my envelopes and made a show of putting my pen back in the inkstand, before spinning my seat around and raising my eyes to meet his. Under my cool gaze, an element of self-consciousness stiffened his sprawling body, and he raised himself up into a more proper, seated position.

Emboldened, I went on. 'But I fear that Her Royal Highness, my mistress the princess, may have had her peace of mind disturbed.' I let out a sigh of my own and knitted my brow in genuine perplexity. 'I do not believe that she is acquainted with the true ... erm, with the truth of your brother's *circumstances*.'

At this he flinched, and he had the grace to look deeply uncomfortable. I noticed a rosy flush appearing on his throat as he rubbed the heels of his hands into his eye sockets, then smoothed back the black, un-British waves of his longish hair.

He seemed at a loss to know how to proceed.

'I believe,' he said eventually, 'that the matter of my brother's ... engagement to the Queen of Portugal is quite well known.'

'Not by me, sir,' I said, refusing to be cowed and continuing to gouge him with my eyes, 'until I heard of it from a mere acquaintance at the ball last night. And not,

267

I believe, by my mistress, unless your brother told her in the early hours. And may I suggest that he was not acting quite as an engaged gentleman should?'

Prince August slumped in his sofa once more, threw back his head and laughed. 'Well, my prim little English miss!' he said much more warmly. 'I must admit that you are right! You are quite formidable! I surrender.'

Now he smiled, and still shaking his head, he leaned forward with his hands upon his knees.

'Between you and me,' he said, glancing over his shoulder towards the door, 'my brother never knows when to stop. He cannot see a girl without wanting to make her fall in love with him. And, to be completely honest, he rather dreads his coming marriage and wants to avoid thinking about it. It was arranged by our Uncle Leopold, you know.'

I sat back and raised the tips of my fingers into a tent. How miserable it must be to be a prince or princess and to have to marry the choice of one's uncle! I returned my gaze to Prince August, wondering what bride might be in store for him, and whether he might like her when the time came.

Perhaps he too was thinking about his own fate. As he sat there, cogitating, I noticed the roses in his cheeks, the gloss in his hair. Yes, this prince, too, was handsome when you got to know him. 'You cannot imagine,' he said eventually, 'how many and heavy are the cares which must be borne by those in a high station in life.'

I wasn't going to let him get away with *that*.

'With great splendour comes great responsibility, though, does it not?' I said steadily. 'I should be most obliged if your brother could see his way to mentioning his engagement to my mistress.'

He coloured again and looked down at his hands.

'Of course,' I went on, 'I do not mean to suggest that the princess has any kind of feelings for your brother beyond those of a respectful relative. A lady never commits herself to a gentleman; it is for him to fall in love with her. But I feel that the situation could be cleared up to everyone's advantage if his engagement were generally known.'

It was a long speech, perhaps longer than I had ever made to anyone outside my immediate circle, but I kept my voice and gaze steady. Only when I had finished did I have to clasp my hands together to keep them from trembling. I would never have spoken so boldly but for the thought that Victoria, my friend, had been deceived, even maliciously tricked, by this man's brother.

He looked down at the floor, thought for a moment, then slowly stood and bowed once more. 'Miss V. Conroy,' he said slowly, 'you speak good sense. I shall see what can be done.'

With a fancy little click of his heels, he turned and was gone.

Trembling, I returned to my desk. But then I felt a breath of air on the back of my neck, and looking up, the door to Victoria's sitting room, off the drawing room, caught my eye. It had been ajar, but now it had swung wide open. There stood a waiflike figure, wan, her hair round her shoulders, a shawl over her nightdress. Victoria stood looking at me, her face an awful picture of woe. She turned, speechlessly, and disappeared back into the shadows.

I heard the thin wail rising from the bedchamber beyond the sitting room. I could picture Victoria burying her face in the mattress to try to stifle the sound, and it broke my heart.

Now Lehzen appeared in the open doorway. 'Yes,' she said, 'we heard everything from the sitting room. And once you had started to speak, there was nothing we could do to expose our presence. *Lieber Gott!* What a mess. He has flirted with her dreadfully.'

She must have seen the distress in my face, for she came forward into the drawing room and laid her hand over mine as it lay on the writing desk. Quickly and quietly she spoke into my ear. 'You did well, my dear,' she said. 'You certainly won that duel of words with Prince August. If only her mother or your father had taken the same trouble to find out the truth and to protect the princess. You have been her true friend this last day.'

She stopped and raised her head. Yes, the sobs were growing louder, becoming almost screams.

'Curse that perfidious prince!' Lehzen said and turned to go, once more, to comfort the weeping princess.

I sighed. It was only a ball, only a setback. Why did she always have to over-react? Once more that dark fear for Victoria's reason came over me. Her mother had such influence on her character, and there were so few of us to counterbalance that love of drama and self-pity.

Chapter 28

Two More Princes

Victoria presented a pitiful sight over the next few weeks. The princes had cut short their visit, departing the day following the ball, but the business with Prince Ferdinand seemed to have put her back into her convalescent state. One day I found her shepherdess dress on the floor of her bedchamber, kicked out of sight under a bureau. 'Look, it's all creased!' I said. 'Shall I send it to be cleaned?'

Victoria gave it a look of distaste. 'Do what you like with it,' she said, turning away as if she could not bear the sight of it. 'Just take it away.'

I also overheard my father and the duchess arguing.

'She needs to learn that life will bring little setbacks,' he snapped.

'But she is so pure, so good! Ach, if only she had a father to protect her, to find out before he came here if the young man's intentions were honourable.'

'Well, your fine brother Leopold should have seen to that, I would have thought. It's his nephew that we are talking about!'

'But Leopold is not here!' she wailed. 'Oh, how defenceless Victoria and I are in this strange country, with no near relations to hand.'

Then the sound of their voices grew still, and I thought it requisite to cough loudly to remind them of my presence in the long gallery. 'Yes, Adams, I know that the post must go,' I said briskly. 'Can you wait one moment while I finish this last letter?'

More and more often I was replying now to letters from Victoria's future subjects sending her their best wishes and hopes that she would soon be queen. Victoria could never settle to such work and let the correspondence build up into great, guilt-making piles of paper, but I actively enjoyed it. I loved reading people's stories, hearing about their families, understanding their problems. I put great care – probably too much care – into my replies, and signed them on behalf of Her Royal Highness the Princess Victoria with as much pride as if it had been my own name.

Her uncle, King William, seemed to disappoint on every level: he was neither energetic nor splendid nor kind. In response to this, most of the letters that came for Victoria at Kensington Palace were simply loyal and loving. Some were crazed and bizarre, written by people who might be ill, but occasionally a more serious missive would pull me up sharp. In particular, I dwelt for a long time over a well-worded warning that the monarchy was a tarnished institution and that civil war in our own country would ensue unless the virginal Victoria, a fresh start, came to the throne and soon. She was, this writer claimed, the monarchy's last hope.

So the weeks went on. The German princes had travelled to Portugal for Ferdinand to do his duty by the bride selected for him by Uncle Leopold, and our lives returned to their normal quiet pattern.

But Uncle Leopold was clearly still working away behind the scenes, and soon we learned that more German cousins were expected at Kensington Palace.

When we gathered one afternoon at the head of the new stone staircase once again to greet a second pair of German cousins, it was like an echo in a minor key of our happy reception of the Princes of Saxe-Coburg-Gotha-Koháry. This new pair of German princes were the sons of yet another of the duchess's brothers. This was the Prince Albert of whom Uncle Leopold had spoken, and his brother Ernest. I rather wished Albert had not come, for it brought back to mind the unwelcome question of Victoria's marriage.

'Leopold!' My father hissed the name to me out of the corner of his mouth as we stood and waited. 'He does not know what he is doing. He sends these German princelings to marry our princess, but believe me, that will never happen.' He seemed to take heart from his own words and puffed out his chest a little. 'You can count on a Conroy for that,' he concluded.

I kept my own counsel, uneasily wishing that he would keep down his voice in case the princess ahead of us might hear.

Adams filled his lungs and spoke in his most sonorous voice as the two young men proceeded up the stairs towards us. 'Princes Ernest and Albert of Saxe-Coburg-Gotha!'

I watched Victoria closely. She had kicked up a great fuss about being made to receive the two new princes today, but her mother had insisted that she be present and correct. Much against the duchess's wishes, she was wearing her black tartan velvet dress.

I knew why she had chosen it. 'If I *have* to go,' she'd grumped, 'I'm wearing my Sir Walter dress.' The dark velvet with its tartan pattern belonged to the windswept, rebellious romance of the Scottish Highlands and our beloved novels of Sir Walter Scott. She always put it on when she was in a stormy mood.

I feared that she was picturing herself as the tragic, jilted fiancée of Prince Ferdinand, forced apart from her lover by the cares of state.

So intent was I upon Victoria, observing her casual, almost dismissive greetings to the visitors, that I failed to pay them much notice for myself. It came as something of a surprise therefore to find the younger prince, Albert, bowing low to me, then taking my hand with real warmth. A pair of blue eyes beneath wavy chestnut hair brushed back from his brow met my own and held them. His mouth quivered slightly, as if with amusement at the ridiculous situation in which we found ourselves. After all, we were drawn up in a formal reception line as if at a grand ball, and there were only the handful of us present.

He smiled so infectiously that I could not restrain myself from smiling back.

As he and his elder brother moved on into the saloon, the pair seemed lively and interested, asking the duchess and my father all sorts of questions about what lay within.

'And is this picture by the master Rembrandt?' Albert asked.

The duchess tinkled. 'As if I should know such things!' she simpered, pleased. 'You must be a knowledgeable young gentleman.'

'Ah, but anyone might see that the room has been furnished with great taste and elegance,' he replied gallantly. 'That must reflect the character of its chatelaine.' The duchess curtsied, and I saw her glance round the room with renewed pride. I noticed that Albert had deftly put her at ease, giving her the attention she always demanded.

I looked at Albert's back, fine and upright in a red military tunic, and noticed that his breeches were very white. Soon he was bowing to Lehzen and speaking to her warmly about her birthplace in Hanover, and now, having discovered his involvement, he was complimenting my father on the colour scheme.

It was Victoria herself who had to give me a little prod to get me moving once more. 'Wake up, moonface!' she whispered. 'They are so soft and girlish compared to my other cousins, are they not? Ernest has rather a soulful face, and Albert is almost beautiful. They look like a couple of angels. Not my idea of handsome.'

I thought privately that soft smiles were much better

than smouldering good looks, and that kindness and politeness were worth far more than arrogance and grandeur. 'Oh, I'm not so sure,' I murmured back at her. 'I've never shared your taste for rogues.'

I hardly joined in the conversation over our drawing room tea and did not presume to sit with Victoria and her two cousins at the round table. I had observed Victoria subtly excluding my father from the group by asking him to fetch the chart with the family tree so that they might see clearly how they were related, and then hardly paying it any attention when he returned. I stayed by myself in a corner, slightly out of sight behind a pillar, and took up some embroidery.

'Have you been long in the service of the princess?'

It was Albert, unexpectedly standing there in front of me, that same merry smile on his lips.

I'd been deeply engaged in my needlework, though, in truth, I had also been lost in a gentle reverie about his very self. I'd had no expectation that the younger brother, my favourite, should pay me special attention. But here he was, come across the room particularly to speak to me.

'Yes, indeed, my whole life, it seems,' I said, stammering.

'I hear that you would have given the princess your life if you could,' he said, in a light and joking tone. 'Your governess has just been telling us of your brave exploits in seeing off an intruder into the palace, back when you were just a little girl.'

I shivered with sheer pride and tried to think of a response that would not seem boastful. But perhaps he took my bashfulness for coldness, for he turned and returned to the communal table.

Yet each time after that when I raised my head from my work, I found that those playful, glowing eyes were upon me. And each time I noticed, I grew stiff and self-conscious. I feared that a blush was ebbing and flowing up and down my throat all afternoon. There was something about this new young prince, with his perfect, self-effacing manners, that was deeply, unsettlingly attractive.

At length there was a call for lamps, the better for the four of them to play a game of cards, and I volunteered quickly to go to fetch them. But as I stepped along the carpeted corridor in search of Adams, I heard a soft tread behind me. I knew who it was even before I had turned to see.

'I shall come to your assistance with the lamps!' Albert said in his low, melodious voice. He stopped and bowed again and placed his hand upon his heart. 'Now that we are alone, let us introduce ourselves less formally. I am

Albert, of Saxe-Coburg-Gotha.' I inclined my head as graciously as I knew how. Of course I knew who he was, and this was hardly an informal introduction, but it was very modest and generous of him to assume that I didn't know his name.

Again I felt a ridiculous smile forcing my cheeks upwards.

I was smiling so broadly that I could hardly speak, but eventually I bowed my head and whispered out the words.

'And I am Victoria.'

For some reason it felt completely natural – as it had never done before – to tell him my name. I had been called 'Miss V' for so long, but I wanted him to know who I really was.

'Victoria,' he said. 'A beautiful name.' I expected him to comment that it was the same as the princess's.

But he didn't.

'Victoria,' he said again slowly, as if savouring it.

I realised that I had allowed myself to become distracted. A bit later than was polite, I curtseyed to thank him for the compliment. But at the very same moment he bowed, and simultaneously our heads, reaching forward, actually clashed slightly. I felt the brush of his hair on my forehead. It could have been immensely awkward, the kind of difficult situation for which a response should be sought in an etiquette book, but Albert simply laughed. So I did too.

'Oh Lord!' he said. 'I hope I have not injured you within seconds of making your acquaintance. Here, let me see.'

He led me along the corridor, despite my protests, to where an oil lamp stood burning on a side table. Under its light he looked at me closely and became so still that my own agitation and protestation was silenced.

'I see you have blue eyes!' he said quietly. 'And I also see that you are not hurt. Indeed, you are quite unblemished and perfect.'

At that moment, I felt a little click inside my chest. I believe that was the first moment in my whole life when my heart truly began to beat. I was worried that the vast thumping sound of it would deafen both him and me.

'Oh, nobody is perfect,' I said at once, which made him smile. At the same time, though, I was thinking that he was very perfection itself.

We went on along the corridor together towards the servants' hall and the lamp room, and now we said nothing as we walked. But I sensed that something important had happened, and I could tell, from his careful tread beside me, that he was still looking at me.

As we drew near to the shadowy place under the curve of the stairs, he stopped me again.

'Excuse me for my ignorance,' he said, 'but am I correct in assuming that you are indeed the Miss Victoria Conroy of whom my Uncle Leopold spoke of back in Germany? Sir John is your father, is that so?'

'Perfectly correct, sir.'

Strangely, I did not mind the impropriety of our standing talking almost in the dark, although if Adams or one of the servants had come past I would have felt deeply discomfited.

'My uncle has often said,' he continued in a soft voice, 'that you are a loyal and devoted friend to the princess. That you will always serve the princess and the country as best you know how.'

Never had I thought to hear such words! And from the mouth of this man who was almost a stranger as well.

'I ... hardly know what to say,' I stammered, again feeling a hot blush rising up my cheeks and towards my hair.

'Say nothing!' he said. 'I can see that it almost pains you to receive praise. That, too, is the sign of a noble, unselfish character.'

We stood there smiling at each other for such a long time that I felt almost dizzy and had to reach up my hand for the balustrade of the stairs. And then the door of the servants' hall was swinging open, and light and voices were spilling out.

'Oh, Adams,' I said, quickly stepping forward, 'we have come for the lamps if you please.'

I hoped he would not see the glow in my cheeks or the sparkle that I knew to have come to my eyes. I hoped that Prince Albert would pay us a very long visit.

Chapter 29

Sir Walter

And so it proved. They stayed for weeks. I had to admit that these two princes were less glamorous than Ferdinand and August, but to me – unlike Victoria – romance was not everything.

I found Ernest to be of good sense, and Albert – why, Albert was well travelled, well educated and delightful. I grew to learn that his burst of lively conversation on the day of the reception was out of character, and that he had forced himself to it in order to make a polite first impression. But that was typical of him, to give of himself.

Each evening, he and I usually found ourselves the most silent members of the family party. But often our eyes would meet and lock as the duchess and the rest went about their lively teasing, scolding, playing and gossiping. Even Victoria could be jollied into laughter on a good day. However, I could also tell that the plaintive, repetitive note in the duchess's conversation pained Albert as it pained me, and sometimes he would be the first in the evening to rise and say that he must go to bed.

'What a grouch my brother is!' Ernest would say. 'Albert the Grouch. It should be his name in the history books. Early to bed, early to rise, makes a grouch happy, wealthy and wise.' It made me smile, for Albert seemed far from grouchy to me. And of course Ernest meant it affectionately, for he was devoted to his younger brother.

One morning I came into the German apartment early, there to find Albert alone in the drawing room and deep in Scott's *The Bride of Lammermoor*.

'Are you also a devotee of Sir Walter?' he asked as he saw me looking at his book. 'Her Royal Highness, my cousin, has lent me this volume, which I am finding most diverting. She says it is a favourite. I was pleased and surprised to discover that she is fond of reading.'

I could not help but smile, for it was my own copy, and Victoria, never a great bookworm, knew the story only because I had read it aloud to her.

Albert instantly noticed my reaction. 'Oh …' he said slowly, 'I believe that I might have understood. Perhaps the book is yours?' He flipped upon the title page. 'Yes, I am right! "Miss V. Conroy", you have written. How enigmatic of you not to share your Christian name, even with Sir Walter.'

'Sir,' I said, 'pray do not mock me. I am of low station. People don't need to know my name.'

'Modest and gentle!' he said. Then he sighed. 'I'm afraid that people do know your name, at least your surname. Please – will you sit?' He got up out of the armchair, patted it to show that I should sit, and positioned himself on a footstool near my knee.

'May I be completely open?' he asked. He waited with his head bowed and his hand upon his heart with continental courtesy until I had begged him to go ahead.

'I have already told you some of what my Uncle Leopold has said about you,' he began. 'He believes that you are to be trusted utterly – a person in a thousand, he says.'

During this speech my eyes had become trained intensely downwards towards my lap, my burning gaze almost searing through the skin on the back of my hands. There was no conceivable way that I could meet his gaze while he was talking in this painful manner.

But at the same time the discomfort was exquisite.

'Say nothing!' Albert said quickly. 'I can see what you

feel.' But now it was his turn to glance towards the ground. 'Yet I'm sorry to say,' he continued, more reluctantly, 'that my uncle does not hold your father in such high regard.'

He lifted his eyes back to mine. I stared back, and despite the shameful stain that must remain in my cheeks from his earlier flattery, I was unable to look away. 'I fear that the princess is not always … well advised,' he said, groping for words, 'by those around her.'

'I cannot help but agree, sir,' I said simply and sincerely. 'I do everything I can to counteract the influence of my father, which is sometimes … overbearing.'

It was the first time, I think, that I had spoken of my fears to anyone who was not Lehzen. Yet here I was, sharing them out loud to someone I had only known for a short time. But then, I reassured myself, Albert was very far from being a stranger. In fact, it felt like I had known him forever. It was a warming thought.

'I can see that it is complicated.' He sighed again. 'I can see that it is difficult for you, this loyalty you feel.'

I nodded. He understood. He was a friend.

But then a less pleasant reflection made me suddenly stand up from the chair and prepare to change the subject. Of course, we could not go on being friends like this when he was married.

'It is my fate, perhaps my burden, to care deeply for the princess,' I said. 'Not only out of duty, but also from affection. I really do want nothing more than her happiness.'

I was thinking now of her wedding to this prince with his mobile mouth and his expressive hands, and for the first time it was a grim prospect. Their marriage would cut me off from both of them.

It was becoming inescapable to me that Prince Albert would be an excellent influence upon Victoria. He was calm; he was wise. Even the duchess could see this.

The next morning, she came into the drawing room as I waited for Victoria, and asked me where he was.

'In the gardens, I believe, Your Grace,' I said.

I had observed him from the window a few moments before, chatting good-naturedly to one of the gardeners. In fact, I had been wondering if I had enough courage to go out to join him there.

'Ah, then I must send Vickelchen outside,' she said. 'She must spend more time with this suitor of hers.' The word 'suitor' came as a little shock, for her daughter's marriage had never been discussed directly between us before. She had spoken as if I were privy to Uncle Leopold's plan and in support of it. I supposed that I was. After all, it was months since he had told me of what he intended. And I could see that Albert was perfect.

'Indeed,' the duchess said to herself, so softly that I could hardly hear. 'You shall not spoil this, Sir John.' She misted the window glass with her breath as she searched outside for her nephew. Perhaps she belatedly realised her indiscretion, for she turned suddenly towards me.

'Miss V!' she said sharply. 'I know that my brother Leopold has confided in you. You must do everything you can to help the match proceed smoothly. That is my royal command. Your father disagrees, but I cannot allow him to wreck it. There have been … painful scenes.'

At that she bustled off to find Victoria. Left by myself, I wondered for a few regretful moments what kind of quarrels and confusions had taken place between them. Then, as if some superior power was exerting its hold over me, I forgot to worry, and my eyes were drawn out of the window once more in search of a dark blue morning coat topped by a curly brown head.

I knew that Victoria herself scarcely gave Albert a second glance. 'Oh, Prince Ferdinand!' she would say to me each morning in the sitting room before her cousins came in to join us. 'Beautiful Prince Ferdinand! When will it stop hurting, Miss V? I have given my heart utterly and forever to Ferdinand. Ferdinand! What a wonderful, romantic name it is.' But she admitted that Prince Ernest, with his lively conversation and good spirits, was a pleasant companion for whiling away the hours.

And each morning I would smile at her and say nothing, though one time I had casually asked her what she thought of Prince Albert.

'Oh, I know that Uncle Leopold wants me to marry him,' she'd said dismissively. 'But he's such a prig! So interested in books and lectures. I could never live with a man like that.'

This had made me both outwardly smile and inwardly wince. She may not have liked it, but it seemed that if Uncle Leopold willed it, then their destiny was to marry.

All at once I felt a little sick inside. The thought made me horribly jealous.

I was beginning to think that it would be utterly delightful to live with a man like Albert. I imagined us sitting each side of the fire in some small apartment like my father's own at Kensington Palace, not in the splendid surroundings of the princess and duchess's rooms; each of us reading a book, discussing what we would have for breakfast the next day … The thought seemed both charming, and very, very wicked. He was to be Victoria's husband! I carefully packed my thoughts away in my mind to turn over later, at night, when I was alone in bed.

I also did not allow myself to dwell on the fact that

this visit must inevitably come to an end. If I thought about it at all, I encouraged myself with the notion that it would become easier and more satisfying once again to concentrate on Victoria's correspondence, her dresses, our meals. I had been skimping my duties, but only because there were so many new things to think about.

But for now, I told myself firmly, I had the excuse that the princes were still here, demanding our attention. For once, I would live from day to day and enjoy each one of them.

Chapter 30

Princess Sophia in Danger

One evening, as spring moved into early summer, the dining table was set and dressed with flowers, and the family were gathered in the drawing room. The duchess tapped me on the shoulder with her fan. 'Miss V,' she said in what, for her, was a low voice. 'We are expecting the Princess Sophia tonight, and dinner is ready. Please go and ask Adams to find out where she is.'

'Of course.'

I gave my curtsey and discreetly wove my way between my father, Prince Ernest and Victoria, who were vigorously discussing horses, and slipped out through the big double doors. I was wearing a new silk dress in very pale primrose yellow, and I thought it quite the prettiest thing I had ever owned. It had been ordered in a hurry last week and delivered just this morning. I had decided that I really needed several more outfits than my rather limited wardrobe contained – after all, Victoria had been telling me for years that my clothes were dull. At last, it seemed, I could dimly perceive what she had been saying.

Out on the landing, I almost bumped into Prince Albert. 'Good evening!' he said, snatching my hand in his strong warm grip and carrying it up to his lips. 'I haven't seen that dress before, have I?'

I bowed my head, chagrined that my little manoeuvre had been detected. I didn't want him to think I had dressed up for him. And yet I was glad he had noticed.

'I am just going to call upon the Princess Sophia across the courtyard,' I explained. 'She is expected to dinner but has not yet arrived. I could send Adams, but I think she would prefer it if I went myself.'

'The lady with the cat?' said Albert. 'She is a friend of mine. Permit me to accompany you.'

I wondered how on earth he had made the acquaintance of the old and rather batty princess. Most young men, I thought, would have run miles rather than permit themselves to be enticed into her musty drawing room. In fact, the imagined thought of the horror on Prince

Ferdinand's face, if summoned to the princess's abode, made me smile.

'Of course,' I said again, leading the way by running lightly down the stairs.

Out in the courtyard, darkness was falling. Now that it was May, the air was much warmer and more fragrant than on the inhospitable March night of the ball. But I detected something of the same atmosphere in the palace, of anticipation, of pleasure to come. The very lamps seemed to wink through the various windows in a friendly fashion, and the geraniums in the pots on the steps seemed to nod in the slight breeze. Or perhaps, as I came to think of it, the pleasure and anticipation lay not in the palace, but in myself, relishing the evening that lay ahead. An evening in the company of Albert.

I led him quickly across the cobbles to the front door of Princess Sophia's apartment, and knocked. There was no reply, which did not surprise me. She was very deaf, and I believed that her still more elderly maid was even deafer.

I made as if to open the door, but Albert gripped my arm. I looked at him in some alarm. 'Can you smell … smoke?' he asked. Together, we craned to look in through the window of her drawing room.

Instantly my good humour fled and my palms tingled with a strange sensation.

The room was full of light, yes, but it was not the friendly light of hearth or lamp. Red, flickering flames were climbing the wall – I could see their very tongues attacking the wallpaper – and the furniture was only dimly to be seen through clouds of smoke.

Even as I looked, there was a crash. Albert had used his shoulder to burst his way through the door, retreating almost at once with his sleeve across his face.

'I can see her!' he said, between retches and coughs caused by the smoke. He stood by me, with his palms placed against the wall, and spat a horrible smoky mixture out of his lungs. 'But I cannot hold my breath for long enough to reach her. It looks like she is lying down on the hearth rug, or where it used to be.'

I gasped and tried to think what to do. 'I'll fetch Adams!'

'No, no, we must be quick.'

I squeezed my stupefied brain into action.

'Take this!'

I snatched off the lace fichu that covered my shoulders. He reached out for it, but I gestured at him to wait. I dipped it into the dish of water left out for the princess's cat.

'Inspired!' he said, clapping the fichu up against his mouth as a kind of mask. Then he turned to face the blaze.

'Albert!'

For an instant he turned, but I could see that he was impatient to throw himself back into the flames. I felt guilty for having stopped him in doing his duty.

'Be careful!'

He smiled. Even amid the heat and hurry and danger of the moment, my heart contracted because he had that smile for me. Then he disappeared into the gloom and the dreadful loud cracks and reports as timber was devoured by flame.

I peered through the window as best as I could from outside, but the smoke was so dense I could barely see a thing. The fire was now making a dull, deep roar, and I could hear crashes that might have been Albert banging into the furniture. I twisted my hands uselessly together. Should I fetch help? But if I left, would Albert burn alive with no one to know where he had gone?

I searched desperately around the courtyard for water, for aid, for anything. But there was nobody, nothing. At last, through the gateway, I saw the soldiers returning from guard duty. It must have been the hour of the end of the watch.

Just as I had done when the intruder came into Victoria's bedroom, I screamed. It was a mixture of 'Help!' and 'Oh!' and 'Fire!' It was a high-pitched sliver of sound that cut through the evening air. One soldier paused and looked round, then they were all running over.

Panting, I waved to summon them to move more quickly. But even then, something knocked against my bare shoulder. Spinning round, I realised that it was the old lady's foot. Albert had Sophia in his arms. His clothes, his hair, all were black. He was breathing hard, and I can tell he was trying not to retch once more. Carefully he laid the old lady down on the cobbles, and I sank down too and cradled her head on my lap. Behind us, the cries and calls of the soldiers told me that they were trying to prepare water supplies before making their way into the blazing building. 'The engine!' I heard, and 'Buckets!'

I met Albert's anxious eyes, which now looked very white in his smutty face. The Princess Sophia had not moved, nor apparently breathed. I placed the back of my hand very close to her lips, and held my own breath, and prayed.

Yes!

There was the faintest breath of air. In a moment or two, she was choking and coughing, and Albert was dripping water from the cat's dish between her lips. She clutched my hand with a powerful grip. 'My dear!' she panted. 'Your young man saved my life, you know. But have you seen my cat? Where is Tiddles?'

Albert was on his feet. 'Tiddles!' he said. 'How could I forget Tiddles?' He went running back inside, calling for the cat.

'It is my own fault,' she said weakly. 'I was sitting too near the fire, and I perhaps took a little snooze, and when I woke the flames were at my apron. I ripped it off but it was too late. Oh! It was awful!'

'But Your Royal Highness, where was your servant?'

Feebly, she waved her hand in the air in a gesture of denial. 'Gone,' she said. 'No … money to pay, my dear,' she said. 'Your father has been so good to me. He has helped me. I get on quite well.'

Not so well now, I thought, looking down at her tired and filthy old face. She closed her eyes. I had the impression that she had retreated into her own world.

But then she surprised me by snapping open her eyes once more.

'I owe so much to you, my dear,' she said, 'for looking after me in my hour of need. I am surrounded here in my home by good, gentle people. There is your kind young man there, who has found Tiddles, and your good, generous papa.'

Albert was kneeling beside us, the cat in his arms, and I could see my father and Adams coming out of the big door of Victoria's apartment. 'Come away, come away,

298

ladies!' my father was saying, taking charge. 'The building is not safe, come away.'

I was glad to let him raise Princess Sophia to her feet and coax her into the duchess's apartment. I was left sitting on the cobbles, but Albert's dirty hand was extended towards me and his strong arm was lifting me up. Now, with the delayed shock, I felt weak, and I leaned upon him heavily as we went. My father and the princess had gone on ahead when Albert suddenly stopped. He lowered his mouth to my hair and stood still, clutching my shoulders. 'Do you know what I thought in there?' he whispered. 'Do you know what kept me going through the smoke? It was the thought of acquitting myself well in your eyes.'

My heart lurched inside me like a wild thing, and all the dirt and sweat and shock melted away. I said nothing, saw nothing but the sight of his steady gaze, which I returned with all my heart.

'Victoria,' he said, 'you make me the best version of myself.'

'Sir!' I whispered at length. 'You must not speak so. It is unfitting. Remember your status.'

He laughed. 'Silly billy!' he said. 'It's too late for that. You know that I love you. And there's no need to say anything. I know that you love me too.' With that, he lowered his lips and planted a kiss on my sooty forehead.

He knew me well enough to know that this would distress me almost as much as it pleased me. So he swiftly walked me on, allowing me no time to protest, and I had to bend my head to hide the crimson tide of pleasure that was rising and spreading and warming me from head to foot.

Chapter 31

Dinner at Windsor

The weeks after Albert and Ernest's departure were sad and drab. I believe that they were harder on me than anyone else in the household, for I had to keep it from everyone that Albert and I had become sincerely attached to each other.

The only thing that lightened my gloom was the feeling that Albert shared my sense of having met a true kindred soul. As he followed his brother down the stairs to the carriage on the very last morning of their stay, he took my hand and drew me aside.

'I entreat you,' he said out of earshot of his brother, 'to permit me to write to you.'

'With pleasure,' I said and smiled.

It was only as his back disappeared out of sight that I gasped with the boldness of what I had done. To enter into a secret correspondence with a young man would ruin my reputation if it were to become known. And it was contrary to the stated wishes of both the duchess and King Leopold of the Belgians, no less.

'What was he saying to you?' asked Victoria curiously, as the carriage drove away.

'Oh, nothing!'

I should have realised that such a response would only encourage her.

'Really, Miss V!' she said. 'Come on. You never have anything scandalous to tell me. What's the secret?'

In the end I told her to leave me alone because I had a headache. And in truth the wretched, miserable experience of the princes' departure had made me physically ill.

'Well, go and lie down, Miss V,' said Victoria. 'You do look pale. I shall have to take care of you. It's just you and me again now, isn't it? Come on, to the sofa and rest, and then later on we'll take Dash out. We haven't taken him for a run together for ages.'

Her unwitting kindness made me feel even worse.

I knew that Albert, too, could see only insurmountable obstacles ahead of us. We could correspond, but it would hardly ease the pain of parting. He could never ask for my hand in marriage. The System would not allow it.

The daily round of pianoforte, walking Dash and writing letters resumed. Once I had revelled in this quiet life, but now it seemed a little tame. Partial relief came in the form of an invitation, in the summer, to Windsor Castle. Now that Victoria was an interesting young lady of seventeen, who had danced at a masquerade, King William the Fourth decided that he wanted to take a look at his niece. In the days before the visit, we at least had the excitement of packing a trunk and preparing dresses.

'Oh!' Victoria said one morning while I was reading and she was opening letters from Germany. The princess was also in correspondence with Albert, I knew, as a cousin and a friend, exactly as her Uncle Leopold would have wished. 'The boys have been to a spa. Swimming! How about that?'

All at once I blushed and hung my head, feeling guiltier and worse than ever. I had so nearly said that I already knew about the trip to Baden Baden. 'I … didn't realise,' I stammered out, 'that Albert could swim.'

'Why should you?' she asked, but idly, scanning the rest of the letter quickly as if it bored her. 'It is surprising. I suppose he is a bit of a drip. I can't imagine he's much good at it.'

'Well, he does ride, *and* shoot, *and* hunt!' I piped up loyally.

'Really?' she asked. 'I never heard him talk about that. Only about boring old books or music or paintings. Yawn. What a pair of goody-goodies you both are. But I'm glad you mentioned it, because, do you realise, it's practically the first thing you've said all morning? Come on, enough reading. Where have we got to with the wretched Windsor dresses?'

It was only with memories of Albert, especially his kiss on the night of the fire, that I consoled myself during the dull hours as Lehzen and I aired and refurbished Victoria's gowns for a reception, a dinner and two nights away. There had been much negotiation, as was standard between the two rival courts of the king and the duchess, about the length of our stay. It had been finally determined as two nights.

Victoria herself was deeply ambivalent. Since our very first visit to Windsor to see the old king, the gloss for her had worn off. She wanted nothing to do with the king and the court, nothing that would remind her of what lay ahead. We had to coax her into the carriage, for appealing to her morality and reminding her of where her duty lay only made things worse.

When finally we climbed in and took the road to the

west, my thoughts could not help but return to the time I had travelled in the opposite direction to begin my life at Kensington Palace. That had been long ago, before I met my dearest friend Victoria, and my dearest Albert. Then, as now, I sat opposite my father. But I pondered on how much stronger and more confident I had become. I knew now that I need not be a slave to my shyness. I still had it – I always would – but when I tried, I could cast it aside.

This time we were heading straight to Windsor Castle itself, a fine, fairy-tale sight as we climbed up the steep road into Windsor town.

'King George the Fourth, bless his selfish old soul, really was quite marvellous at devising buildings,' said my father, admiring the turrets and towers against the sky.

'Yes,' the duchess was quick to respond. 'That is why he was so tight with his money that he never gave the future queen her rightful allowance!'

Once we had been shown to our rooms in the castle, I quickly went to find Victoria, hardly stopping to wash my hands and certainly without a pause to rest. I was very worried about her and about how she would behave during this stay.

As was only right for the princess, she had been given a vast room, and it was to be found along a wide, curved corridor. I discovered her standing and staring out of the window. There was a tremendous view over the great park below, with its avenue of trees marching up and up towards the sky. Merely the thought of walking along that seemingly endless avenue made me tired. And Victoria herself appeared still to be in a particularly sombre frame of mind.

'Are you thinking about the time when you will come to live here yourself?' I asked lightly, not wanting to intrude, but wanting to help if I could.

She turned and threw herself down upon the small armchair near the window. 'Yes, I am,' she said. 'It's splendid, isn't it? So much more magnificent than Kensington Palace. But almost … like a cage. I won't be able to walk in that park without many eyes looking at me from this great barrack of a building. This must be one of a hundred windows.'

'But, Victoria,' I pointed out, 'ever since you were a baby you've had people watching you. You, more than anyone, are used to it.'

'But at Kensington Palace I had you and Lehzen, and there are no crowds of people there unless we hold a party. Here it will be different. Everything will be different. I shall be quite alone.'

She sat unusually quietly, still looking out at the trees.

In her face I could see traces of the ghostly, ghastly little girl I had first met at Kensington Palace. 'I shall not leave you all alone if I can help it,' I whispered to myself, and clenched my fists.

'You know, there's only nine months to my eighteenth birthday now,' she said, turning suddenly as if reading my mind. 'Everyone knows. Don't pretend that your father and Uncle Leopold – and other people too, I'm sure – don't keep calendars and count the days down.'

It was true. I could not deny that I had often seen my father looking in his pocketbook after dinner and checking off another passing day. I knew without being told that he was hoping the old king would die before Victoria's eighteenth birthday so that there would be a regency. I needed no reminding that the duchess and he would then step forward as powers behind the throne.

'Exactly, and I don't think that the king will die tomorrow,' I said. 'He may be old and sick, but I'm sure that he will live another nine months. You will rule for yourself, as *you* want to, as a grown-up. I'm certain of that.'

She smiled a sad little smile. 'You're right,' she said. 'I believe that the very thought of a regency makes my uncle the king cling on to life, so little does he want my mother and your father to rule.'

I also believed this to be true, for my father was not

popular at court. I knew that we had to be more careful than ever of assassins, intruders, chills, illnesses and, more subtly, a loss of confidence that could reduce her chances of success.

'Of course your uncle will live until at least then,' I said with more warmth than I felt. 'He is a tough old sailor, is he not? He sailed in the Royal Navy before he was king. And you wouldn't be alone in any case. Lehzen and I will come with you, if you will have us, and in due course you will marry.'

'Marry.' Her eyes turned away and roamed back out of the window, towards the trees. 'They all want me to marry,' she said. 'But I have met the only man I could ever marry, and he is gone away.'

It pained me to think of Uncle Leopold's plan for Victoria and Albert, but I could not resist the chance of mentioning his name. 'But you know your cousin Albert is your uncle's choice. Have you changed your mind at all?' I closed my eyes as if they were tired while I waited for her answer. I did not want her to be able to read my expression.

'Well, he's perfectly nice,' she conceded. 'But he's too quiet. He likes going to bed too early. Do you know what, Miss V? He reminds me of you. You're good for me; he'd be good for me; I know that. But I don't always want things that are good for me. Sometimes I want things that are BAD.'

She was right about Albert's love of early hours. When in recent weeks Victoria had been ragging and raging late at night and insisting that we should all stay up late, I had often wished that Albert had been there with his quiet, clever way of breaking up the party and allowing everyone else to retire. I had seen for myself that he had a knack of persuading her to do the thoughtful and sensible thing without the usual dramatic scenes.

'But, Victoria!' I could not help responding. 'I'm not just like … medicine for you, am I? I'm not always such a prim little miss as you make out, you know.'

'Oh yes, you are,' she said. 'Far too good to live on earth really. You ought truly to be an angel. You make me sit up straighter. But I still love you, you know, you dear old thing. We are like two old prisoners in a jail, are we not? We're used to each other – after all, we've shared a cell for a long time now.'

With that she threw an arm around me and gave me a bold, smacking kiss. It was the sort of thing her mother did the whole time, but Victoria could somehow imbue such a light action with real warmth of feeling. When Jane had done this kind of thing, years ago, it had made me rigid with tension. But with Victoria it was easy to squeeze her back.

'Ergh!'

With one of her strange, wild swings of mood, she pushed me away, leaned her head forward between her knees and began tearing at her hair. 'I wish I were an ordinary girl! With dozens of gentlemen calling upon me and asking my hand in marriage, and me refusing them all!'

This was exactly the sort of thing that could damage her irreparably if anyone else heard her. 'Oh, nonsense,' I said. 'Your uncle will choose well for you. And come on, it's time to dress.'

'No,' she said, 'I won't dress. I don't want to go to the stupid dinner with all those stupid, stuffy courtiers. You must go in my place.'

'Victoria!' I cried. 'Don't be silly. Come on, you really must pull yourself together.'

'Pull yourself together, behave properly, that's always, always the way, isn't it?' she said wildly. She began stripping off her dress, and was soon leaping about the room in her petticoat and pantaloons. 'I'm not going,' she shrieked. 'I can't go and sit there, good as gold, to be looked at. I really can't. Honestly, Miss V, the only way I could get through it would be to take some of mother's drops. Go and get them for me if you want me to go.'

I stared at her aghast. Then she leapt into the enormous bed and buried her head under the pillow. She lay there, silent.

I really was flummoxed. I was used to such displays, but at a time like this! With the king and his court waiting for us within the hour! I felt almost angry at her, as she placed me in a most trying position, but it was also tragic to see her so unhappy. What was I to do?

As I stood there uncertainly, hoping that Victoria would change her mind, the duchess came bustling in. But she had as little success as I in making Victoria talk, let alone dress. Her hot temper was quickly roused, and she spoke sharply to Victoria in German.

'There's nothing for it.' Finally some words came distantly from under the counterpane, and at the sound the duchess froze. 'Miss V will have to go in my place. Otherwise there will be an empty seat and a scandal, and the king will think that you, Mother, cannot be trusted to look after me at all.' Victoria's voice was buried beneath the pillow, but we heard her clearly enough.

Dismayed, the duchess and I stared at each other.

'Vickelchen!' she begged. 'Please do not kill me with embarrassment. Please do me the credit of appearing like a good princess should.'

311

At that Victoria poked her head out from under the covers.

'Mother!' she said. 'You don't understand. I am *not* a good princess. I really cannot go down. My nerves will not let me. You must go, with Miss V, and all will be well.'

The duchess seized my elbow in a steely grip.

'Get ready,' she hissed. 'Curl your hair. We will be at the top table. We will be far from the eyes of the crowd, and King William has not seen his niece since she has been grown up.'

I turned to her, embarrassed that she would recommend such a crazy course of action. But then I remembered just how crazy she was.

'Go on, Miss V,' came a little voice from the bed. 'Please. Go and play my part for me. Don't make me take the drops.'

I stood, dithering.

'You're letting us all down,' I said to Victoria sharply, perhaps as sharply as I'd ever spoken to her.

'Please!' She begged me again. 'Please! *Don't make me take the drops.*'

It was the mention of the drops that did it. I succumbed to the two powerful personalities.

As soon as she saw my tentative, doubting nod of agreement, the duchess was pushing and pulling me into

Victoria's silver gown. It fitted so well it was almost made for me. But it was cut lower on the shoulders than I would ever have permitted in a gown of my own.

'Look at your neck!' the duchess said encouragingly. 'It is as long as a swan's. You will be very fine. Here, rings.'

I dropped one of them as I tried in my haste to thrust them too quickly on to my fingers. My eye caught my own familiar hands, bejewelled and lying against the backdrop of a skirt of rich, lustrous silver.

But there was no time to contemplate how odd they looked there.

'Tiara!' The duchess was back in front of me, more urgent than any lady's maid would ever dare to be, imperiously gesturing me to bow my head for the reception of diamonds. Her hands were here, there and everywhere in a blur of motion, tweaking and thrusting my hair into place. 'I wish,' she said, through gritted teeth, 'that it was this easy to dress Vickelchen.'

All too soon it was done, and I was standing uncertainly in the middle of the room without even having had the chance to examine myself in the looking glass.

'There, Miss V! Now turn round and let me have one last check.'

Anxiously the duchess inspected my dress, smoothed my hair.

She smiled.

I passed the test.

'You *do* look like her,' she said, half pleased, half amazed. 'You have always served us well, Vickelchen and I,' she went on, imploring me with her big, bold eyes. I could see that they were bright with tears, and that it was only with a frantic, blinking effort that she was able to keep the liquid from spilling over. 'Serve us now!' she begged again. 'Play your part!'

She turned decisively and led the way from the room. Then there was nothing for it but to follow her along the corridor, past the footmen, down the stairs. I kept close behind her, almost stepping on her train, my eyes on the floor. I was an impostor! This was a deception! Surely we would never carry it off. I felt my old enemy, my blush, starting to colour my cheeks. Nothing kept me walking but my memory of Victoria begging me to go down in her place.

At the bottom of the stairs, by some mismanagement of the household staff, there stood gathered a group of maids and porters. The duchess tut-tutted, but they parted like waves at our approach, and there was a general bending of the knees in curtseys. Then, from behind us as we passed, a young voice piped up.

'God bless you, Princess Victoria!' it said.

The young housemaid who had spoken was instantly shushed by her companions. These were well-trained servants who knew that they were to be seen and not heard. But somehow they did have their own way of expressing approbation. There was a murmur, or susurration, from among them, and I felt that they were pleased. As I walked away in the duchess's wake, I straightened my back. I felt their hopeful eyes upon me, and their collective gaze strengthened my spine.

As we reached the very door of the drawing room, it occurred to me with a sickening jolt that a moment of great danger lay ahead.

My father would be there.

With seconds to go I prepared myself. *Look for him at once*, I told myself, just as a pair of footmen in powdered wigs, as if from the palace in the story of *Cinderella*, bowed and threw wide the double doors.

I saw before me a glittering crowd filling a rich, dim interior, a blue evening sky still softly glowing behind the vast windows of the drawing room.

The colourful blur soon began to separate itself into individual figures, and there he was. His mouth was open in an expression of amazement, and his brows were coming down to wrinkle his forehead into deep, black creases. Of course he was angry. The System did not allow such perilous tricks as this.

But I sensed the duchess ahead of me giving him a quelling look, and I gave him the tiniest shake of the head. He slowly closed his open mouth. He said nothing.

But as soon as he had the chance, he came slinking up behind me. 'In the Lord's name, what is going on, Miss V? Is this some silly girls' game?'

'It is by the wish of the princess,' I said drily, and without further ado, stepped forward to greet another courtier who tottered towards me in unsuitable shoes and too many pearls.

For the rest of the evening, I had very little to do apart from to smile and look pleased as a succession of elderly ladies and gentlemen were introduced to me, all of them peering at me through their quizzing glasses or taking my hand limply in cold fingers and letting it drop. If anyone paused to talk, I deflected attention away from myself with polite questions to the speaker.

The old king was the next challenge, perhaps the biggest threat of all to our carrying off our deception. First he spoke to the duchess, as shortly as was compatible with politeness. I could see her back bristle up like a cat's at the lack of respect.

Then she was turning and shoving me forward, and I was curtseying as deeply as I ever had done.

But as I rose and looked at him, he seemed scarcely able to make me out in the gloom of the great drawing room, lit by rather too few oil lamps. As he peered, I received an impression of geniality but disinterest.

'Is that my niece?' he croaked. 'Welcome, my dear. *You* are always welcome here at the castle. What a pretty dress.'

Then the ordeal was over, we moved on and into the crowd. Suddenly my stays felt tight. I realised that I had been holding my breath ever since we had entered the drawing room, and had only now let it out.

As the duchess and I led the procession out of the drawing room through to dinner, I found myself strangely proud of my performance. After all, to stand and smile, to listen and nod, had been my life, a life of service. That is what these people wanted of their princess, someone to take their hands and ask them questions and make them feel good about themselves.

I could do this. I could do this.

It was such a tragedy that Victoria, the real princess, could not.

Chapter 32

Where Is the Money?

After that strange evening living the life of a princess, I'd soon had enough of the stiff and formal ways at Windsor Castle. We managed throughout the visit to keep Victoria's nervous attack a secret, and she did eventually get out of bed and go to ride out in the park.

'Thank you, Miss V,' she said. I was handing her the hat that went with her navy blue habit, and she took my hand as well as the hat itself. 'Thank you,' she said again, as sombre as I had seen her even in these sombre days. 'You are a true sister to help me like you do. I shall never forget it.'

It was a relief to all of us to return to quiet Kensington

Palace. Its gardens were now in the heavy scented stage of summer, and the year was beginning to turn. One evening I found myself passing the front door of Princess Sophia's temporary new apartment. It was in fact very old and very poky, but she had moved here while the smoking mess of her own abode was cleared up.

I decided to tap on the door very gently, and to leave at once if there was no reply.

But to my surprise, she opened the door immediately and stood there twisting her apron in her hands. She seemed to have taken to doing all the cooking and cleaning herself. I had even asked my father why he had not done more to provide her with domestic help. 'She admires you so much, you know,' I had reminded him.

'Ridiculous old woman,' he had muttered. 'I have spent far too much time already pandering to her needs.' I had not dared to press him further.

'Oh, my dear, come in,' she now said in her anxious, fluttery voice. 'Do sit down.' She looked around her helplessly. 'Now, I have some tea or maybe some seltzer water, or, stay a moment, maybe that is gone ...' She trailed off, confused.

'No, Your Royal Highness,' I said, 'I beg you to sit down. I shall make us both some tea.' So I bustled into her tiny kitchen and gave a sharp kick to the range, and in no time had a kettle boiling. I found some stale seed cake and put it on to a grimy plate.

When I brought in the tea, I noticed that her hands looked terribly fragile, like the twigs of a birch tree in winter.

'Oh, that's better!' she cried, nibbling her cake. 'It has been so hard, my dear, since the news. Doubtless your father has told you?'

'News? I'm afraid not,' I answered tentatively. I didn't sip my own tea because I wasn't quite sure when the cup had last been washed, and I didn't want to risk it.

'Oh!' she sighed, and dabbed up even the crumbs of the cake with her finger. 'I thought that the news of my humiliation would be all around the palace by now. Any gossip here travels so fast.'

I knew that myself. Despite the palace's sleepy aspect, a deep throb of life pulsed in its veins, life that was indiscernible to the eye but none the less powerful for that.

'It's the railway company,' she said. 'If you ask your fine papa, he will tell you, I'm sure, of the unfortunate turn of events. Needless to say no blame is attached to him. He was advised, on very good authority, that I could double my fortune if I invested it all in the new Wales-to-Scotland Railway Company. I thought it was too good to be true – oh, how I wish I had heeded my own judgement!'

'A railway company? Your fortune?' I asked incredulously.

'Yes, dear, a company run by fools and madmen, so it turns out. They have spent all the money, yes, all! My own, and the money of many other private investors too. All is lost. We were too slow, you see. The Grand Junction Railway has beaten us and taken all the new investors and all the profit.'

I twisted my untouched teacup round in its saucer.

It seemed plausible, and certainly her penury was plain enough. But this was shocking. And something about it did not quite ring true.

But no, I thought, surely not. This could not be the answer to the question that had bothered Lehzen and I for months. Whence had the money come for the grand remodelling of Victoria's apartment at Kensington Palace? No, of course there been no dishonesty.

And yet the thought was now inside my head, like a mouse crept into the cellar of a building.

'But, my dear,' she said more briskly, 'you don't wish to hear my troubles. Tell me about that fine young man of yours. Are you engaged yet?'

I felt a fiery blush rise at once to the very roots of my hair. This was indeed torture, or would have been if I hadn't been thinking so hard about money. An engagement! No one should even know or guess about Albert and me. What if my father were to hear?

I felt a rising tide of consternation, which made me leap up from the tea table and begin to pace about. What if King Leopold were to discover? Everyone would be furious if it were to come out.

'I could see that matters were well advanced between you on the evening he saved my life from the fire.'

I slowly shook my head.

'I fear there has been … a misunderstanding,' I said. 'The prince … well, I have nothing to do with the prince. That would be quite wrong.'

But although her eyes were dim and old, she detected something off in my response.

'Oh, my dear,' she said reproachfully. 'You don't mean to say you've refused him? Alas, you need your mamma at a time like this to advise you. A gentleman, even Sir John your father, can never quite understand a young lady's feelings. But you must, you know, you must accept him. He is a perfect match and loves you dearly, that much is clear. I only wish the Princess Victoria could find someone half as good.'

I could hardly begin to tell her what obstacles lay in the way of a match between Albert and myself: the disapproval of Uncle Leopold, his plan for Victoria to marry

Albert, the impossibility of my marrying and leaving Victoria to the mercy of my father …

The thought pulled me up short. My father. What had my father done?

The old lady could see that I was dismayed, and I had no words to answer her. Instead, she came over, placed one hand on my shoulder and with the other chucked me tenderly right under the chin. 'It will be all right, my dear!' she said, raising my head up so as to meet her eyes. 'I might have no money, but I don't need it at this time of life. And you have something much more valuable than money anyway. You have the love of a good man.'

With that, or perhaps it was her earlier reference to my mother, she felled me. I leaned forward on my hands and wept as I had never wept before.

I knew all too well that the System would keep me apart from Albert. The System, my father's creation.

For weeks, all through the stay at Windsor, I had tried to pretend that everything was fine, that Albert and I could one day see each other again. But I had been pretending to myself. Deep down I knew that we would never be together. Although the kind old princess would have been aghast had she known it, it seemed to me that her words were cruel, heartless almost.

Had I really found Albert only to discover that I had to leave him? The System was hurting me. It was hurting Victoria. And now I had a horrible fear that it had hurt this kind old lady as well.

In fact, what good lay in my father's System at all?

Chapter 33

Letters from Germany

When Princess Sophia had asked me if there was an engagement between Albert and myself, I had answered truthfully in the negative. But my words skirted very close to being an untruth. For pressed close to my heart under my bodice was a letter from him. If its existence were known by the world, our correspondence would have been taken as a sign that we were engaged. And yet we were not.

Back in my own room, after leaving Princess Sophia's apartment, I looked out at the gardens below once more. As I opened the window, I reflected upon how much time had passed since I first sat here. Then the palace had seemed alien and cold; now I was close to its warm, innermost workings. Despite my worries and my concerns – and my deep new fear about the Princess Sophia's money – I realised I had become truly part of the System. I had internalised it, lived my life by it.

Once again I took the thin packet of Albert's letters from the front of my dress. My flesh had heated it very slightly, and each one was growing worn from where I had unfolded and refolded it.

Germany.

Victoria,

I hope that I may have the privilege of using the name that stands for you: victorious, alive. No one seeing your little figure and your little blue eyes would know how strong the spirit is within. It has been one of the great joys of my life to make your acquaintance in the last few weeks. I hope I do not offend or presume when I say that the world is a better place for having you within it.

Albert

Italy.

Victoria,

How happy your letter made me! How wildly my heart beat! I have been singing all day, the same song that we played together on the piano. Ernest and the rest have been asking me what has happened. I can hardly answer. The answer, should I have made it is this. I am in love! In love! With the sweetest girl in the whole of the British Isles.

Albert

Germany.

Victoria,

You are right that Uncle Leopold has plans. You are right that the Princess Victoria is in a position of great danger and great responsibility. I know how well you have served her. But I am not as willing as you are to do what my uncle says.

Albert

Postscript: I cannot see that my duty requires me to give you up.

Germany.

Victoria,

My dear heart. I long to see your little face again, and to kiss it. You are so good, so true, so pure. Like the flame of a candle burning bright. I know that I can trust you. I wish that you would do me the honour of making me the proudest man in the world. I would be that man should you consent to be my wife.

Albert

I knew that some time I would have to answer this most recent letter and that it would be the hardest letter I would ever have to write. I longed to consult someone. I even longed to tell all to Victoria, to share the burden with my friend. But she was the last person in the world with whom I could discuss Albert.

I looked down on the gardens once more, and a movement caught my eye. It was Victoria herself, in a pink dress, head down, walking disconsolately between the trees, Dash at her heel. Her head was bowed. Her small figure looked completely alone. She must have been thinking of the trials that lay before her. It gave me a pang of guilt. After all, how could I possibly weigh my concerns alongside hers? The stability of a whole country would soon rest in her hands.

My heart clutched with pity. I would give anything, all my own strength, to help her.

And then the decision became very simple: for she needed help and it was in my power to offer it. Uncle Leopold was right. A good, steady, trustworthy cousin like Albert would be the very thing to get her through the coming trial.

But where did that leave me? It left me, unfortunately, quite alone.

I sat at my writing desk and took up my pen, but I could not bring myself to begin. I had a sudden vision of Albert opening my letter, and of his face falling in disappointment. Surely this could not be the right thing to do?

Tears were running down my face. I gave up the task.

Half an hour later, I made a second attempt. This time I made a mad dash at it, scribbling as fast as I could before I lost my nerve.

Albert,

You are too good to me. Your impetuous, fine nature leads you to say things that are not true. Your letter paid me the finest compliment I have ever received. But I cannot accept your offer. My duty is to a certain person, and she needs you more than I do. The alternative is her failure, which would place the nation at risk of rule by a dangerous brute. You must do as your Uncle Leopold has planned. I shall miss your love greatly, but it is the right, the only thing to do.

Victoria

Then I sealed it, addressed it and presented the messiest, least careful letter I had ever written to Mrs Keen to take to the post.

Then I sobbed again as if my heart would break.

Chapter 34

'I Love You'

A few days later I told my father that I needed to get away. 'I've been here for so long,' I said. 'I should like to see Mamma and home once more. I think I'd like to rest up while the king is still quite well, so I'm good and strong for when … well, for you-know-what.' It was thus that we had taken to speaking of the king's death and Victoria's becoming queen.

'Oh!' he said. 'There's no doubt that you look a little pale and peaky. And it might be as well that you pay a visit to Arborfield before your mother completely forgets who you are. I suppose I could probably spare the carriage. But then, there is the princess to consider. Will she let you go? And what have you been doing with yourself to get worn out? I suspect you of eating ices in the early hours and getting indigestion.'

I hardly had the patience to make a civil answer and glowered at him across the marmalade dish. 'The System,' I said, 'will hardly fall apart, will it, if I go home for a few days?'

'Well, possibly not,' he admitted. 'But as the time grows shorter, the danger grows greater.'

I knew what he meant: the ever-shortening time between now and Victoria's eighteenth birthday. We heard reports daily of the worsening health of the king. If he were to die, there would have to be a regency. There was talk of nothing else but of regencies, and of who would be regent.

I was so sick of thinking about it all that the very word gave me a headache.

Mainly I just wanted to get out of his sight. He was always saying that you could 'count on a Conroy', but he had discounted the Princess Sophia so utterly. At the very least he had been reckless; at worst he had stolen her fortune. I sat there simmering with resentment.

'All right,' he said at last. 'I can see that you are under the weather, and your losing your health will not best serve the princess. A few days in the country will perhaps restore the roses to your cheek. By the way, this letter arrived for you this morning. Who can be writing to you from Germany?'

I bowed my head as the blood pulsed shamefully up and down my veins. 'I believe ...' I began, but faltered. Somehow, from somewhere, I gathered the wit to lie. 'I believe it is from Baron Stockmar, the tutor who came with the Princes Ernest and Albert, as you may remember. He promised me the lyrics of that ancient German song we learned together when the princes were here.'

I was not used to lying outright to my father. I expected him to detect me at once. But there was nothing but silence as he turned over the pages of his paper.

'Miss V!' he said at last, without even looking up. 'You are a funny little thing. You should really have been a professor or an archivist, not the lady-in-waiting to a future queen.'

You think you know me, Papa, I thought silently. *You think I am just a mouse. The truth would surprise you.*

'Well, thank you, Papa,' was what I said out loud. 'Thank you for the offer of the carriage. I shall go and pack.'

'Oh, but finish your breakfast!' His words trailed after me, but I was already halfway up the stairs.

I was barely in my room, banging the door and leaning my back against it, before I was turning the letter from

Germany over in my hands and raising it to my lips to give it a kiss despite myself.

'*Germany. Dearest Victoria …*' Even the very first words in that dear familiar hand made my heart beat faster. I glanced around the room, feeling for some reason that I was being watched. This was underhand, illicit behaviour. I was working against the System by reading this letter, by the very act of holding it in my hand.

But then I remembered that Albert might be hurt, might be sad. I desperately needed to know how he was, and concern made me read on.

I simply don't accept what you say. You cannot refuse me, however much love and duty you owe to the princess. You see, I don't love her, I love you. I don't accept your answer. I know that we shall end up as husband and beloved wife. I beg that you will not think me impertinent, but this is too important for me to say less than I mean.

I take upon myself the honour of signing as your own constant

Albert.

An awful trembling overcame me. I had tried to be so strong, but Albert had been stronger. He had simply disregarded my good advice. My head told me that this could not end well, but my heart leapt with excitement.

All I wanted was to be quiet, alone, to think over his letter, to read it over and over again.

I turned to my chest of drawers. How perfect it was that I had already made plans to go to Arborfield. I began packing quickly, deftly, with excitement. I picked up a necklace that Victoria had given me. Victoria! In my haste, I had almost forgotten Victoria. How could I say goodbye to her?

I sat down on my bed, disconsolate. This is where we had sat together and she had told me that we were sisters. Well, in revelling in the joy that Albert's letter had brought me, I wasn't acting as a good sister should.

Yet how could I remain here to be so tortured by doubts and anxieties?

It was no good. I had to go. I had to go home at last.

PART FOUR

AT ARBORFIELD HALL

Chapter 35

Mr Grouch

Three days later, I was back at home at Arborfield Hall, and in some ways it was as if I had never left. There was the piano, and – oh! – the very same books on the schoolroom table. But then I noticed the place by the window frame where my old governess, Miss Moore, had marked my height with a pencil. I stood near it. I was taller now, much, much taller.

'Ah, Miss V,' my mother said, as I went into her room. 'What's the weather like outside? Is it raining?'

I wanted to shout that I had been away for seven years. Seven years! Surely she had noticed?

For a moment, just as if I were ten once again, I felt

unable to summon up the words. 'Yes, Mamma, it's raining,' was what came out.

Now she was looking at me closely, almost with her full attention. 'You've changed your hair,' she said eventually. 'Ringlets. Like Jane.'

'It's more than my hair that has changed,' I said, approaching her bed in expectation of further questions.

But she rolled away so that I couldn't see her face. I drooped. Mr White the butler and our old cook had been more pleased to see me than she was. From the back she seemed to look exactly as I remembered, except for maybe a further paling of her skin and fading of her own hair.

Then I saw it.

By her bed, on the table, stood a green bottle.

I recognised it as soon as my eye fell on it. I had seen a bottle like that before. I had seen it in the hands of the duchess when she was distressed or anxious, and I knew my father provided it.

Had he led both of them to the drops they drank so deeply? Was my mother really so sleepy as she seemed – or was this somehow his fault as well?

At that moment, I decided I would sit with her every single morning, and try to get her to take an interest in the world.

As I leaned over and looked at her lying on the pillows,

her eyelashes fluttering upon her cheek, I felt like I was the mother and she the vulnerable little girl. It made my heart ache in a newly unpleasant way.

I sighed.

I crept out and softly closed the door. Like everything else at Arborfield, it swung smoothly on its oiled hinges, falling into its frame with barely a click.

After a few overtures, the Arborfield servants left me alone, and I took to my old solitary round of walks in the shrubbery, piano practice and long hours sitting with my mother, book in hand. I sadly missed Dash, as I had left him behind to comfort Victoria.

My mother continued hardly to register that I was there, but I think that as the days went by she began to like having me in the room. I read aloud letters from my brothers, now serving in the army all over the world. Once, she even took my hand and smiled. It was peaceful, sitting there beside her, and slowly, gradually, I began to feel I was doing her some good.

But her reactions were so weak, her progress so slow. As the days grew into weeks, I started to feel angry that my father was still controlling my mother through his bottle, even though he was far away from us. He would *not* control us any longer, I decided. He could not know that, each day, I stealthily removed the green bottle from my mother's room and tipped away half an inch or so of its contents, filling up the gap again with water. As the days went by, the green bottle's contents gradually grew weaker and weaker. My mother seemed not to notice, and I vowed that when at last it was all water, I would tell her and promise her that she didn't need it any more.

I felt that this was really important, and that only I could do it. And yet with nearly every post, a letter arrived from Victoria full of complaints and her constant suggestions that I should return. Sometimes the letters hardly made sense, and I feared that her own health was declining alongside her uncle the king's. I was torn. I began to think that perhaps my duty lay there too. She would need me as the king's end drew near.

But I could not quite bring myself to write to my father to say that I was coming back to the palace.

April was almost May before something happened to shake me out of my dream-like state. I had begun to dwell often on the fact that it was nearly a whole year since, on that Kensington Palace staircase, I had first laid eyes on Albert. I was now quite old enough to be married, and indeed a letter had recently come announcing Jane's engagement. 'At last!' was all that my mother had to say.

One evening I was all alone in the drawing room, my mother having gone up to bed.

And of course I was thinking of him. I always was.

With a start, I realised that there had been a knock, and that I had said 'Come in!' mechanically, without even thinking about it. Mr White was in the room, closing the door behind him and turning to me with a bow. 'A young … gentleman to see you, miss. Should I ask Maria to summon Lady Conroy? He seems to have arrived with luggage.'

'Oh!' I rapidly turned to the fireplace and picked up the tongs so that he would not see my face. 'No, White, no need to disturb my mother.' I thought quickly. 'Did he give a name?'

'Of course, miss. I believe it was Grooch, or Grotch, or something of that nature. He seems, miss, to be a *foreigner.*'

Where had I heard that name before? Of course, it was what Prince Ernest always called Albert. 'Albert the Grouch' was his name for his brother. My heart almost stopped beating. Albert? Was this – hope against hope – Albert, come to see me?

But at the same time I almost had to laugh at White's distaste. I was in complete disarray and urgently tried to gather my scattered thoughts. 'Oh, that's all right,' I eventually managed to say. 'I was expecting Mr Grouch. But not tonight. Maybe a letter has gone astray or some

343

travel arrangement has collapsed. Please ask Maria to prepare the blue guest room.'

He bowed and turned, and instantly my hands flew to my hair and dress. Was it smooth? Was my dress straight? Was this really the person I thought it might be?

Had White guessed the reason I had selected the blue room for Mr Grouch? The answer was that it was next door to my own, and I wanted to be as near as possible to my 'foreign' visitor.

There was conversation in the hallway, and I swallowed an imprecation to the Almighty as I heard the housemaid's voice. They were interfering in my arrangements! 'No need, no, please do not disturb Lady Conroy,' he was saying. 'I am already well acquainted with Miss V. Conroy, from the palace, you know.'

That was his voice. It *was* him!

Then he was bounding into the room. For a moment we both stood on the hearthrug, trembling and looking at each other. White softly closed the door. At the exact same moment, Albert and I both laughed, and we hurled ourselves into each other's arms.

We hugged tightly, but in the end I became very sad and still. It was a completely unfamiliar feeling to have arms tightly wrapped around me in a great big bear hug. I loved it, but feared the moment it would end.

Then he thrust me away from him and scanned every inch of me, looking for change. 'A year has made a vast difference!' he said. 'You used to be ugly, but you are now almost pretty.' I hung my head. I loved and hated being teased by him. But I could give as good as I got. It was *Albert*; he would not mind.

'And you!' I said. 'You are almost tall now. I believe you have grown up. Is that a beard?'

Sheepishly, he ran his hand over his chin.

'Almost,' he said. 'And I'm sorry now I teased you. I know you hate it. My Victoria,' he continued seriously, 'you are the most beautiful woman in the world! Now, come sit with me and tell me everything.'

But we could neither of us remain seated for long. We paced the rug, I showed him the dank view out of the window, and he poked the fire to warm up my hands, which he said were too cold.

'And why is your mother in bed at this early hour?' he asked eventually. 'It's only eight o'clock. Is she an invalid?'

I had observed that at Arborfield this was the sort of question that casual acquaintances never ever asked, for my mother's ill health was shrouded in mystery. But I could deny Albert nothing, and tell him nothing but the truth.

'Well, she takes drops from a bottle. Every day. They make her very sleepy. I am trying to stop her; we are cutting down. I think … I think my father likes to keep her that way. He gives the same drops to the duchess when she is … you know … too …'

'Too dramatic, you mean?'

I nodded silently. I felt a wave of relief followed at once by fresh anxiety. For in speaking openly about these doubts for the first time, I realised how convinced I was of their truth.

'But this is very dangerous!' Albert went on. 'It must be laudanum. Once you start taking it, it's very difficult to stop.'

I had suspected this for some time. But my father … he got the bottles from the chemist, and he seemed so *right* about everything. Except when he seemed so wrong.

'Victoria,' Albert said seriously, putting his hands on my shoulders. 'You should know that my parents are not … quite normal, either. My mother has left us. She preferred another man. My father has taken up with mistresses. I think that you and I are in something of the same position.'

'Albert, I really don't know …' I trailed off, miserable. But his face was very close, his eyes very insistent that I should continue. 'I really don't believe my father is a good man. Not just mistaken or misguided or overbearing. You know I have thought those things before. But now I think he might be wrong … almost evil.'

I found I was panting slightly as I spoke, this admission torn from me only by a love of the truth and a need to speak it to Albert.

'I have the same doubt,' he said at once. 'But don't be frightened. You are strong. You will manage. And I will help you.' He cradled my head on his chest. I could feel his heartbeat. The slow hypnotic pace of it gradually stilled my fears, and a soporific peace stole over me, almost like the benison of laudanum itself.

The tap at the door sounded like thunder, and guiltily we sprang apart. 'Come in!' Albert said, much too loudly. Maria, our housemaid, was there with the evening tea. The sight of two cups rather than one on the tray gave me such a radiant glow of happiness that I could scarcely hide my smile.

'The room is all ready, miss,' she said, hardly able to keep her eyes off this mysterious stranger who had arrived so suddenly and unexpectedly.

'Thank you, Maria,' I said crisply, and there was nothing for her to do but to leave.

We giggled.

'I have caused a commotion in this household, have I not,' Albert said, 'by walking up the drive out of nowhere?'

'Indeed you have, but given that for so many years I have been so good, so very, very good, I think I am allowed to be a little bit bad for once, and to have a gentleman caller.'

We sat drinking our tea. He sipped first from his own cup, then from mine, then from his own again, watching me sternly until I performed the same absurd little ceremony.

'Victoria,' he said seriously. 'You are certainly allowed to be bad this once. You deny yourself so much for other people. That's why I admire you. And I have something to tell you. I have been with the Princess Victoria. I have come to tell you that you must return to the palace.'

'Is it the king?' I asked, quickly putting down my cup. But I was a little uncertain. Surely if the king were dead, he would have told me straight away.

'No,' he said. 'It is not the king. It is something else. It is not for me to tell you, though. She must tell you herself.'

Silence fell. I knew at once what he meant. After the excitement of our meeting, the serious question of our future lay between us. My stomach felt like it was falling into a deep chasm. So it had come so soon, this horrible question of his marriage, Uncle Leopold's marriage … Victoria's marriage.

I schooled myself.

'When is the wedding to be?' I asked in a small voice.

Of course, she wanted to tell me all about it, to make

preparations. With a heavy heart I realised that she probably wanted me to be her bridesmaid. It was sweet, so bittersweet, of her.

'It's not that,' he said quickly, seeing my distress. 'No, not that at all.'

'But what can it be?' I cried out. I was almost shouting in my anguish. 'What can she have to say to me?'

'Dearest,' he said, flying over and seizing me again in his arms. 'You are strong, stronger than anyone else I know. You must be strong now. I would tell you if I could, but I cannot. It is a matter of honour. But look at me. Look at me.'

I raised my red, smarting eyes to his face.

It was true that he looked happy and calm.

'Something has happened,' he said. 'She knows I am here with you. She is happy for me to be here, happy, I tell you. Will you trust me? Will you trust me and go back to Kensington Palace to discover what awaits there?'

I stared at him. My face must have been a picture of consternation. What could he mean?

But then I saw the tiniest pinprick of light in the darkness that had surrounded me for many months. Albert believed in the future. It was written on his face. And if he believed, I could believe too.

'Yes,' I said. 'I will.'

Chapter 36

Return to Kensington Palace

It was some days later, and I was on my way back to the palace, alone in the carriage. I'm sure that I looked just the same as when I had travelled the other way, to Arborfield Hall: neat, discreet, tidily dressed. But then I had been in the blackest despair. Now a powerful feeling, like lightning or the crashing of waves, flowed through me. I was no longer alone; I had my two dear friends. I did not know what was happening, but I had faith in them both.

It was now full June, and the trees and meadows were glossy with the glow of summer. Out on the streets, it seemed that the British people were also aglow with enthusiasm for the young princess. Like me, Victoria was now safely eighteen years old. There was a sense – perhaps it was indecorous – but there was a sense nonetheless that the old king could safely die. There would be no regency. My father would never rule.

Reports from Windsor suggested that King William the Fourth believed the same thing himself. Now he was sinking fast, as if his furious venom against the duchess and my father was the only thing that had kept him going so long.

As we passed into the high street of Kensington, I could hear the newspaper sellers shouting out: 'King's 'ealth! King in decline! Latest!' and 'Our fair young queen-to-be! All the news!' There were ladies shopping, tradesmen's carts delivering groceries, soldiers from the barracks walking at their leisurely, off-duty pace. They looked happy and serene in the sunshine.

Watching their faces, I thought, *You know nothing, nothing, you happy people. You don't know what has to be done to make sure there is no dispute or regency or civil war. You don't know what it will cost your princess to serve you.*

But then, nor did I know myself quite what was going on at the palace. I felt a little faint with nerves and the strain of thinking about what this mystery could be. I also felt shaky with plain old hunger. I had hardly been able to eat since Albert's secret early morning departure after his night at Arborfield Hall, striding off down the misty drive and disappearing between the trees.

Back at the palace, I went at once to the German apartment without pausing to change my travelling dress, abandoning my luggage to be dealt with later. Adams let me in, refusing to meet my eye. My heart lurched. *He knows what you're up to!* yelled an insistent voice in my head. *Everybody knows you have been with Albert! You are shamed!*

But a rival, more sensible voice piped up to tell me that this was just Adams' usual polite deference. Still, I was disturbed.

Once I was inside, Victoria herself came skipping down the great staircase to meet me.

'Oh!' she shrieked. 'Miss V! You have been so long! Dash and I have missed you so much!' To my surprise, she threw her arms around me and covered me with kisses until I laughed and begged for mercy.

Then she grew grave and sat me down next to her on the stairs. 'It's time,' she said very quietly. She glanced up and down the staircase, but no servants were in sight. 'It's time to tell you. I know you will say yes.'

'Say yes to what, Victoria?' I asked, laughing a little, for she was so happy and confident.

'It's a plan. Albert and I have formed it. Well, I formed

it, and then Albert agreed it would work. So it's not just a wild fancy.' She saw me start at the mention of his name.

'Yes, yes,' she said quickly. 'I know *all* about you and Albert. Why didn't you tell me sooner, you silly thing? Anyway, that's what makes it all so beautiful.'

My brain simply refused to work. 'Victoria,' I said almost crossly. 'What *are* you talking about? What's going on?'

'Shh!' she said, glancing up and down. It was so unlike her to be worried about making a sound that I knew for real that she was about to propose something deadly serious. 'I think we're safer here on the stairs,' she explained. 'Who knows who might be listening at the door if we go into the drawing room? At least here we can see people coming.'

Indeed, as she spoke we heard the tramp of feet outside as the guards were changed in the courtyard. We waited until the little ceremony was over. My heart began to hammer in my chest, louder and louder, at the prospect of what she might say.

'Here's the plan,' she said, when the sounds had at last passed away. 'You have known for some time, I think, that I can never be queen.'

I made a stifled little sound of disagreement, but she shushed me at once.

353

'You try to believe in me,' she went on, 'I know that, and I love you for it. But I cannot take the throne. YOU must take it for me.'

I sat there on the stairs. I could hardly take it in. Was she mad? Had she fallen into madness at last? I gazed at her, horrified.

It must have been all too obvious what I was thinking.

'Oh, no, I've not gone bonkers,' she laughed. 'Consider this. One result of the System is that no one knows exactly what I look like, although the truth is that I look like you. Or that you look like me. We're practically identical. Everyone at Windsor Castle was deceived – you saw that, didn't you? You will marry Albert and take my place on the throne. And you will be happy.'

'Victoria,' I said. 'That would be selfish of me. You know I can't do that.'

'It's not a question of selfishness,' she said.

She was being so quiet and grave I hardly knew her.

'Everyone knows that a good queen is *not* selfish. That's why you must be queen, and I must not. And indeed, it would be selfish of you to refuse. Because if you do, George Cumberland will be king, and there will be civil war. People will be killed.'

She was right. She could see it in my face that I knew it.

354

'You see that you *have* to take them both, don't you? The throne and Albert. The two go together. It all fits.'

'Wait!' I said. 'I need time to think.'

'No, you don't,' she said. 'You think too much. I've done the thinking this time, for us both – with Albert's help, of course. He will get you through it. My mother and your father are upstairs together now. This evening we will tell them the plan. You do agree to it, don't you?'

At that I faltered.

'Victoria,' I began uncertainly. I had felt brave and bold in the carriage, with the memory of Albert fresh in my mind, but now my confidence receded. 'I really cannot do this. You *must* take the throne. You have no need to fear. You will do the right thing, and after a time, when you get used to it, doing the job well will give you pleasure. I promise. You always know your own mind.'

'I do know my own mind. I've thought about it, I've decided what's best and I've made this decision myself. It's true that, as Lehzen says ...' She paused, so that I could join in chanting the familiar phrase from years of lessons and drills: 'It's better to be wicked than to be weak!' we concluded together.

She laughed, almost clapping her hands. But then her smile faded.

'Come on, Miss V,' she said. 'You know you will do it

better than I would. You care so much about right and wrong, and you are so modest and devoted to serving other people. I ... I just haven't got it in me. And I really don't want to give up my throne to my cousin George. I want to give it to you.'

'But even if I said yes, what will *you* do?' I asked, astonished that I had not really thought of this before.

'Well, I shall go and live *your* old life,' said Victoria, with a twinkle in her eye. 'I shall go and taste the pleasures of country life at Arborfield Hall, and quarrel constantly with your father, and get the better of him, I'm sure. And soon Sir John Conroy's younger daughter, who nobody knows and who nobody has seen since she was a child, will come out into society and have a gay time. Who knows where life will then take her?'

In saying all this she grew fresh and glowing once more. I could see why she wanted to be free of the terrible burden of queenship. I could see that I could carry it, bear it, better than her.

'Come on,' she said, standing and holding out her hand.

I paused, still seated on the steps, conscious that this was a moment of fatal decision. It was bigger than Albert, bigger than anything.

'But, Victoria,' I said, 'what about my father? You

know how … dominant he is, how powerful. He just won't let us do this.'

Victoria quickly knelt by my side, there on the stairs, and peered closely at my face.

'Deep down, Miss V,' she said, 'deep, deep down inside, you *do* know that your father is a cruel bully. Don't you? Don't you? You have the upper hand over him. He can deny you nothing after what he has done to you. He has kept you a prisoner, here, in the palace, for ever so many years.'

At this I could only hang my head and acknowledge the truth of her words.

'Come on,' she said again. 'This is the finest thing that you can do for me, dear friend. And for my mother: she needs to be rescued. If he says a word against it, we will tell the world how he has mistreated her all these years. And your own mother, remember her as well. And – Albert. Don't forget Albert.'

I certainly could not forget Albert, for any moment of any hour of any day.

And so I got to my feet, and together we began to climb the stairs.

As we went, Victoria beside me chuckled.

'What is it?' I asked.

'At last,' she said with glee, 'we're going to beat the System!'

Chapter 37

A New Reign

At five o'clock the next morning I was woken by a tapping at the door of Victoria's old bedroom. I had not slept here since the night of the intruder, years ago. Then I was a visitor, now it was my own. The sun was already up. The tapping was meek, almost obsequious, but I sat up at once, completely awake.

The terrible interview in the old schoolroom, late the previous evening, had drained me completely. My father's anger, the duchess's tears, Victoria's cold, focused rage at the two of them, had left me feeling nothing but dread and lethargy. Ugly words had been spoken, ugly threats made.

But then, when it was all over, I had crept through

here into the bedroom and found Lehzen sitting, waiting, on the bed.

On seeing me, she'd smiled.

'Ah, Victoria,' she said. 'You must rest now. It seems likely that your uncle will die before morning, and it could be that tomorrow your reign will begin. May God bless you and watch over you tonight. I will be next door. You must let me know how I can best help.'

Her words left me speechless. I remembered the conversation we had had once before in the woods near Ramsgate, and I wondered how much Lehzen had planted the seed of the plan in Victoria's mind. How many people had been working against the System? Perhaps it was not just three of us, but four. It occurred to me that there were now only two people left who truly believed in the System: my father and the duchess.

Perhaps even the duchess was losing confidence in it, too. My father's rage against her at her failure to control her daughter had been truly horrible.

Lehzen had lifted a finger to her lips, getting up from the bed. 'No need to say anything at all, my dear,' she said. 'Now let me help you off with those shoes.'

And so soothed, contrary to all my expectations, I'd drifted off to sleep.

Now I pushed my feet back into my shoes, for I was

not sure where Victoria's bedroom slippers might be. That knock, so gentle and weak, hardly sounded like Lehzen. I was right. When I tugged open the huge, heavy door, it was the duchess. Her hair was all up in curl papers and her Chinese dressing gown gaudy in gold and red. But her eyes were red and her manner strangely subdued.

'The news has come,' she almost whispered. 'The king is dead. God bless you, my dear, you are now the queen.'

At that she shuffled across the room and opened up the curtains. A long finger of early sunlight found its way into the gloomy chamber, and I saw that dawn had come to the gardens below. 'The archbishop is waiting for you downstairs,' she said.

I could not quite keep up the pretence.

'Duchess …' I began.

'Mother!' she said kindly. 'You must call me "Mother", especially when we are in public together. And I feel for you as a mother for her child. It is a great, great thing that you do for my girl.'

After the threats and tantrums and tears of yesterday evening, I was stunned at her change of heart.

'Yes,' she said, smiling at the consternation on my face. And I saw that this morning, as she had not yet had the chance to paint her face, there was a child-like serenity and a certain dignity to it. 'I have thought all through the night and talked to Victoria, and I see that you are acting for the best for us all. I have had enough, my dear, of your father, Sir John, although I say it as should not. He has not served us well, and I am no longer going to be his creature. My daughter and I will survive. With your help.'

It was the longest and calmest speech I had ever heard from her, and it did me good. I took the white dressing gown that she held out to me.

'Now,' she said, 'put it on. The Lord Chamberlain is here. And the Archbishop of Canterbury. I tried to spare you, but they won't see me. They insist on seeing you, and you alone.'

Belting the white gown around myself, I left her and passed down the steep staircase, the one Victoria had never been allowed to descend without holding someone's hand.

It was steep and my heart was beating wildly, and I thought I might slip. But I imagined Albert's voice in my head. 'Victoria,' he said, 'you can manage this.'

In the corridor, I paused. There was a strange footman there, in livery, standing up straight, so straight he could hardly have been breathing.

When he saw me there in my dressing gown, he instantly bowed and gestured to the door of the little drawing room.

'This way,' he said. 'I have put them in here, Your Majesty.'

Your Majesty.

I heard the words with a lurch of the heart. But I would soon be hearing them again. Many times.

Two hours later, I had met a succession of men in black – grave and solemn – each of them eager to kiss my hand and give me their condolences upon my late uncle's demise.

I had to pinch myself occasionally, for I found myself beginning to believe that I was bereaved, and that the death of a strange old man had indeed had a profound effect on my spirits. After my dressing-gowned meeting with the Lord Chamberlain, I had changed into a black dress obtained for Victoria in preparation for this eventuality.

With the duchess and Lehzen, I had given orders for the removal of our things from Kensington Palace. We had decided to make a new beginning at Buckingham Palace, where none of the old servants would wonder which of two very similar girls was wearing the Crown.

I was in the old schoolroom, pointing out to the maids which things should be packed, when yet another unfamiliar footman came in, with the announcement of yet another visitor.

'Sir John Conroy!'

I looked at Lehzen in consternation, but her face was impassive. She gave me a stately nod, as if to say: *Here is the real test. I know you will pass.*

My father was bowing down low before me and kissing my hand. I wanted to snatch it back, but it seemed too undignified. I found him hateful now, his hair too slick, his manner too bold. I remembered my mother lying on the couch, and the duchess looking sad and childlike as she contemplated life free from his clutches.

Every fibre in me rebelled against his bluff, confident front, marching into the apartment as if he owned it.

'Ah, Miss V,' he said loftily. 'I have run up here to say that, upon mature consideration, I accept the deception. I see the necessity. And the Other Party sends her love and best wishes, and says she will spend this morning reading a novel in bed. Perhaps it is really for the best.'

I stood silent, unwilling to acknowledge what would now be a secret between us all, and should no longer be spoken of.

'However,' he said, and here he finally appeared to notice Lehzen, and bowed to her, 'I have come with a certain demand in return for my discretion on the matter.'

I saw Lehzen start forward, almost as if to strike him. But she subsided and turned quickly on her heel.

I knew that I had to fight my own battles.

'There is to be no treaty between us, Sir John,' I said clearly and boldly, gathering all my strength.

'I think that you will require a steady private secretary beside you,' he said as if I had not spoken, and resting an elbow possessively upon the mantelpiece. 'You are inexperienced; you require a man of business to help you make the decisions which will be matters of life and death. A little miss like you cannot be all alone on the throne.'

Ah. He did not know it, but he had made it easy for me.

I would *not* be alone on my throne.

'Thank you, Sir John,' I said. 'But the duchess and I release you from our employment. We have our own advisors now, advisors from Germany and our family connections there.' I did not say Albert's name, but the thought of him gave me strength. 'And the Princess Sophia, of course,' I added. 'She is familiar with all the business of a court.'

He grew pale with rage at this, and an ugly, angry snarl escaped his lips.

'As – I – said – last – night, Miss V,' he panted, now

discomposed and breathing harder, 'I see some advantage to this plot, but you must not get too high-handed. You need the support of a secretary, of a father, to carry this off.'

'I need no support,' I said, although my knees were now trembling under the pressure of the emotion I felt. 'I need none of your green bottles, Sir John. I am not your creature. I am your queen. And my name is Victoria.'

For the first time in my life, I had left my father speechless. He stood, staring, as if he had been turned into stone.

Lehzen coughed.

'Her Majesty,' she said coldly, 'now wishes to be alone with her household.'

My father looked steadily at me, and now, recovering himself slightly, he raised one eyebrow. I dreaded and feared what he would say next. I had stood up so well so far, but he still had the power to wound me, perhaps fatally.

But what I saw in his eyes was the barest flicker of amusement. When he spoke, it was under his breath.

'Well, I'll be blowed,' he said quietly, gathering up his cane into his hand. 'You can certainly count on a Conroy. She means it. The mouse means it.'

Without further ceremony, he turned to go.

'Sir John!'

At first I thought it was the parrot. But it was Lehzen croaking out a final warning to my father.

'Ah, indeed, I forgot.'

He turned back and, placing his hat over his heart, cocked out a leg and bowed down low before me.

'Your Majesty,' he said solemnly. 'May I have leave to withdraw?'

'You may,' I said. 'I give you leave to retire.'

As soon as the door closed behind him, I knew that the worst was over. As if enjoying a gleam of sunlight after a storm, I allowed my mind for a moment to travel to Albert in Germany, and to the joy waiting for me there. Perhaps a letter, soon a visit. How long would we have to wait until our wedding? Surely Victoria would be there too, in her role as Miss V. Conroy, bridesmaid.

And that is how my reign began.

Epilogue

Why I Wrote This Book

If you visit Kensington Palace today, you can see the room where Queen Victoria was born. You might visit the bedroom where she woke up on that May morning to learn that her uncle was dead. You will certainly walk through the Red Saloon, where the eighteen-year-old queen held her first Privy Council meeting.

As one of the curators at Kensington Palace, I've long been intrigued by Queen Victoria, our most celebrated palace character. Most people think of her as a grandmother in black, looking rather like a potato, and immensely old, tired and fat.

But she wasn't always like that. In her youth she was passionate, joyful and a lover of dancing. I say that she's 'intriguing' though, because it's hard to work out whether she's a saint or a sinner. She had a powerful sense of duty, yet she could be ridiculously intolerant of other people's failings. She's full of contradictions. But the person you are as an adult is shaped by your childhood, and I started to think that some of the secrets of Queen Victoria's character might lie locked up in the Kensington Palace of her youth. She was brought up there in a curious state of strict seclusion which was intended to keep her safe, secure and untainted by the unpopularity of her Hanoverian uncles who were kings before her.

The architect of 'the System' was, in truth, Victoria's mother's comptroller, Sir John Conroy. Victoria thought of him as her arch-enemy and nemesis. She called him the 'Arch-Fiend' and the 'Monster and Demon Incarnate'. The best that can be said for him is that he created the abysmal conditions in which the young queen's character was challenged and strengthened. The Kensington System – a real name for a real thing – is seen as the fiery furnace in which was forged the steel in Victoria's soul. And Sir John Conroy did have a real daughter, called Victoria, with whom he forced the young princess to play.

But the trouble the historians face is that most of the evidence for what it was really like to live under 'the System' comes from Queen Victoria *herself*, in her letters and diaries.

And we also know that Queen Victoria tended to self-pity and to melodrama. What if we can't really trust and believe in her to report the truth?

I began to imagine an alternative course of events at Kensington Palace, where everything was *not* what it seemed. What if Sir John Conroy's daughter, Victoria Conroy, was not really Princess Victoria's enemy – as she claims in her diary – but her friend?

Once I had asked myself these questions, I decided to create a parallel universe where some of the 'known facts' of history get turned on their head. This is something that's fun to think about, but impossible to do in a normal history book … so that's why I wrote a novel instead. I hope you enjoyed reading it as much as I enjoyed writing it.

Acknowledgements

I would like to thank all my Historic Royal Palaces colleagues at Kensington Palace, Queen Victoria's childhood home, for our many conversations about her over the years. A.N. Wilson's excellent *Victoria: A Life* (2014), especially the chapter in which he speculates on Conroy's motives, set off a train of thought that led to my counter-factual approach. Other people to whom I'm extremely grateful are Catherine Clarke, Hilary Van Dusen and Hannah Sheppard, as well as Helen Vick, Helen Szirtes, Katie Everson, Jenny Beer, Lizz Skelly, Charlotte Armstrong and everyone else at Bloomsbury. Most of all, though, I'm indebted to Zoe Griffiths and Hannah Sandford.